Dear Casey . . .

by

June Patrick Gibbs

To Mary Beth
with my Kindest regards,
June
5-20-12

TENNESSEE VALLEY
Publishing®

2007

Published by:

Tennessee Valley Publishing
PO Box 52527
Knoxville, Tennessee 37950-2527

Printed and bound in the United States of America.

Library of Congress Control Number: 2007928141

ISBN: 978-1-932604-46-7

Cover art: Elizabeth Polfus.
Visit Elizabeth's Web site at www.elizabethpolfus.com

It's like singing on a boat during a terrible storm at sea. You can't stop the raging storm, but singing can change the hearts and spirits of the people who are together on that ship.

– from *Bird by Bird* by Anne Lamott

With special thanks . . .

. . . to Richard Dew, whom I entrusted with my first draft of this book. You know the "painful pleasure" of trying to write about a child who left too soon. Thank you for your friendship and for making helpful suggestions both about this book and about how to survive. I will forever remember you for striving so hard to help the rest of us, while honoring the memory of your son. I didn't know Brad, but I feel like I do – through you.

. . . to Ted Wampler. Thank you for reviewing this book. Most of all, though, thank you for the example you set. I have watched you since the first time I walked into a Compassionate Friends meeting and have seen firsthand the way you help others, even though you have a broken heart yourself because your beloved Mary Lee is not here. Your words and actions have helped so many people, including me.

. . . to Rose Thompson. Thank you for reading my manuscript and for sharing your thoughts from a mother's perspective. All the conversations we've had through the years leave me feeling blessed to know such a kind, caring and graceful person. Evan would be proud of his mom for making a difference in the lives of so many people after his death.

. . . to Elizabeth Polfus. Thank you for creating the cover of this book. Your artwork leaves me speechless. You were Casey's friend, and now you're mine.

. . . and to my husband Steve and my daughters Nikki and Erin. How can I say how much I appreciate you? Thank you for rolling up your sleeves and walking with me on this journey. You give me a reason to go on. I love you so much.

Introduction

My daughter, Erica Casey Shelton, died when she was 14 years old. She was the passenger in a car driven by her 17-year-old cousin. The accident happened in 1996.

I began writing to Casey almost immediately. It was something that helped me. When I wrote these letters to my child on pieces of notepaper or jotted down my thoughts on napkins, scraps of paper or whatever was convenient at the time, I had no clue that someday I would even think about letting other people read them. I wrote the letters at home, at work, in the car – anywhere I happened to be when the mood struck. Sharing them is something I've had to think about long and hard. I wrote from my heart. They're so personal. So private. My grief was private. No one, not even my husband Steve who saw me every day, knew the degree.

Prologue

July 25, 1996. When I got home from work that afternoon, it seemed like a good time to clean the refrigerator – one of the chores I dislike most and don't do very often. My youngest daughter, 14-year-old Casey, and I were the only ones left at home. On that particular evening, she was at my mom's house in Petros, about 20 miles from our home in Oak Ridge, Tennessee, spending the night with her "granny." Jennifer, my sister's 17-year-old daughter, was there too.

Erin, my middle child, had just gotten married three weeks ago and was now in Oak Ridge with her new husband Brad. Nikki, my oldest, was in Nashville attending summer classes after her second year at Vanderbilt University. Their father and I had been divorced for nine years, so it had been just us girls for quite a while.

I had finally finished with the refrigerator and was vacuuming when Erin called. She was upset because the photographer had lost almost all the pictures from her wedding. Forgetting the housework, I went to her apartment to see what few photos she had and to console her. When I returned home, I had a message from Steve, my fiancé, whom I planned to marry in April 1997. I returned his call and while we were chatting, the call waiting alerted me to another call. I clicked over. It was my brother Pat who lived in the same town as my mom. He said Casey and Jennifer had been in a car wreck and had been airlifted to the University of Tennessee Hospital by LIFESTAR, the emergency medical helicopter. That was all he knew since the roads were blocked and he had been unable to get to the scene of the wreck.

I clicked back to Steve and screamed that Casey had been in a wreck and had been taken to UT Hospital and to call Erin and her dad to let them know. Just as I hung up the phone, it rang again. It was David, Jennifer's dad. He had received the same call. He told me to stay home and he and my sister would pick me up on their way to the hospital. Since they had to wait for someone to take care of their 10-year-old son, I said I couldn't wait. I was going on to the hospital. He insisted I go with them, so we agreed that I would drive to their house while the sitter was coming.

As I ran out of my house to go to Casey, I dropped to my knees on the porch and asked God, "Please, *please* let Casey be OK," little knowing that she was already in His arms.

Dear Casey . . .

by

June Patrick Gibbs

*C*asey is my daughter. Casey was my daughter. No, Casey *is* my daughter. Casey is my daughter, and she will always be my daughter. I loved Casey from the moment I knew she existed – which was October 7, 1981, the date my pregnancy test was positive. I first "saw" her on February 5, 1982, in a sonogram picture while she was still inside my body. That day I saw the outline of a wee little baby who was growing larger and stronger every day. Then I got to really see her on June 3, 1982, the night she was born at 8:27 p.m. at Oak Ridge Hospital.

I got to love and be with Casey for 14 years, 1 month and 22 days. Then a car accident took her away. I last saw her on July 24, 1996. She went to be with God the next day, July 25, 1996. The hospital where she had been born just 14 years, 1 month and 22 days earlier was the hospital where she was taken after the wreck and where I was told the news that Casey had not survived the car wreck, news that would forever change my life.

Not long before Casey went to heaven, she asked me how I pictured her in the future. I told her that because her sisters Nikki and Erin are a littler older than she, that they would probably have the first children and that she would be their children's favorite aunt. I told her I could picture her taking her little nieces and nephews to ball games and playing with them, and they would love her so much and want to be with her all the time. Then I told her I pictured her having lots of animals and then children of her own – probably boys since our own family was entirely girls. She liked my picture, and so did I. Casey always told me when she was little that when she grew up she was going to buy us a house at the beach and we'd have horses there. The beach was for me and the horses were for her. We would be so happy. I really liked her picture.

But our pictures didn't get the chance to develop. Casey died before nephews and nieces could be born, before she could have children and a

*beach house and horses of her own. She packed a lot of life into 14
years, but in many ways it seemed to me that her life was only beginning.*

*This is a story about Casey. I'm writing it for Casey's nieces and
nephews who will someday be a part of our family. I want them to know
Casey. And I'm writing it for me, because I don't want to ever forget
anything about Casey.*

I can't do this.

I don't know when I wrote the words above, because the sheet of paper
is undated. It was probably sometime in 1997. I wrote a lot that year. But
that's all I could write on my first attempt to write a story about Casey.
The pages attached to that sheet are blank.

But it's 2007 now, and I'm going to try again. Today, Casey's nephews
and nieces that I had only imagined 10 years ago, are real. Three little
boys – Caden, Conlin and Jacob – and three little girls – Caroline, Olivia
and Charlotte. Their mothers tell them about their Aunt Casey who lives
in heaven. But I want to tell them even more. And there are other people
I want to tell about Casey. I know there are so many grieving parents out
there – I personally know a lot of them – and I want to share Casey's
life, and my experience in dealing with her death, with them. I have
learned so much about grief since Casey died. Maybe something in my
experience can help others see their way through.

I started writing letters to Casey soon after she died. I would write a
letter to Casey, or just jot down a note about whatever was going on at
the time, fold it and place it in a box. I had never looked at these letters
and notes again until I started working on this book. Re-reading them, I
can see that I have come a long way. I still grieve for Casey every day. I
think of her many times every day. It's just not as raw now. The bruise
on my heart is still there; I feel it when something touches it. But I have
adjusted – not recovered, not found closure. Just adjusted. I hope by
sharing our story – Casey's and mine – that we can offer hope to other
moms and dads, sisters and brothers, grandparents and friends who have
suffered the loss of a dear, precious person in their life. And you can
also get a glimpse of who Casey was.

I can't forget a lady with long blond hair and wearing a red dress who came to the funeral home on Saturday night. She said she didn't know me and I didn't know her, but she wanted to tell me how sorry she was. She hugged me very hard, for a very long time. She was different; something about her hug was different than all the other hugs I received. Was she an angel?

This is a dream I had on July 27/28, 1996, after returning from the receiving of friends at the funeral home: *I was in a city at dawn. Graffiti was on buildings and I strained to see what the graffiti said. A van with a black man inside was parked in front of a building. I had to look through the windows of the van to see the graffiti. The black man was asleep, but he raised up, tipped his hat and said, "Good morning." Then I saw graffiti that read "Jacob is resting in the bosom of Abraham."* I wonder what that dream meant.

August 3, 1996
Steve took me to the Chimneys in the Smokies. The Chimneys has a section of huge rocks in the middle of a mountain steam. We had gone there before just to enjoy the peace and quiet. This time I crossed over the stream and sat on a big rock and cried and cried. I kept staring at a leaf on a tree, and it waved to me. It was Casey waving to me. It made me feel better.

I feel fortunate that I soon began to have dreams of Casey. I've learned that not all bereaved parents do. My dreams were sometimes puzzling, sometimes comforting. Sometimes they left me feeling sad; sometimes they left me with a warm feeling. But always they were a way for me to spend time with Casey, something I desperately wanted to do.

September 1996
I dreamed what I think was my first dream of Casey. We were together in a house picking out her bedroom. Just us. It was normal. It felt good. We just looked through rooms, picking which one she would have.

Dear Casey, Do you remember how you played your harmonica on the way to Granny's? I do. I want to hear you play again. I will. And we'll laugh and I will be so happy again. You are my little ladybug. I love you! – Mom

September 21, 1996
Sleeping in the room with Nikki, it's like you are in the room. Nikki breathes like you breathed. I can hear you. My Casey.

❧

September 21/22, 1996
I dreamed of Casey while I was spending the night with Nikki in Nashville. In the dream I was on my way back home from my mother's and I had stopped at a white house. Casey, Erin and Jennifer were there. Jennifer was walking in front of bleachers at the house, with Casey behind her. Erin said Jennifer had won the "Best Sport" Award. I asked why Jennifer won. Why didn't Casey? Erin said, "Mom, don't you know what happened to Casey?" She couldn't see Casey there. I was the only one who saw Casey. This has troubled me.

❧

September 22, 1996
Dear Casey, Today I missed you so much. The sadness I feel makes me queasy and unable to speak and like throwing up. I just want to collapse, and I don't care if I ever get up. Nikki and I were on the Vanderbilt campus. You were always with me there. Why aren't you with me, Casey? We passed the Rec Center. You always liked that place. Nikki and I talked about how you always wanted to climb that rock wall that's just inside the door. That's when I missed you so much. I thought I can't drive home without Casey. I don't want to go home without Casey. I want Casey! But I did drive home. I still imagine you asking, "Where are we?" as I go across Rockwood Mountain. And I answer aloud, "Rockwood Mountain" four or five times because that's how many times you always asked. Going to and from Nashville, it struck me that I-40 is not even the same anymore. It was familiar with you; now I could be anywhere in the world. It doesn't look the same. I look over at your empty seat and I even reach over and pretend I can touch you. Passing by Watt Road on the way home, I am flooded with memories. You played some of your last ball games at the fields there. I look over at the turn and say, "I love you, Casey. I was so proud of you." From Watt Road to Westin Place, where I live now, I cry huge tears that flow down my face onto my neck. For the first time, I scream. I ask God, "Why?" I tell God I don't understand and I want you back and I love you so much. And I ask God to be with me.

❧

When she was little, Casey called the moon the "cookie moon." I used to tell her what she got from me was her love of nature. She loved the outdoors, the sky. We went outside in the spring to see the Comet Hyakutake, the "Great Comet of 1996" that won't be visible again for thousands of years. She looked at the stars with me. We looked at clouds and pointed out shapes to each other. On the way to the state ball tournament on July 19th, I said I saw a frilly little poodle and she immediately saw it too. We connected so much. She saw things I saw. She loved corny jokes just like I do. Nikki and Erin would say we hung around together too much, because we laughed at the same things while others just groaned.

❦

Casey always put a dot inside the C of her name. It was her trademark.

❦

October 5, 1996
I went on a long walk around the neighborhood. I passed two houses with dalmatians in the yard. Casey was going to name her dalmatian "Jake." I saw lots of houses decorated for Halloween and fall. Casey liked Halloween.

❦

October 8, 1996
Steve called me at work today and said he thought of us – you and me – when he walked into work this morning and saw the beautiful sky. The moon was shining and the North Star was "an arm's length away." He said he thought of us again when he was outside around one o'clock in the afternoon and noticed that the sky was pure blue with not a cloud in it. He said it must be so beautiful where you are and he's almost jealous. He doesn't want to leave me or his children, but he's ready to go. He said I had made him start looking at the sky. Looking at the sky. Remember when I always told you that's what you got from me? You always looked at the sky with me. I look at your picture that is in my eye's view when I work at my computer, and I smile at you. You're seeing the sky from the other side. I can't wait to see it with you. I really miss you, Casey. When I allow myself to think about your not being here, I can't bear it. You are in my heart forever and will be with me wherever I am. You left your little footprint there on my heart. I asked God to please let you know how much I love you, and I believe He's told me you know.

❦

October 10, 1996
Dear Casey, Last night I was reading Dr. Dew's book about his son
Brad. He said that after three years, he didn't remember exactly what
Brad looked like without looking at his picture. And he didn't remember
exactly how his voice sounded. That scares me.

I met with Ron Ingram, our pastor, yesterday afternoon. He just listens
and told me he'll always be here. He told me a lady whose son had died
told him it was two-and-a-half years before she felt like she was OK. But
he acknowledged that her child was older and "was not sleeping in the
next room" when it happened. He asked me if I still just want to go to
sleep, and I said yes. He asked me how often I feel this way, and I said
daily. He reminds me every week that other people need me around and
really love me. I know that. I wouldn't want to hurt them. But I do wish I
was with you.

I asked Ron what he thinks you're doing. I spend a lot of time wondering
what you're doing. He thinks in heaven you do what you like to do.

I told Ron I asked God to tell you I love you and I felt a real peace that
says, "I will" and "She knows you love her." I want you to <u>know</u> I love
you. I can't wait to see you again. I miss you. Stay with me.

October 10, 1996
Today I glanced up at your picture and thought about the freckles across
the bridge of your nose. They were so cute. And your eyes. You have the
most beautiful eyes. Even when you were a baby, everyone commented
about your eyes. So blue and clear. So big too.

I think about the times you'd go swimming at your dad's and come home
so sunburned. I worried that someday you'd get cancer. You won't ever
have to have cancer or any of those bad things.

October 14, 1996
Dear Casey, Yesterday Steve, Erin and I attended our second
Compassionate Friends meeting. Again, it was so draining but I'm glad
we went. I heard people express the same kind of feelings I have. I hurt
for them too. Someone said their child's name is like music to their ears,
although people around them may be afraid to say it for fear of upsetting

them. I, too, love to hear your name. I love to talk about you. I will always talk about you.

Someone said in the Compassionate Friends meeting that they built a special place in their home for their child's memory but then weren't able to even go in that room for awhile after they'd finished it. I have a very hard time going in the sports room. I helped fix it up, but then can't seem to go in it and look at your posters and trophies and shoes and jerseys and gloves. Someone else said they have a picture of their child with a candle beside it and light the candle whenever all the family is there. Another lady said she can't bear to look at her child's pictures, although she really wants to. That's a problem I don't have. I love to look at your pictures. I am so glad I have them.

Erin has lots of pictures of you on her entertainment center. I always look at them. She took a picture of you and her together to the Compassionate Friends meeting yesterday. She sat there looking at you and wiping any smudges off the frame. She said on the way home she just wanted to pass the picture around so everyone would see you and she wanted to spend the whole meeting time "just talking about Casey." She loves you so very much and is so sad. At the first meeting we attended, a lady was there who had lost her sister, and she and Erin had connected. This month Erin had taken your picture to show her, but she wasn't there. Her mother was though and she asked Erin if she could see the picture. That was kind.

Saturday I told Steve and Erin about a few days before the accident when you had told me you wanted some hot tamales. I bought a can of hot tamales and fixed them for your supper. You ate them, and then with a silly little look on your face said, "Mom, these were good, but I was talking about hot tamales candy." I will always remember that when I see a bag of hot tamales candy at the store or theater. If I could bring some hot tamales candy to heaven to you, I would.

❦

October 15, 1996
Dear Casey, I was thinking about you and how much you liked Halloween last night when Steve and I had gone out for a walk. I told Steve I want to ignore Halloween this year, go to a movie and just let it pass by. The night air and night sky felt like Halloween last night. Last

year you went to Becky Rich's house and trick-or-treated with her in her neighborhood. By the time I picked you up, your bag was loaded. You always – every year – let me have any of your candy I wanted. And you selected the Tootsie Rolls and gave them to me because you knew I liked them. You were always good to me, Casey. And in so many little ways. For Easter 1995 you gave me an Easter basket. That is the most precious gift I have ever in my life received. I burst into tears when you gave it to me. You liked that. You spent every penny you had on the basket and gave it to me. Casey, please know it is my favorite possession, even more precious to me than my stuffed monkey, Debbie. You are so precious to me. So very, very, very precious. I want you back.

I have the wooden flower box you made me for Mother's Day in 1995. It was special then but even more so now. I remember how you worked on it. I can still hear you hammering. Mr. Edmond remembers too. He told me he wanted to help but you wouldn't let him because it had to be just from you. You borrowed wood and nails and paint from him. I remember too that you got mad at Nikki and Erin because they bought me a flower box the following Christmas. You said they'd just stolen the idea from you.

Thinking of you making the flower box makes me also think of the time you and I put together the book shelf. You were really mechanically inclined. I couldn't have done it without you. We spread the pieces out on the driveway and put it together. And remember when we assembled our new vacuum cleaner? I couldn't have done that without you either. You don't even have to read instructions. You just know how to do things like that. I need for you to be here to help me put things together, Casey. And remember how you and Steve assembled Nikki's daybed this summer in the house she was going to be living in in Nashville while she went to summer school? Steve has mentioned that several times. You're just good at knowing how to put things together. So talented.

Another of your talents was your knowledge of snakes. I could ask you any question about snakes and you knew the answer. I'd get mad at you for not knowing or caring about spelling or English or the other "school" stuff, and then I'd remember about all the stuff you did know and care about. Somebody said something the other day about dalmatians being white at birth and then developing black spots. I didn't know that, and they said, "Don't you remember Casey telling us about that?" Erin gave you a leash, she told me, to walk the dogs in heaven. I can see you now.

Casey, I am sorry for fussing and scolding you about any bad grades you made in school – sort of. In one way I wish I'd never, ever said a harsh word to you, but in another way I'm glad I cared enough about you to expect the best from you. I was being a mom when I fussed at you. It never meant I didn't love you. You just didn't care as much about your school subjects as I thought you should. You probably had it right. Not me. I'm sorry I fussed at you.

You know something? You were just 14 but you went to college (with me), you played basketball on the Vanderbilt court (with Nikki), and you played high school fast-pitch (with Erin). Pretty good for a 14-year-old.

I was thinking about your braces. You didn't want them. Isn't it ironic that I put it off and you were supposed to go in on August 5th to begin the process? So you didn't have to wear them. You won that one, Little Girl. I always called you girls "Little Girl" when I was fussing about something or the other. You probably laughed behind my back. I hope you did. I wish I'd never fussed or raised my voice.

I miss you, Casey. – Love, Mom

October 17, 1996
Dear Casey, Erin and I talked about you for a long time last night. She had had a hard day. When we hung up, we had both laughed and cried. We laughed remembering all the things you gave us to laugh about, and we cried because we miss you so much and wish we could just have you back with us. We talked about how you were a religious person. You were really one of God's children who seemed, in looking back, to be preparing to go back and live in God's house. Your drawings, your writings, your wish to have a crucifix for your 13th birthday (which you got and kept hanging above your bed), the cross you always wore around your neck, the other crosses you kept neatly lined up in your room – so many symbols of your tie to God. I gave your crucifix to Granny, and she told me she put it above her bed. I gave the cross I carried with me to our pastor at the hospital that awful night, and he

said he would make sure it was with you. You wore your necklace, and I was assured your necklace and my cross would be on top of your ashes, with you. I think Granny had given you your cross necklace. I know it was very special to you. You wore it always.

At Erin's wedding, you looked so pretty. We laughed as we remembered that Erin insisted you remove all the band-aids from your leg and ankle that day because they took away from your beauty. You really did look gorgeous. I'll never forget when I walked into the church parlor and saw you. You were beautiful. Absolutely beautiful. Your hair was in a French twist, and Nikki had put makeup on you. You were stunning. Everybody thought so. I look at the pictures and see a glimpse of your appearance that was to come. I guess my most frequent pictures of you in my mind's eye, though, are of a little girl in a t-shirt and shorts. My little girl who was taller than I and so proud of it, but still my little girl. I love you, my little girl. I love you so much. – Love, Mom

❧

October 22, 1996
My Dear Little Casey, When Steve and I got married on Saturday, I felt your presence very strongly. I wanted you to be a part of it and I believe with all my heart that you were. While we were standing in front of the minister, I looked to my left at Nikki and Erin who were standing there beside me and I felt you too. I visualized you standing there with your sisters. I had thought that I couldn't get through the ceremony and I had prayed that God would be with me and help me – and He did, because He allowed me to feel you. I carried the Bible I had given you for Easter three years ago, and I had your pictures inside. I kissed them before we walked to the area for the ceremony. I had another picture of you inside my underclothes next to my heart. The sunflowers Erin, Nikki, Ginger and I held represented <u>you</u>. Steve and I took a sunflower and placed at the cemetery on Saturday morning. That was real hard and hurt. I feel so frustrated. Why did this happen? Why aren't you here with me? When I write this and say this, I feel so angry and frustrated and like my head will explode, and the tears burn.

Steve showed me on our drive to Kentucky that he had the little golfing bear that you had given him, in his pocket. I thought that was really sweet. He truly loved you, Casey.

Sunday night we went to a movie in Lexington. A few rows ahead of us sat a girl about your age, with a ball cap on and she wore glasses. It reminded me of you, and I couldn't quit staring. She was sitting with a boy about her age, and I felt just a sense of sadness that you wouldn't be doing that too. I remembered your boyfriend – Bret – and how we teased you (and you liked it). I saw you holding hands at the basketball game and remembered the way you said you'd kissed! I remember telling Nikki about that on the phone and her relaying it to her roommates. Her little sister had kissed a boy. No! I have a feeling that you would have been a knock-out, but still a little tomboy at heart. The perfect combination. In fact, you were headed that way. You were so beautiful.

When you were born, you were the most beautiful baby I'd ever seen. You had lots of dark hair. I remember a dream I had when I was pregnant with you. I was walking down the hall of a hospital. As I passed in front of the nursery, a baby girl raised up and waved at me. I knew you were going to be a little baby girl. I told your dad that. The baby girl in my dream had lots of hair and a ribbon in it. When you were born – and before I had seen you – Dr. Darling said, "This baby has so much hair, you'll need to put a ribbon in it." I couldn't believe he said that.

When I got up Saturday morning, I was combing my hair and it came back to me that I had dreamed that you were combing my hair. I would like to think you were helping me get ready for my wedding. I love you, Casey. – Love, Mom

October 23, 1996
Dear Casey, We are approaching three months since you left. I keep thinking of Thursdays and twenty-fifths of months. Those "anniversaries" are harder days than "everyday" days. You were also born on a Thursday, though. I went by your niche yesterday. Your sunflower I had left on Saturday was there, but it had fallen and dried out. I set it upright and kept looking at it and thinking about you. It would move a little – the wind, I suppose – but I felt like it was you communicating with me, just like I felt you did through the leaves at the Chimneys and the leaves outside the church window.

The second time I went back to church, I kept staring at a leaf outside the window. Only one leaf moved. It waved to me. It was like you waving to me.

I feel your presence very strongly, more strongly as time goes on. I like that. I was so numb at first I couldn't even feel God's presence. But that is growing stronger too. I took a walk at work yesterday just to get some fresh air and clear my mind some. I found myself crying, thinking of you, just as the tears sting my eyes as I write this. I ran into three friends who all expressed their care and told me they pray for us. Sometimes I have a real strong urge to leave behind everything I know and that was a part of life – <u>our</u> life. It just seems like it would be easier to be amid strangers. Then I wouldn't have to talk or respond or be caught off-guard by innocent remarks that make me think of something that hurts.

There are still some things I can't do. I can't go to ball games or to see Jennifer or to Petros. I've been in Oak Ridge some, but I don't like to be there. I can't go back by our house. I've told your friends Lesley and Brittney that I'll spend some time with them, but I dread it in some ways. I want them to be alive and happy and safe, but I want you too. It seems to underscore my loss to see your friends or even to see girls your age that I don't even know. I really want you back. I wish we could go back to this time last year. If you had to leave on July 25th, I wish the world had ended on July 24th and I could have gone with you and so could all the other people we love. Life is so different without you. I wasn't finished mothering you. I liked being your mother. I hope you know that. – Love, Mom

❧

October 24, 1996
When I awoke, I had been dreaming that I was on my stomach and riding what looked like an oversized skateboard (like the kiddie ride at Opryland). I was traveling faster and faster on my stomach on this board on the highway. I remember going through Oliver Springs and turning at the traffic light. I remember going faster and faster and faster. Then all of a sudden I was in Stephens, and I told Jennifer – I don't know where she had come from – that I hadn't been to Petros since the accident and I didn't feel like going on. I got off the skateboard and woke up.

❧

October 25, 1996
I woke up at four a.m. and couldn't go back to sleep. This is three
months today. I feel so strange on these "anniversaries." Three months.

❧

October 25, 1996
Dear Casey, You are so often on my mind. It's been three months. I
remember you just as though I saw you yesterday. I pray that God will
never let me lose that memory.

It seems that you were picked just when you were blooming. Like a
beautiful flower.

I saw an expression yesterday that seems so appropriate. It was in an
article about a little seven-year-old boy who had been killed in Italy. His
parents had donated his organs and that led to much more awareness of
the need to donate organs. It was called the "Christopher Effect" (I
think it was "Christopher") by his mother. I thought of the "Casey
Effect." That's the fun-loving, loyal, so-good-in-your-heart, everybody-
loved-you effect you had that still lives on and will never die.
"Everybody loved Casey." I've said that so many times. And I've heard
other people say it. What a girl you were. You affected and touched so
many lives. Babies, little children, your own age friends, grownups –
everybody loved Casey. Kristen carries your picture in her backpack.
D.J. carries the ticket stub from "The Nutty Professor" that you had
gone to see with him and his sister. I carry you in my heart. You will
always be a part of me. I love you so much. I will be happy to see you
again! Heaven is real. God is real. I will see you again. – Love, Mom

❧

October 25, 1996
Remembering. On Tuesday, July 23, 1996, I went out at lunchtime and
got Casey the Alanis Morissette tape she had been wanting. She was
really happy to get it. She wrote down some words to one of the songs
and gave to me while I was cooking our supper. It's strange that instead
of going straight to Granny's when I got off work and eating with her, I
had said to Casey, "Let's just have a chili bun here," and we did. While
I fixed the chili buns, her dad called and talked to Casey. She said they
were going to spend more time together. He called that evening, just out
of the blue. Twenty minutes later and we would have been gone, on our
way to Granny's. At Granny's, Casey helped Judy and Dickey Justice

put a freezer in Granny's kitchen. Judy is our much-loved cousin. Years ago, when Casey was a toddler, Judy had sewn little cheerleader outfits for the girls.

I remember that Tuesday night at Granny's, we watched the Olympics. Jennifer arrived. She had been at Roane State registering for classes. Casey had been watching the Olympics and listening to her Alanis Morissette tape through her headphones. She was happy when Jennifer got there. I remember Jennifer went into the bathroom, and Casey got in the closet next to it so she could scare Jennifer when she came out of the bathroom. Casey loved to do that.

On Wednesday, July 24th, Granny used Mozell's clothesline. Casey went with her. While Granny either hung up or took down the clothes, Casey sat on the porch and visited with Lawrence, Granny's brother. Lawrence is elderly and has bone cancer, but he stood in line at Weatherford's to pay his respects to Casey. When he finally reached me after at least an hour, he told me he had gotten to know Casey that day on the porch.

I went back to Granny's after getting off work on Wednesday, and Steve went with me. I took Casey another change of clothes because she wanted to stay longer, especially since Jennifer was going to be there. We ate supper with Granny, and then Casey and Jennifer went to the ballfield to play basketball for awhile. When Steve and I got ready to leave, we started up the road to the ballfield so I could tell Casey goodbye, but we met Casey and Jennifer in Jennifer's car coming down the highway. We all turned around and parked in the parking lot at Gunter's Store. Casey got out of Jennifer's car and came to me. We hugged and kissed goodbye. I still see Casey in red shorts and a t-shirt. What were to be my last words to Casey were "I love you." And her last words to me were "I love you."

The next evening, my brother Pat, his wife Rachel and their son Michael ate supper at my mother's. Rachel told me Casey was in such good spirits that evening. She and Jennifer were laughing and cutting up. Granny told me that for the two days they were there, she had not gotten on Casey or Jennifer for anything – and she was very glad that she hadn't. She had bought them strawberries. Casey and Jennifer and Michael played basketball at the field with a group of other kids.

Michael went home afterwards, but Casey and Jennifer apparently went on to Petros-Joyner School. Why? They were on their way back to Granny's from there when the wreck happened.

❦

October 28, 1996
Dear Casey, Today I was thinking about your games at the State Tournament just a week before this happened. You and I drove to Gallatin on Friday, July 19th. I can still see you riding in the front seat beside me. I really miss you in the car. Sometimes I reach over and pretend I can touch you. You and I spent a lot of time in the car. You named the car "Jordan." On our trip that Friday, you listened to tapes. I remember us looking at clouds that day too. It was a real blue sky with lots of puffy white clouds that we could imagine as various things. Our room at the Shoney's Inn in Gallatin wasn't much, but we didn't spend a lot of time there anyway. We got supper at Wendy's across the street and then went on to Hendersonville in a caravan with the other players for Kern Memorial United Methodist Church. You played a really good game that night, and Kern won. One of your coaches, Harold Harder (whom you nicknamed "Loafy"), had given you all hats with "Kern – We're On A Mission" on them. You wore yours and looked so cute.

On Saturday, the 20th, you played two games, both in the rain. Kurt brought Nikki to see you play. Kern lost both games, but you made a great play in the second game and scored. I made a picture of you running in to home, but I did something really stupid and lost those pictures by opening the camera and exposing them when I was trying to remove the unfinished roll. Your dad was having the pictures developed on July 26th, and I just unthinkingly pulled the roll out, something I knew better than to do. I wish I had those pictures of you.

After the second game that Saturday, you and I headed back to Oak Ridge. It rained all the way. We stopped at the Cracker Barrel in Cookeville for supper. I think we both had vegetable plates that included dumplings, but I know we had pie. You had lemon pie and tried to get me to eat some because it was sour. I remember we wandered around after we ate and looked at all the stuff Cracker Barrel sells. I remember we looked at a stuffed lamb there. When we got ready to leave, you asked me if you could drive, just out of the parking lot. I remember saying, "Now, like you think I'm going to let you drive!" You were always bugging me to let you drive. One time I had let you drive in the empty parking lot at TTU and another time in the empty parking lot at Willow Brook. So you got to drive a little anyway.

You had told me about a dream you had about my dad a few months before this happened. You asked me what he looked like, and I told you he looked a lot like you, with dark hair and blue eyes. Now you are playing ball with him. I know you are. I know he is so happy to have you with him. Two shortstops.

Baby girl – my K-K. I love you so! – Love, Mom

October 29, 1996
Dear Casey, I had the most wonderful idea yesterday as I drove home from work. After I am cremated, I want your ashes and my ashes to be taken together and spread at the beach. Hilton Head, South Carolina, or Pawley's Island, South Carolina, or Myrtle Beach, South Carolina, or New Smyrna Beach, Florida, are my choices because those are the beaches we were on together. I love this idea because you said <u>we</u> would live at the beach someday.

Oak Ridge Memorial Park is holding niche #77 for me (next to you). We won't need that, though, since I've had this other idea that really makes me feel quite happy.

You know, Casey, I had never ever thought about you or Nikki or Erin going to heaven before me. The service for you was really <u>my</u> service – what I wanted done for <u>me</u>, not you. I wish with all my heart it had been me, that the service had been for me, that the accident had been me – not you.

We'll be on that beach together. I love you! – Mom

October 29, 1996
"I pray to Him and He responds through the people He has placed around me. . . . I've experienced peace through the prayers of others and I've seen God actually answer my prayers through those people." –
Dave Dravecky, pitcher for the San Francisco Giants

I like this. It's how I feel. When I thought I just couldn't go on, I thought, "I don't <u>have</u> to do this myself. There are so many people praying for me. They're taking care of me." God was always there. I seemed to shut down, like there was a curtain between me and God. I found it hard to talk to Him, and I didn't much feel His presence. But I knew others were praying for me. So many people told me that. Then, later, I felt like God had really hurt too that Casey was in an accident. He hurt for me too. This comforted me. I felt like the unending rain from the night of July 25th until the next Thursday were God's tears for us. Somewhere along the way I felt God again. I know Casey is with Him, and they're with me. I love you, God. I love you, Casey.

October 30, 1996
Dear Casey, Yesterday when I got home, I had received a letter from Becky Rich. It was a real sweet letter, and she had sent me a Freshmen Basketball schedule and asked me to come to a game. She had sent messages from Lindsay, Brandi and Eliza too. I was so deeply touched. She told me "who was going with who" and about high school. I miss you so, Casey, and the letter somehow underscored my loss. I could not look at the basketball schedule.

I went by your niche at the cemetery before I went home. Yesterday was a real hard day. As I drove, I thought, "This should not have happened!" That really frustrates me. I can't change it. I want you back. I want this time last year back. I want my little daughter back. I want my little daughter who had grown into a teenager so full of life and fun back. I want you with me. <u>This</u> is where you should be. Then I think of times I've been told not to use "should." I don't know the right "should." Only God knows. For now, I can only feel you <u>should</u> be here with me. That's what I want with all my heart and soul.

When Steve and I were at the UT football game Saturday, I saw a little girl two rows in front of us. Her hands reminded me of yours, and I couldn't quit looking at her. I sit in the seat you sat in last fall when Steve took you to the Homecoming game. I sit there and think of you. I just felt sick the whole time. Our friends we tailgate with were so nice to me, but I just felt sick. I didn't want to be there. It didn't feel right to be there. Nothing feels right.

My mind is full of pictures of you. I think of the way you pointed your finger, scrunched up your nose and closed your eyes. I think of the way you'd stand tall beside me and call me "Shorty." I think of the way you always read cereal boxes while you ate cereal. I think of the way you liked to find the hidden pictures in the Mini-Page section of the newspaper. I think of how good – no, excellent – you were at working puzzles. That always amazed me. You could work a huge puzzle when you were just a little bitty girl. You were so good at that.

I remember one evening not long ago when you and I went to LaSalle Park and shot basketball. You made fun of the way I shot, and I said I was going to go home if you continued to make fun of me. So you told me to go ahead and shoot my way, but you still laughed at me. We had fun that night. You were much better than I. You were good at every sport you tried. You liked to go to the ballfield behind Willow Brook Elementary School and play "rolly bat" after supper. We had fun there too. I wish I'd gone every time you asked. We flew kites there too when you were little – probably five or six years old. I remember you would cry and get mad if I let a lot of string take the kite too high. You were sure it would snap and be gone forever.

Willow Brook Elementary School. That reminds me of the time we went there on a Friday morning to watch Nikki and Erin's assembly program. You weren't in school yet. All the little kids were gathered around you after the program, then they returned to their classrooms and somehow in all the hubbub we lost you. I was frantic. I ran out to the parking lot. Mr. Walker, the principal, announced on the intercom that we were looking for you. Everybody was looking for you. As I ran back up the steps to the front of the building, a child on the second floor was pointing to the fire hydrant beside the shrubbery. There you sat – perched on the fire hydrant looking at one of your little books you'd taken with you. It was the little book that had a fuzzy pink poodle on the front. (Why do I remember that?) That's such a scary and funny memory. I can still see you. I love you. – Love, Mom

🍎

October 31, 1996
Today I was listening to a tape of an interview I had done at work. I could hear a thunderstorm in the background. The date of the interview was June 12, 1996. You would have been attending the Lady Wildcats

Basketball Camp that day, or it might have been your last day of school. Seems like it was your last day of school because school didn't get out as early this year as normal due to all the missed days because of snow. I think that Wednesday, June 12th, was the last day. That would have been the day the school got to go to the Oak Ridge outdoor pool. You went. I had given you a new swimsuit and coverup for your birthday, and you wore the swimsuit. It was navy and white striped, with a yellow Tweety Bird on front. You never wore the coverup. When I was going through your things, I noticed it still had the tags attached. Erin took it to keep. I don't know if you didn't like the coverup or what. You never said anything about it.

You were a little waterdog when you were little. You weren't afraid of anything – once you got past the summer I enrolled you in ACAC swimming lessons and you screamed and hated it so that I talked to the lady instructor and we decided to withdraw you from the class. You must have been three, I guess. On your own, you loved the water – just not swimming lessons. Later, when we lived in Cookeville you completed a swimming course at the pool at the apartments where we lived. You were six then. I think Erin has the little card you received. When you got older, you lost interest in swimming. You said it was because you couldn't see. I could relate to that. Without glasses or contacts, you're kind of in your own world at the pool, and it's not a lot of fun. When you were between roughly six and eleven, though, you liked to swim. You went to your dad's pool most Sundays. You'd come home so sunburned, and I'd get so mad. I can still see your little red face. It made those huge eyes of yours look like pools of clear blue water themselves.

When I began this letter, I was thinking about how you liked storms. I remember us sitting on the porch or standing at the door or window and just watching it storm. You were never afraid. You liked storms – just like me. You know, the only thing I ever saw you afraid of was for a short period of time when you were two or three you were afraid of airplanes, or the noise they make. You could be outside playing and a plane would fly over and you were frantic to get inside the house.

Thinking about when you were little . . . you got a little black dog for your birthday when you were three. We got it from Yvette Roberts. We named it "Barkley." You loved that dog. One day he got out of the yard and ran away. He was gone for awhile, then out of nowhere he appeared on the patio. Then sometime later he left again and we didn't see him anymore. Someday I'll write about your other dog, Shay. Someday we'll have to talk about Shay.

This may be strange, but yesterday I looked in the mirror and searched my face for traces of you. I guess our personalities were more alike than our looks.

I love you, baby. Happy Halloween. – Love, Mom

❦

November 5, 1996
Sometimes I can look at Casey's picture and it takes my breath away. I can't believe what happened and that she is not with me.

❦

November 5, 1996
Dear Casey, Today is November 5, 1996. I was sitting here trying to work, and I just kept thinking about when you were in the fourth grade at Willow Brook and played the bass fiddle in the school strings orchestra. That was so very funny. We had just moved back to Oak Ridge from Cookeville and you had started the fourth grade. Of all the instruments in the band, you chose to play the bass fiddle. It was much larger than you. Your strings teacher was delighted that you wanted to play it. You were the only one at Willow Brook who did. The school system owned the instrument and you could take it home on weekends to practice. That's what was so funny. Every Friday afternoon I would pick you up from ECC (Extended Child Care) at school after I got off work, and we would struggle to get that bass fiddle in our little Honda. It took up the whole back seat. Then on Monday morning, back we went to school with that bass fiddle – except this time Nikki and Erin were in the car with you and me and the bass fiddle. Gosh, that was a wonderful time. You were so cute playing it.

You had a concert one time, and I paid you five dollars to wear a skirt for it. When you walked in, all the kids said, "Look at Casey! She's wearing a dress!" You were so embarrassed. After the concert, Ms. Damiano, the teacher, laughingly told me she understood she owed me five dollars for getting you to wear a dress. I guess you had told the kids, and they had told her.

I don't know if the novelty of the bass fiddle wore off or just why, but you decided the strings orchestra was not your thing.

When you got to Robertsville Middle School, you joined the chorus. You seemed to enjoy singing, and you were in several programs. For one, you dressed in a long pioneer-style dress and wore your hair in a bun. We had rented your dress from the Oak Ridge Playhouse. I remember you wore my brown granny-style boots. Those were the boots you always made fun of. I wore them often and you'd see me and start humming the music from the "Wizard of Oz" that always played when the wicked witch was onscreen. They had sort of pointed toes so I guess that's why you thought they looked like witch's shoes, not that you thought I was a witch. Anyway, you wore them for the performance.

I love you so, Casey. You made my life so happy. I wish I had done more to show you how very very much I loved having you in my life. I hope you knew. I really miss you so very much. I can't let myself think about my sadness for long because I don't think I can stand it. So I go on. Life with Steve and Nikki and Erin keeps me going and is good. But sometimes I feel like I'm just living until I can die and see you. Life is so different. It's so up and down. I can be OK one minute and <u>not</u> OK the next. Sometimes I think I'm pretty strong, but sometimes I don't think I'm as strong as other people might think I am. If I had ever imagined life without you, I would not have thought I could go on. But I am going on. How am I going on? God is keeping me going on, and He is using Steve and Erin and Nikki to help me. I don't understand much of anything anymore. I know you're OK though. That really helps me keep going on. I just wish I could see you and talk with you and hug you and kiss you and never let you go. – Love, Mom

☙

November 8, 1996
Dear Casey, Sometimes I can almost pretend the accident didn't happen and that you're just away for awhile and will be home soon. Sometimes all I can think about is the accident. Sometimes I do nothing but think of you. Sometimes I just cry. Sometimes I just look at your pictures. Sometimes some of the memories are more than I can bear and I have to let it go. Sometimes I'm afraid I'll wake up during the night. Sometimes I can't look at places we've been together. Sometimes I don't think I can stand it. Sometimes I think I see someone who resembles you. Sometimes

I think about picking you up from all those practices at Robertsville. Sometimes I can't think of those times because it hurts too much.

Yesterday I was talking about you with a friend. She said that when I talk about you, she sees you in me. That made me very happy. Always be there, Casey. I love you, little girl. – Mom

❦

I remember getting so MAD the first time I went to buy flowers to place at the cemetery. I left the store without buying anything. I looked at sunflowers and had almost decided what I wanted you to have, then I just felt furious that you were dead and I was buying flowers to take to your niche at the cemetery. I got so mad and upset. I just left the store, without flowers.

❦

November 11, 1996
Dear Casey, Today I was talking about you with a friend at work and something was said that struck a chord. My friend said something to the effect that all of this is a puzzle but that someday we'll know how the pieces all fit. I just thought of how you were always the best and fastest puzzle worker I'd ever seen. You beat us to seeing how the puzzle fits. I've told Nikki and Erin several times that you just beat us to heaven. You always wanted to do everything first and be the fastest. You just beat us there. This is like that – you solved the puzzle first. You know more than we. You are literally seeing God. You have answers to some things that we only have questions about. You will be the person who can tell me so much when I see you again. I'll bet God will say, "Casey, here comes your mom. Why don't you sit down with her and tell her all the wondrous things you have learned!" I'll be learning from you. I'll be so happy to be sitting with you again. Just the thought of seeing your precious face and hugging you again fills my heart with joy. And we will never ever have to be apart again.

I dreamed of you again. Like every dream I've had, you were just there and it was natural (except for the one dream I had that upset me because I was the only one who saw you). Steve has said that my dreams of you allow me to spend time with you. I love that thought. In this dream, you were telling me about a room you were fixing up for me. It was sort of like the minister's sermon from the week before where he talked about God preparing a place for us. Well, you were telling me of the room you were fixing for me. I love that dream. I loved hearing you talk to me. I love you, little girl of mine. – Love, Mom

P.S. A lady at Compassionate Friends told me yesterday that her priest said heaven would be boring without teenagers.

November 12, 1996
Dear Casey, Today I read something that was of comfort to me. "Whatever heaven is and wherever it is, Jesus believed in it, and I think He knew something I don't know." I think of you so many times during the day and night. I really believe in heaven and I really believe you are there. That helps me. I want you to be with <u>me</u>, but what better place could you be? I think so many times of how it will be to see you again. I want to see you first. I'm sure God/Jesus will understand that. I love you, little Casey. – Love, Mom

November 15, 1996
Dear Casey, I went to see Jennifer on Wednesday. Today is Friday. I haven't written you because I've been very hurt, angry, confused, unsettled. I didn't want to convey that to you for some reason. This probably sounds strange. But, anyway, it was hard for me to write you. I didn't feel like I could. It's certainly not because I didn't think of you. I think of you constantly. Good thoughts. Happy times. Sad memories. Sad thoughts. Always of you. I look at your pictures beside my computer and over my desk and on my desk tons of times each day. I love you so much. I miss you so much.

Last night Steve was standing in the bedroom and when I walked through the door, he stuck his hand out and scared me. Just like something you'd do. I told him he'd get paid back. Just a short time later, he was painting the bathroom and he called me to come look at the ladybug perched on the mirror. Then a short time later he called me to come help him clean up the mess he'd made because his paint bucket spilled. It was all over him, the cabinet, the floor. He said that was his payback from the ladybug (you) for pulling a joke on me. That was <u>your</u> area of expertise. I loved it that the ladybug – a real ladybug – was there. I loved it that your little spirit was in that ladybug. We talked about how you were probably laughing. I can just imagine that you *were. I loved that feeling. Love you, baby. Love you, my little girl. Love you, K-K. Love you forever – Mom*

On November 13th when I went to see Jennifer, I was really nervous. During all the months she was in UT Hospital after the wreck, I visited regularly. But I had never gone into the room to see her. I just always sat in the waiting room. And I prayed for her. Honest, from the heart, appeals to God to please heal her and let her live. When she was finally able to be moved to a rehabilitation facility, I decided it was time for me to see her. To talk to her. For her to talk to me. I didn't know how the conversation would go. Dr. Friedman, a psychologist at work with whom I met regularly, suggested that I prepare myself for how I would react if she cried, if she was upset, if she asked me to forgive her. And so I did that. I was prepared to tell her that I knew she would never have hurt Casey on purpose. But I didn't get a chance to say that, because the one reaction I hadn't prepared for is what happened. She said nothing about the wreck. Nothing about Casey. So I didn't say anything either about the wreck or about Casey.

November 19, 1996
Dear K-K, This past Saturday, I spent the whole day going through your backpacks from the seventh and eighth grades. You hadn't cleaned either of them out. Surprise! You were such a little packrat. I loved looking at your "stuff," and I learned even more about you. I especially loved the journal you had kept in one of your classes. It covered December 1995 - February 1996. I loved reading that I was one of your heroes. You were and are one of mine. I hope you know that.

You had so much stuff. I even found a dollar bill, folded as you always did, and four quarters here and there. I'm sure that was four times you forgot to return the change. I'd always give you two dollars each morning for the bus and lunch, and you'd give me back a quarter at the end of the day. I found a funny story you'd written about leaves growing out from under your fingernails. I found a story you'd written about how Brittney was your "bestest" friend. You had doodles and drawings on everything. I don't think a single piece of schoolwork lacked a picture of some kind. You were really something, Casey. I love who you were.

I was so engrossed in looking at your things and reading your papers that hours flew by and I didn't even notice. When I started to pack your things in a box, that's when the anguish hit me. I should not be doing this. This should not have happened. It breaks my heart and I feel like I can't stand it. I want you here, with me. I wish I could change this. I want you here, Casey. I want you back. I want to go back to last November and for time to stand still <u>there</u>.

Today as I passed by the cemetery park on my way to work, I looked toward your niche and I felt such a sense of sadness. Such a sense of THERE'S ABSOLUTELY NOTHING I CAN DO TO CHANGE THINGS! Such a sense of WHY DID THIS HAPPEN? Such a sense of WHY CASEY? WHY NOT ME, INSTEAD OF CASEY? CASEY HAD SO MUCH LIVING TO DO!

I remember a time last spring that was so much fun. You and I and Steve were playing cards. You and I ganged up on Steve and made fun of him for complaining about something. You were so funny. You got a Magic Marker and drew tears on your face and my face. You made little mustaches for us to wear, like Steve's. You talked about writing graffiti on his truck. We all laughed so much. You were so clever. After Steve had left, I told you that you were really good at that. And you were. That was a specialty. You were clever and sharp as a tack. And so funny.

I love the happy memories you gave me, Casey. Thank you for those. Thank you for being my little girl. Thank you for being a part of my life that was one of the very best parts. You will always <u>always</u> be a part of me and a part of my life. As long as I am alive, a part of you will be alive. I love you. I miss you. – Love, Mom

P.S. Remember how we called you "Casey Louise"? You'd even answer to that. "Casey Louise."

November 26, 1996
Dear Casey, On Saturday, I brought Brittney and Lesley home with me and we spent the afternoon talking about you. I thought I would die driving to Brittney's. The only times I ever went to Brittney's were to drop you off or pick you up. Pulling in her driveway and seeing the rope hanging from the tree that you used to play on, the trampoline that you

spent so many hours having fun on, the basketball goal you shot so many baskets at, the fields around her house where you spent so many fun-filled days – all the thoughts of you crashed in on me. Brittney loved you so. My heart aches for her. She lost her best friend. She said she told her dad that she wanted to go hunting, and he told her she could ask a friend to go with them. She told her dad she didn't have a friend anymore who would do that. She told me that her dad had let you and her shoot his guns, with his supervision of course. She said you had a good aim. I hate guns, so I guess that's why you never told me you'd shot a gun. I would have had a fit. Yet, now, I'm glad you got to do that. I'm glad he let you. Erin told me that you had told her about shooting at targets and cans.

Brittney told me she had put some clown band-aids with you at the funeral home because you two loved clown band-aids. That just broke my heart. I knew she had written a note, two notes actually, and placed beside you, but I didn't know about the clown band-aids.

I gave Brittney the little angel ceramic box I had given you this past Valentine's Day. I also gave her two of your crosses and your sunshine earrings. Someday when I can go through more of your things, I'll give her more. I know you'd like that and she'll take care of whatever it is forever.

Brittney told me again of the way you wouldn't ride her four-wheeler the last time you were at her house. She said I had told you to not ride it, so you wouldn't – even though Brittney said she tried to get you to because I'd never find out. I was so proud of you, Casey. I am proud of you, Casey.

I can just see you running in the fields next to where Brittney lives. Even Brittney's house doesn't look the same anymore though. The fields, or trails, where you rode go-carts are growing up because the land is for sale. The trampoline looks deserted. Brittney said it's been a long time since she's jumped on it. Remember how you went home after school with Brittney in fifth grade? She lived at her grandmother's then. You called her grandmother "Nanny" too. You had a ball there. I'd come by after work to get you and you'd be dirty or wet from head to toe. And you loved her dogs. Those were good days, Casey. I wish we could go back to them.

Lesley told me of some mischief you and she got into together. Lesley said Erin Hinton told her she shouldn't be telling me of stuff like that. I don't care though. As long as you didn't get hurt or hurt somebody, I'm glad you were lively and playful. I know Ron Ingram told me that the stories I told of your mischief made him love you even more. I told him about how all your teachers at Robertsville at one time or another called me in for a conference because you talked too much. You were apparently the class clown. Even the teachers said you were funny, you just disturbed the class though. Every one, without exception, told me what a great kid you were and how much they liked you – but could I get you to quiet down during class? And please speak to you about turning assignments in on time?

All the stuff you did only endears you to me that much more. You really lived. You were a good person, but not a goody-goody. I really liked you. I ask God to let you know that I love you. – Love, Mom

November 26, 1996
Dear Casey, Yesterday was hard. It has been four months. I haven't seen you in four months. This whole situation was unthinkable until four months ago. Now it's all I seem to think about. It was unspeakable, yet now I speak of it. It was unbearable. It still seems unbearable, yet I am bearing it. How can I bear losing you? Only with God's help, and even then it is <u>very</u> hard. I love you, baby. I miss you. – Love, Mom

December 4, 1996
Dear, dear, Casey, There is this great big part of me that is missing, and it is you. I love you. – Mom

December 9, 1996
Casey, my little Casey, Sometimes I feel utter despair. I miss you more with every day. And with every day I feel what in some ways feels worse. I can't stop thinking of how this just couldn't have happened. We should be going to your ball games. We should be together. I miss you. I miss our life. You were my very life, Casey. I didn't even know how much. I knew I loved you dearly, but I never ever thought you wouldn't be with me. I guess I never really knew just how much my heart and soul revolved around you and Nikki and Erin. Now you're not here for me to see and hear and hug. I want so much to see you and hear you and hug

*you and never ever let you go. I love you and will love you forever. –
Mom*

❧

December 13, 1996
*Dear K-K, It's not Christmas without you here. I thought this morning of
you spending your first Christmas in heaven. I wonder what that would
be like.*

*Steve has bought me a locket to wear that I will put the locks of your
hair in. I intend to put that locket around my neck on Christmas Day,
and I will wear it every day for the rest of my life. Then it can be placed
on the top of my ashes in my urn for the trip – with your ashes – to the
beach where we will be scattered together. I have told Steve and Nikki
and Erin of my wishes for us to be scattered together on the beach, and
they have agreed.*

*I think of you so very often. I see you walking into the kitchen wearing
your purple pajamas with feet. I see your long hair and I see you
wearing your glasses since you just got up. I hear you saying, "Hey," or
"What ya doing?" I see you pouring a bowl of cereal. You loved cereal.
Waffle Crisp was your favorite, but I think you'd eat any kind of cereal. I
miss buying cereal. You liked tacos and Petro's and pasta in a can (like
Spaghettios and ABCs) and salsa, Happy Meals and Chicken McNuggets
from McDonald's, rainbow sherbet from Baskin Robbins and Slushies
from Weigel's. You liked eating at the Hungry Bunch with Granny. You
liked Alice Springs chicken at the Outback. You liked pizza. You prided
yourself on eating hot peppers, the hotter the better. You liked Gatorade
and Kool-Aid and any of the fruit drinks that came in individual glass
bottles. You liked Toaster Strudel. You really weren't a picky eater.
You'd eat about anything I cooked.*

*I remember when you were seven, eight and nine you loved fried
chicken. For your seventh birthday, when we lived in Cookeville, we
invited the family to come to our apartment for your birthday party. It
was a Sunday and I fried chicken all morning. You ate nine chicken legs
that day! We laughed so many times about that. For your birthday that
year, you got an aquarium and angel fish. It was really a pretty
aquarium. You were pretty good about taking care of fish. You won a
goldfish at a carnival at Sycamore Elementary School that year. It was*

one of those fish in a plastic bag that usually dies before you get it home. Yours lasted forever! You wanted some of those little newts that look like miniature dinosaurs. We checked them out, but I vetoed the idea when I found out we'd need to put glass or plexiglass over the top of the aquarium because the newts could crawl out.

I remember one day in Cookeville you were outside playing with a dog. I asked a lady who was talking with you who the dog belonged to. She said it was your dog. You had told her it was yours! She didn't know you were my little girl and that you were just <u>wishing</u> it was yours. I have pictures of you playing with a dog on our front porch. You had put a rope around it and dragged it up the steps, then put lawn chairs around the entrance to the porch so it couldn't get away. You'd cover it up and lay down with it when it took a nap.

I can still see you playing at our apartment in Cookeville. Riding your little bike. Swinging. Swimming. Playing with any animal you could corral. The second summer we were there, in 1990, you played softball for the team sponsored by Woodmen of the World. You were the catcher. I hated that. I was afraid you'd get hurt by somebody's bat. Why is it that you and Erin always liked catching? It just scared me to death. You were <u>so</u> cute in your little uniform. Lime green and white pants, shirts, socks and hat.

We moved back to Oak Ridge when you were in the fourth grade. You really liked fifth grade because your teacher, Ms. Stevens, had snakes in the room. You and Brittney were the animal helpers. You loved that. I remember you talked about Felicia, Monroe and Elvis (the snakes) all the time. Sixth grade was when you went to Robertsville. You hated seventh grade, mostly because you hated your Spanish class, but by eighth grade you were at the top of the world and seemed really happy.

Oh, Casey. My heart hurts so. I wish this hadn't happened. If only I could have you back. – Love you forever, Mom

❦

December 13, 1996
Dear Casey, I came across something today that referred to an explosion that had almost deafened one of the engineers where the accident happened. It made me think of when you were in first grade. I

was sent a note that suggested I have your hearing tested because the screening at school indicated there might be some problem with your hearing. I made an appointment with an audiologist. I can still see you in his booth, raising your hands when you heard a sound. The audiologist, after testing you, said he found nothing at all wrong with your hearing. That was great news. You said something really funny on the way home. We were driving along and all of a sudden you asked, "Did you hear that?" I said I didn't hear anything, and you said, "That's exactly what it sounded like!"

That makes me think of another first grade story. You had a few bumps on your arm or something, and Gail said maybe it was chickenpox. I didn't think so, so I sent you on to school. The teacher called me to come and get you because you said your aunt said you had chickenpox and she was a doctor. (Gail worked in the pharmacy at the hospital at the time.) So you stayed home for a few days with the "chickenpox," which I didn't think was the chickenpox. Two years later when you were in the third grade, you <u>really</u> got the chickenpox. You were covered this time and there was no doubt about it. I remember getting you little things to entertain yourself with. That's when I gave you the little journal to write in. I found it this summer with your things. What you wrote, that I can read, is precious beyond words.

Casey, I see you with chickenpox, and I see you raising your little arms in the hearing booth. I will always see you in my mind. I pray the Lord will always let me see you in my mind until I can see you with my eyes again. I love you, my precious, precious little girl. – Love, Mom

❦

December 18, 1996
Dear Casey, I have many good people in my life, but I feel empty without you in it. I don't want to ignore or not appreciate all I have left, but often, so very often, I only think of what I have lost. I would be very happy with life if only you were here. I feel so angry sometimes that you were here for only 14 years. You should have been 100 before you left. That's what I think. That's what I wanted. I wanted you to grow up and be an oceanographer or vet and live somewhere where you could have all the animals you wanted. I wanted to see you as an adult, to see your children, to die myself before you did. I don't understand why this did not happen as I dreamed and hoped it would. I know with all my heart

that you are with God and that makes me happy, but why couldn't you have gone home to God later – much later? I see God as our Father. I see you as His child – but my child too. I wish God would have let you stay with me longer. Why didn't He? It hurts me so.

I have been thinking of you so much. Today the thought of lambs made me cry. You knew my favorite animal was a lamb, and you encouraged that. You told me when we stopped in Cookeville on July 20th on the way home from the ball tournament that you were going to get me a lamb for Christmas.

Casey, you are my little lamb. When I pray, I often ask God to tell you for me that I love you so much. – Love, Mom

My favorite Bible verse is Isaiah 40:11. "He tends his flock like a shepherd: He gathers the lambs in his arms and carries them close to his heart; he gently leads those that have young." I think this is such a beautiful verse. You are a little lamb that God has in his arms, close to his heart. And I am a mother God gently leads.

January 8, 1997
Dearest Casey, I know this is the first letter to you I have written this new year, and the first in several weeks. Getting through the holidays without you was very hard. I couldn't seem to write. But you were always in my mind, always in my heart, always in my very soul. Many times I've wished I could just go to sleep and wake up months later with amnesia. Then I wouldn't be sad or hurt or feel so just uncaring. I just can't seem to care about anything. I go through the motions, but inside I feel hollow.

Many things happened during the time I didn't write. I went to Mom's (Granny's) house the Sunday before Christmas – by the back road so I wouldn't have to see where the car wreck happened. I could see you in her house. I could see you hiding in the hallway closet to scare someone coming out of the bathroom. On Christmas Eve, Steve and I went to Chattanooga and passed the day. We went to a movie that night. We had all of downtown Chattanooga practically to ourselves. It was really sad. I felt really sad. I took an extra Tylenol PM so I wouldn't wake up early on Christmas morning. I just wanted to sleep and not be aware or remember past Christmas mornings when my little girls made Christmas so happy. I thought about you all the time. I really miss you, Casey. So very, very much. On New Year's Eve, Granny came to spend the night. She loved you so much. We sat at the kitchen table and just cried. I felt closer to her that day than in a long time.

Last Saturday Nikki and Kurt and Steve and I went to the Smokies. I stood at the rocks in the Chimneys and saw you having such a good time there, climbing the rocks and crossing over the creek to the other side and yelling for me to come over. I was crying and Nikki came over to me and said, without my having said a word, "I see what you do. Casey would have loved this." The night Nikki came home from school for the holiday break, she and I sat in the kitchen and talked and cried into the early hours of the morning. She struggles to deal with losing her little sister "K-K." Erin and I have always drawn from each other. We talk of you every time we are together or on the phone. I don't know what I'd do without her. She helps me so. She was so very crazy about you. On Christmas Day, she told me she believes you were an angel sent to earth. Casey, your two sisters loved you dearly. When the three of you were little, Nikki and Erin fought with each <u>other</u> – but both loved <u>you</u>. It will be such a wonderful, wonderful day when we're all together again.

We had a Christmas tree just for you this year. Every year we're going to add a special ornament. This year I got you an angel that has "Dear Daughter" engraved on it. Steve put the dalmatian ornament he had bought for you last year, that we keep in the curio cabinet now, on the tree. Nikki put a bird in honor of that silly bird you always put on the tree, Erin and Brad put a tiger because it just looks like something you'd like, and Ginger sent an angel she had engraved with "Casey - Our Angel." Of course we put your mouse on there too. I never looked at our Christmas decorations, never even opened the box – but somehow that silly mouse was out, just like its purpose was to go on the tree forever, even this year. When I had gone to our house in Oak Ridge after our things had been moved out and I had moved to Knoxville, that silly little gray mouse was lying in the yard. I guess it had fallen out of a box during the move. I picked it up because I knew it was yours.

I love you so much, Casey. – ❤ forever, Mom

☙

January 9, 1997

Dear Casey, Do you know that in my office I have the picture you drew years ago of Clifford the dog, the modern artwork you did, the Valentine you gave me that says "I love you very much" on the back, and six pictures of you? I hope I told you that I've had these things for years, in whatever office I've worked in, because they are precious to me. If I didn't tell you I had parts of you in my office – and that I always have – I hope you know.

Today I was thinking that someday I want to write a book about you. I think I'll call it "Heaven Is Much Closer to Me Now."

Life does not have the meaning it once had for me, Casey, since you are not here with me. You really impacted my life, Casey. I didn't even know how much. I think of how I felt when my dad died in 1974. It hurt so much. I think of how I felt only last spring when my best friend Kathy died. I thought I couldn't be sadder. But, although I loved my dad and Kathy so much – very, very much – it does not compare with losing you and how I <u>long</u> to see you and hear you and hug you. When I think of seeing you again, that makes me so happy. What a wonderful wonderful day that will be. I must believe and live as God wants me to because I want to see not only Him but you too. I know you are with God, Casey, and I know you are safe – one of His little lambs. I love you, baby. – Love, Mom

January 10, 1997

Dearest Casey, I need to get some blue flowers to take to your niche to replace your Christmas tree. I went by last week to replace the tree with sunflowers, but the red looked so good (there are lots of red ribbons and flowers at the park) that I didn't want to remove the tree with its red velvet ribbons. You loved blue. We should have something blue. Your favorite color. Actually your favorite shade of blue was cerulean. I remember the exact color because you pointed it out to me one night. It's the deep deep blue the sky gets sometimes before dark.

You know one thing you taught me was not to be afraid of death. Thank you for that, Casey. I always kind of had the creeps about it, even though I believe in God. You taught me many things. It's good not to be afraid of death. My eyes water up when I think about dying and getting to see you again. I can imagine saying, "I get to go see my little Casey!"

I looked at your bridesmaid's dress in the closet. I can see you in that dress. You looked so beautiful. So much older than normal. You had the prettiest eyes in the world. Sometimes I wonder if they took your contacts out. I am so glad you were not buried. I could not stand to think of your body in the ground. I could not bear that. When we receive our new glorified bodies at resurrection I'm sure God will manage to scoop all our ashes up. I'll be cremated too.

I have a new necklace. It's a locket and I have locks of your hair inside. I intend to wear it every day of my life. Maybe I'll give it to a little granddaughter named Casey if we get one, or maybe I'll leave instructions to put it on top of my ashes, like your crosses are for you.

You loved crosses. I gave Brittney some of your crosses. She was very pleased. She said she has a brush with your hair in it, and it's special to her. I have a special love chest, a cedar chest, for your special things I kept. Your other clothes and stuffed animals, after Erin and Nikki took what they wanted, we gave to Goodwill so some other children could benefit from them. Your bikes I gave to Mr. Edmond. He'll see that someone who could enjoy them will have them, I know. Your Jesus on the cross that you wanted for your 13th birthday, I gave to Granny. She has it over her bed, just like you had it over your bed.

I'm sitting here looking at your picture. You had really pretty eyebrows. Freckles on your nose. A face that was becoming oval-shaped. You were scheduled to go to the orthodontist on August 5th to get fitted for braces. Bet you're chuckling over not having to go. You're so pretty. But your heart and character were even prettier. A beautiful, beautiful child of God. I can imagine God introducing you and saying, "This is Casey, my daughter, and I am so pleased with her."

This is how you drew your suns: (upturned lips with curls) Your artwork was great. You doodled on every piece of homework and every piece of paper in your path.

There are so many things I love about you. I miss you. I love you. – Mom

❧

January 13, 1997
Dear Casey, I miss you so much! I've thought of you many, many, many times today. I can't get you out of my mind. Not that I would even want to though. Erin and I went to Compassionate Friends yesterday afternoon. Today I was thinking about the group there and replaying in my mind the circle of parents in the group. I could envision replacing that circle with the children that all of us represent. It would be a great circle of children. Both sexes, all ages. In December when we all brought pictures of our children and set the pictures on a table and lit a candle in front, it struck me what a good-looking group of children you were. So full of life. So much left of lives to be lived. Such promise. All cut short for various reasons.

Yesterday we sat next to Richard and Jean Dew. In the circle I envisioned, you would have been sitting next to Brad Dew. I'll bet he would have liked you and you would have liked him. He loved sports, fishing, his family, his friends – just like you. And his parents love him so much. Just like we love you. Perhaps you've met Brad in heaven. I hope so. You two could talk about us, like we talk about you. I thought of other people in the circle. Maybe you've met Mary Lee Hitch, the Wamplers' daughter. She'd love you.

It's strange how the world really is a small place. Brad Dew's grandfather and Mr. Edmond, who I sort of view as a surrogate grandfather for you, were fishing buddies. I remember how sad Mr. Edmond was when his fishing buddy died. And I still see the hurt and tears he shed over you. But you'll see each other again. The two people I'd stake my life on going to heaven are you and Mr. Edmond.

I love you, little girl. I love you so very much! I miss you. – Love, Mom

❧

January 15, 1997
Dear Casey, I had been dreaming about you when I woke up this morning. I was so peaceful. You were a baby and I was giving you a bath. I can still just see your little head. In my dream you were about six months old. I tried to go back to sleep and dream more, but I couldn't.

Drats! (You pretended to hate it when I said "Drats!" – so I said it all the time.)

Yesterday I went to UT with Erin to find all the buildings she'll have classes in this semester. She is doing great in school. I am really proud of her – just as you always were. She goes to school, works, and now she and Brad are buying land to build a house. It's a beautiful piece of property.

We were talking yesterday about you, of course. For some reason, Erin remembered the little red shirt you wore when you were little that had two pockets on it and the time you had grapes in one pocket and diced onions in the other. You'd reach in your pocket and eat whichever you wanted, a grape or an onion. We just laughed about that memory.

Another thing I was thinking about was how much you liked Michael Jordan (basketball), Troy Aikman (football), Steve Avery (baseball) and John Michael Montgomery (music). You also had gotten to really like Alanis Morissette, the singer. On the Tuesday before the accident, I had stopped on my way home from work and got her tape for you, which you played and played. You wrote down some of the words to one of her songs and gave to me. The song was "Isn't It Ironic?" I'll keep those words forever. In some ways, that was ironic.

You also liked "Beavis and Butthead" on TV. I couldn't stand that and fussed at you for liking them. You liked "Saturday Night Live" on TV too. You especially loved the Spartan cheerleaders (Craig and Arianna) spoof. You and Elizabeth Polfus mimicked the cheerleaders perfectly. You were so funny. You'd say: "Who's that Spartan (fill in the blank)?" "It's me, it's me." "Who's that Spartan (something that rhymed with the first line)?" "It's me, it's me." Then, in unison, "Uh-huh, uh-huh. Uh-huh, uh-huh, uh-huh."

And you liked "Nick at Night," cartoons, football, basketball and MTV. You loved "The Lion King" movie. One movie that you watched over and over through the years was "Wizard of Oz." You also liked "Beetlejuice." Actually you saw several movies during July. You, Steve and I went to see "Independence Day" (you sat with Sara Harder at the *theater, almost on the front row); you and I saw "The Nutty Professor" on July 11th; and you, Steve and I saw "Phenomenon" on July 21st.*

Erin reminded me not long ago of the way you and I did our "Bullwinkle and Rocky" routine. You did one voice and I did the other. You loved it too when I would tell you stories about my monkey, Debbie – "Debbie stories" – and you'd beg me to do Debbie's voice. I made up stories about Debbie and her little red-haired friend named Sabrina. You loved those stories. We did that a lot when we lived in Cookeville.

Someday I'll write down the story of Ko-Ko, your big stuffed panda. I'm not sure how you spelled it. Now, I can hug Ko-Ko and almost feel you. I love you, K-K! I really miss you. – Love Always and Forever, Mom

January 16, 1997
Dear Casey, When I left work the afternoon of July 25th, my desk calendar with an inspirational saying for each day was turned to July 25th. When I returned to work a little over two weeks later, it was still sitting on July 25th. That's where it remains today. I've never felt any desire to move it forward. Maybe, symbolically, time ended for me on July 25th too.

The saying for that day was: "We are not at our best when we are perched at the summit; we are at our best climbing – even when the way is steep."

I keep climbing, Casey, but the way is so steep. I can't undo what happened to you. The summit doesn't exist anymore. Just enduring and hurting and crying, but climbing all the while – to not go down or backwards any farther. Just to get through the pain, through my life, without causing others to hurt or suffer any more than they do, because of me. To try to help Nikki and Erin get through their pain. To try to be a good Christian. To get to see you again and to thank God in person for loving us and taking care of you and of me too.

Casey, right now I am feeling such anger. Maybe I can call on the example of your goodness toward others to help me work through this.

I love you, my little girl. I miss you so. Sometimes I feel like I can't breathe when I think of how I miss you. – ♥ Forever, Mom

January 21, 1997
Dearest Casey, Tomorrow I have a dental appointment with Dr. Ruyl. I
dread going there so much because I was rarely at his office without you
being there too. You always looked for the book "Popcorn" in his
waiting area. When you were little, I would read it to you while we
waited. Then when you could read yourself, you'd always read it.

I love you, Baby Girl. I miss you so much and in so many ways, in so
many settings, every day of my life. Casey, this does not seem real. – I ❤
you, Mom

January 23, 1997
Dear Casey, I went to Dr. Ruyl yesterday for a cleaning and checkup.
The magazines had been straightened up in the waiting room, and there
on top of everything was "Popcorn" by Frank Asch. It must have looked
funny for a 44-year-old woman to be sitting there reading that little
book, but that's exactly what I did. And I thought, "This is for you,
Casey."

The story is about a little bear named Sam. His parents went out to a
Halloween party. As soon as they left, Sam made himself a costume and
called up all his friends to come over for a party. He told them all to
bring a snack. So, as it turned out, everyone brought popcorn. He put it
in a big kettle and popped it. There was so much popcorn that it filled
the house. All the friends ate and ate till they couldn't eat another bite.
Sam finished off the last bite, the friends left, and Sam went to bed.
About that time, his parents returned home. They had brought a surprise
for Sam. Popcorn!

Casey, someday I'll tell that little story to your nieces and nephews, and
I'll tell them why it's so special.

Last night I finished reading "The Christmas Box." Linda Mrochek
Jones gave me the book last week, because she said it reminded her of
me. Actually, there are more similarities than she could even know. The
mother lost her little girl, Andrea, and grieved for so long until at the
end of the story she died and got to be reunited with Andrea. The mother
wrote love letters to her little girl and placed them in a special box, the
Christmas box, and took them to Andrea's grave. On Andrea's

tombstone was engraved "Our Little Angel," just like on yours is "Our Little Ladybug." And I put your letters in a special box too. The story stresses that love was the first Christmas gift. God sent his Son whom He loved very much so that all of us could return home to Him, where He wants us. I just want you back with me. But since we can't do that, I'll just remember what David in the Bible said about how his son couldn't return to him, but he could go to him. So, someday, I'll come to you. That will be such a wonderful, wonderful day.

Last night Erin was telling me about her new classes for this semester. She said she'd had to write a paper in English class about a place. I asked her what she wrote about, and she said she wrote about your funeral at our church. That makes me so sad.

Little Casey, I love you so much. I will love you forever. – Always and Always Love, Mom

January 27, 1997
Dear Casey, My heart aches so and sometimes I cry that I just can't stand this. There is a sadness inside me that reaches to the very depths of my soul. I can't describe in words how the loss of you <u>feels</u>.

Yesterday in church while the minister prayed, I just closed my eyes and imagined leaning on God's chest with His arms around me. Somehow I seemed to <u>feel</u> God say, "It's OK. Casey is with me, and I'm taking care of her." That made me feel peaceful. Yesterday, I didn't think I could go to church. Friday, January 24th, was a tough day and night to get through because I couldn't stop thinking about it being six months since I had seen you and kissed you for what I didn't know at the time would be the last time. I sat in the living room and held onto Ko-Ko until early in the morning. I stretched out on our couch and tried to remember you lying there, right outside my bedroom door, all those times. But the couch doesn't even feel the same anymore. Nothing, no matter how hard I try to imagine it or will it, feels the same anymore. Nothing. Saturday, the 25th. Six months time has passed, but it feels like just yesterday to me. Sunday, the 26th. Six months since the day we were making funeral arrangements. Six months since I went shopping to find you socks and underwear to wear beneath Erin's uniform that would be the last clothes you wore. Now it's Monday, the 27th. Six months since Weatherford's *and feeling "I can't do this!!! Casey could not die!!! Not Casey. Please, God, not Casey!!!!!"*

Last year on January 26th, you were so alive and happy and excited. It was the Robertsville Middle School vs. Jefferson Middle School basketball game played in the high school gym. It was the night I made the picture of you that now sits on my mantel and in the school's trophy case. They're retiring your number and jersey tomorrow night in a ceremony dedicated to you. I feel my heart will break. Please, God, let this not be real. I love you, Little Ladybug. – Mom

❧

January 28, 1997
Dear, Dear Casey, Tonight Robertsville is going to honor your memory at a ceremony during the basketball game. That is just a sign of the impact your life made, Casey. You were loved and respected by so many, many people of all ages. I thank God that He let me be your mother. I want to be there for the ceremony, but I just can't do it. My heart will be there, just as your spirit will be there. Steve and Erin and your dad will be there. I've worried that you would be disappointed if I didn't go, but now I know you understand. I feel in many ways that my spirit has joined with yours. So although we won't be there physically, spiritually we will.

You are my little girl, my youngest daughter, and I miss you so. Sometimes I glance at your pictures in my office and the force of the loss takes my breath away. It just lasts for an instant, and then an incredible sadness fills my whole body. I just feel so sad. Months ago I could be crying but saying words at the same time to try to make sense of the whole thing. But now I don't even try to say words to try to make sense of this. I just feel sad. I have flashes of anger at whoever or whatever caused that car to hit that tree. Why did that happen? Why? But most often what I feel is just sad. Robertsville should not be retiring your number. You should be ALIVE and wearing it. Running up and down the basketball court. Alive. Alive. I love you, Casey. – Forever, Mom

❧

This is a transcript of the ceremony at Robertsville on January 28, 1997: *"This evening the Robertsville Middle School Lady Rams basketball players and Coach Jamie Petrie would like to present a memorial to Casey Shelton, a member of the Robertsville Lady Rams basketball team from 1994-1996.*

"Casey was a happy-go-lucky Robertsville student who was a leader in every sense of the word and demonstrated enthusiasm for everything that she did. She was born on June 3, 1982, and died July 25, 1996, in a tragic automobile accident. Casey's picture, the basketball jersey she wore at Robertsville Middle School, and a plaque will be placed in the trophy case at Robertsville in Casey's memory. The plaque reads that Casey was a friend, student, and teammate – a winner on and off the court.

"The arm bands worn by the team members this year are in memory of Casey. Last spring, Casey became a member of the Oak Ridge High School Lady Wildcat Freshman Basketball team and is now on God's team."

❦

February 5, 1997
Dear Casey, When I look at the date, I think back to February 5, 1982. I had an ultrasound that day. I was pregnant with you. I "saw" you that day for the very first time. You, of course, were teeny-tiny but nonetheless alive and well. It was so exciting! I looked at that ultrasound picture only a few days ago. I believe I can see your little face.

I haven't written for a few days. I have been having such a hard time. I am so sad and troubled. I just don't understand why this had to happen. Why are you not here?

More and more now I want to know details and how the car wreck happened. This is what a newspaper account said: "According to Tennessee Highway Patrol reports, Jennifer was driving a 1988 Toyota Tercel north on 116 about a mile from state Highway 62 in Petros when the car went out of control on a curve, went off the road and hit a tree.

"Kerry Osborne, a Morgan County Ambulance Service paramedic, said this morning that the accident happened about 9 p.m. He said the car slammed into the tree and the passenger side of the car wrapped around the tree in a U-shape. Both girls were trapped in the car for about 45 minutes, he said."

You were an innocent child. Why did you have to die? Not you, Casey. Not you! – Mom

❦

February 10, 1997
Dear K-K, I read today that a remembered joy is a stabbing pain the
first time you remember it. Sometimes I will remember something about
you and I have to stop the memory because I can't go any further with it
because of the pain. Today I could just see you as my little six-year-old
in your tiny little blue jeans and green pullover knit shirt. "I can't go on
with that memory," I think, but really it does continue on and in my
heart. I want every *memory of you I can possibly have, even if my heart*
hurts and I feel so sad. That's worth the picture in my mind. So, please,
pop in anytime, my dear little girl. Please don't ever let me forget
anything about you. Let me see you in my mind. Please ask God, for me,
to never take my precious memories of my precious little girl. I love you!
– Mom

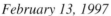

February 13, 1997
Dear Casey, Today as Clyde and I interviewed a Ph.D. weapons
engineer at work, I could not focus at all on the interview because you
were so on my mind. I was remembering random things about you.
Thinking about the balloon I'd get this afternoon to put on your niche
for Valentine's Day. Thinking about the way you looked last summer –
so lanky and with such long pretty hair. Thinking about the way you
looked as a little girl. Seeing you *and not seeing much else around me. I*
started to take a piece of paper out and just start writing you a letter
then and there, interview or no interview. But I figured I should pay
attention to the interview as best I could.

At one point, the interviewee told about something he'd done in the
1950s that's still around. I made the comment that he had left a mark.
He liked that. Then I thought of how you left a mark. Only 14 years old
and loved by so many, many people. Respected. Looked up to. I cannot
wait to see you again. I just don't dread dying anymore at all – all
because of you. I will spend my time on earth as God plans, and I don't
want to be away from Steve or Nikki or Erin, but I so *want to see you*
and be with you. That's such a wonderful, peaceful, HAPPY thought. I
love you, Little Ladybug. I miss you so much. – Love you forever and
ever, Mom

February 17, 1997

Dear Casey, Feelings of "I cannot stand this!" wash over me and I don't know how I can bear this. Casey, little Casey, why did you have to go? I would have gladly, happily, willingly died if only you could have lived. What would we do without God and our faith that you really are OK, even better than we are? I see pretty things sometimes and want you to see them. The only way I can deal with the sadness is to believe that you are seeing even prettier things.

Last night I dreamed that I had taken you to school late and the teacher made you sit in the hall. I awoke in such a sad state of mind and am still trying to shake it. When I took my shower this morning to get ready for work, I couldn't seem to stop thinking about all the times you got hurt. The times you really did have to sit in the hall at school because you'd talked in class or done something to disturb the class. I don't think you cared; in fact, I think it was a badge of honor for you to be sent out of the classroom, the way you and Liz and Lindsay and all you girls talked and laughed about when you'd all get in trouble at school. Maybe the dream just upset me. I don't want to think you ever got your feelings hurt. But I know better. I wish you'd never ever got hurt.

Yesterday I was thinking about if I could just have you back I would never take my eyes off you. I would keep you right beside me. I would be so happy. When I think of someday seeing you again, I cannot imagine the joy I will feel. I want to see you, Casey, so much that I think I cannot stand this! Casey, I do not understand why you were in that accident. I cannot believe that this time last year was our last February together.

Yesterday as Steve and I drove back home from Ginger's, I saw a cloud in the shape of a buffalo and I just started to cry because I thought of how you would have seen the buffalo too.

Steve and I put a big red heart balloon on your niche for Valentine's Day. It says "I love you." We put it there on February 13th right before dark and in the rain. What a sad sight we must have been. How sad I felt. But how happy I felt to kiss and hug the balloon and release it enough to float. How happy I felt to think, "Casey will like this."

Right before we got the balloon, we had stopped at the Sagebrush and ordered a salad. While we waited for our food, the basketball team came in the restaurant. Seeing those girls broke my heart. You should be there! You should be part of that team, not part of God's team. (Forgive me, God, but I know you understand my heart.) I left and went to the car while Steve got the salads to go. If only my tears could bring you back and undo that terrible night in July. If only this had not happened.

Steve went in the store and got the biggest, reddest, shiniest balloon they had. We drove to the "park." I remember thinking "I can't stand this!" I can't even stand to say the word "cemetery." That's why I call it the "park." I can't stand to think of my little girl's ashes being there. Why, God, why? I wish with all my heart and soul that God had let the accident be me, not you. There was so much life ahead of you. So much to do. You were just beginning to bloom. Why, God?

Casey, stay in my heart. Stay in my soul. Stay in my thoughts. Stay with me forever. I cannot bear to let you go. I love you so much. I can't even tell you how much I love you. Of all the little girls in the whole world, I'm glad I got you. – Love, love, love, Mom

❦

February 17, 1997
Dear Casey, I don't know whether I wrote you about this or not, but a few weeks back in church, I closed my eyes and imagined standing in front of God with my head on His chest and His arms around me. That was the most peaceful feeling. But the best part was when I felt God say to me, "She's OK. I've got her. She's with me." Casey, you can't imagine what that did for me. You are with God. You are OK. You are alive with God.

Now, when I feel so bad, I use that memory to help. God has you. I love you so much. – Mom

❦

February 19, 1997
Dear Casey, The world is a better place because you lived in it. You made me, as well as many others, happier because of your goodness. You developed your character and you developed your soul in 14 short years – a character and soul that surely pleased God. I hope I can be as good as you, Casey. I want to be as good as you. You had so many fine

traits. Your heart was so tender and so caring. You were good to
everyone. You didn't talk bad or ugly about anybody. You were not
caught up in material possessions. You were just happy to be alive.
Happy to help others. A wonderful example for us all. Casey, I am so
glad you are my daughter. You will live forever in me. I only wish I
could see and hear and hug you. I can in my mind, in my memories, and
I do all the time. Months ago I was so worried that I would forget
something about you. Now I don't worry about that. My memories just
keep getting sharper.

I love you so much, little girl. I really miss you. – Forever, Mom

☙

February 20, 1997
Dear Casey, For some reason today I was remembering how much you
loved playing with little figures or figurines. You always did. Even when
you were very little, you could amuse yourself for hours playing with
little animals and people and stuff. You had quite a collection. Erin has
kept them.

You gave everything a name. How you remembered all their names, I'll
never know – but you did. You'd line them up, tell me what you'd named
them, then quiz me to see if I could remember. Of course I never could –
which you thought was funny. You had tons of little animals and all the
stuff that went with them. One little cat I remember in particular. Its
name is "John," and it doesn't belong to any set. It was just a single
little tiny pink cat that you seemed to have forever. John is real special
to me now.

When we lived in Cookeville, you had a rabbit's foot collection. You got
them from the quarter machines in K-Mart and places like that. When
I'd be all stressed out about an upcoming test in school, you'd give me a
rabbit's foot to carry – which I did. I don't know where all those little
rabbits' feet are. I really wish I did. Thank you for doing that, Casey.

We used to call you "Baby Luck" because when you were little you
seemed to always bring luck to whoever you were teaming up with when
we played games. We'd say, "Casey, give us some baby luck."
Occasionally even after you got up to the ripe old teenage years, we'd
still ask you to give us some "baby luck."

You were the most beautiful little baby. Big blue eyes and a head of dark hair. So beautiful. I can still see you especially wearing a tiny little yellow dress and then again in a little red sleeper that you crawled around in. Casey, you seem like a dream to me. You were here and then gone. Not long enough. Not long enough. I love you! – Mom

February 25, 1997

Dear Casey, my little girl, It was seven months ago today. In some ways a lifetime ago; in other ways only yesterday. The weather has been warm for a week, with flowers already blooming and frog sounds filling the air. You liked that. It reminds me of you, but it makes me sad that you're not here to hear and see. I just try to remember that you are seeing and hearing far more beautiful things. Still it's sad to me.

I don't look forward to spring. That's when you played fast-pitch and slow-pitch last year and should have been playing this year. I avoided basketball this winter – not watching it or reading anything about it. The thought of ballfields makes me feel so sad. I want to see you playing ball. <u>I want to see you</u>! Are you playing ball with my dad, your grandpa? I remember the dream you told me about – that you were playing ball with my dad, your grandfather. I told you that you look like him – dark hair, blue eyes, a similar forehead. He must be so very happy to have you there. That is a happy thought for me. I read a story yesterday about a doctor who lost her newborn child but she "saw" her father in heaven welcoming the little one to heaven and holding his hand. I would imagine you had many special people, and angels, on your journey too.

Casey, I miss you so. I still can't believe this happened. I wish it could have been me instead of you. I would give my life for you without even having to think about it.

I hope you know how much I love you and how glad I was and am to be your mother. I love you, Ladybug.– Love always, Mom

February 27, 1997

Dear Casey, I spent a long time last night looking at pictures of you. There's a picture of you when you'd just turned one year old. I can look at that picture and remember how your chubby little cheeks felt and how you smelled that wonderful baby smell. You were such a beautiful baby and you grew into such a beautiful teenager. I know you were going to be an absolutely beautiful young lady. Even more beautiful on the inside than out, if possible. And I loved that about you.

I could hardly look at pictures of ballplayers in the backgrounds of some pictures we had made recently. I feel such a flash of anger and despair that you won't get a chance to go on. "Why? Why?" my heart screams. Please don't let this be real.

I looked at pictures of you walking in the ocean and on the beach with your sisters. Such perfect sisters. Such a good life, in spite of obstacles we had to overcome but did. You never asked for anything, either as a little girl or as a young teenager. Casey, you were such a caring, good, decent person. I truly appreciate that you made my life simpler, not harder.

I remember when you were six or seven years old and you sang a really, really funny version of "John Henry." You'd make your voice so funny when you'd say, "Lord, Lord." We'd all laugh at you. You'd get requests all the time to sing that song, and you always would.

I think of the funny blue Converse tennis shoes you wore. They were too big and looked like clown's shoes, but you liked them.

I think about the time I came home from work and you wanted me to open the mailbox. You'd put the cat inside. I remember how you "wore" that cat draped over your shoulders. You went through a period of loving boots and hats when you were around three or four years old. We have funny pictures. Thank goodness for our pictures.

Today I was thinking about your birthday. Someday I wanted to take you horseback riding because that's what you wanted to do. I would give anything if I'd made that happen for you. I also wish I'd taken you to Gatlinburg. You told me one time you'd never been there. I didn't realize that. I think you had before you could remember it, but maybe not. That hadn't occurred to me. I wish I'd taken you there. We would have done that probably last Christmas. I am sorry we didn't go there, Casey.

I'm really glad that you and I had the chance to be together at the two state softball tournaments. Our trip to Columbia in July 1995 and then our trip to Hendersonville in July 1996 are precious memories to me. How could you be playing ball one Saturday (July 20th) and be at Weatherford's Funeral Home the next Saturday? How? Why? Why did this happen? I can't do anything about this. If only I could undo this.

Casey, I love you so much and always will. I miss you. – Love, Mom

❦

February 28, 1997
Dear Casey, Today I was talking about you with a person at work. I told how you planned to be a vet or oceanographer and to build us a place at the ocean where we could live. I remember horses being in that scenario too. You know something, Casey? When you told me that plan, I could see it too. I could see us doing that. Wouldn't that have been grand? Maybe you would have grown up to want to do some other work and to live in some other location – but I loved your dream, your plan. I love it that you included me. It was a little girl's dream that sure made her mom happy. You made me happy, Casey. I loved being your mother. I <u>love</u> being your mother. I will always be your mother. You will always be my little girl. You will always be a part of me.

Today I ran across the expression "fierce and fragile" in an article I was reading. I like that expression. It describes you, and it describes me.

I think about you all the time. I wonder what you're doing. I miss you. I love you. – Mom

❦

March 3, 1997
Dear Casey, I was just thinking about this time last year. I remember on March 4th that you, Steve and I went to Padgett Field in Knox County to watch Erin's first fast-pitch scrimmage game. I can still see you there. You were really a fan of Erin's. Remember the times you and she would throw the ball to each other? You said she threw so hard – which really impressed you even if it stung your hand.

I feel so . . . I can't even think of a word for it . . . when I think about you not being here to do the things – like playing ball with the high school team yourself – that I know were in your future. I really miss the life you *gave me. I miss you and our life so much. I want you back, Casey! I want you back! I want you back! How can I bear this? If I truly didn't know that you are in a wonderful place and that I can be with you again, I don't know what I would do. I don't know sometimes now how I am living with what happened. I would never have thought I could. I remember telling you that I would die if anything ever happened to you. I <u>said</u> that to you less than two weeks before the accident. Why haven't I died? I really wouldn't mind at all. Losing a child is said to be the worst thing that can happen. It is. It really is. All I really want now is for nothing to happen to Nikki and Erin. That's all that really truly matters to me. If I can make it through the rest of my life without losing them, life will have given me what I really want for the remainder of my days after losing you.*

For some reason your friends have been on my mind. Brittney, of course, was first with you. You met in fourth grade and became big buddies. Your friendship survived Brittney's moving several times and going to different schools. I remember both of you saying that you had never, not once, even said a cross word to each other. That's <u>so</u> neat. You always had a good time with her, whatever you were doing. You got to do things with her that probably otherwise you'd never got to do. You raced on go-carts, jumped on trampolines – and Brittney told me last fall that her dad had let you shoot a gun, and that you were a good shot. You'd never told me about that. Good thing! Brittney's dad took you and Brittney fishing and hunting too. You liked that.

Saturday I was in Wynn's Sporting Goods with Steve, and I thought I couldn't bear being in that store. I was fine until I wandered into the fishing section. I was flooded with memories of how you liked to fish. Remember your tackle box? Your fishing rods? Your fishing hat that I pinned lures on? The way you laughed when I caught a tiny little fish and swore I'd never do it again? The time you cast your line but hooked my arm in the process? You and I went fishing on your 13th birthday. And we went fishing on another of your birthdays too – I think it was your 11th. I'm really glad we did. I hated fishing, but I'm really glad you and I went fishing. Thank you, Casey, for so many happy memories. You made life good. You made it fun. Thank you for being my little girl. Thank you for being a part of me and for sharing a part of <u>you</u> with me. You will always be a part of me. Always. You were really neat.

Back to your friends. Liz Polfus had become your best Oak Ridge friend in the last year. She had just moved here from Seattle, and you two had so much in common. You even looked alike. You also liked Becky Rich a lot. And Stephanie and Lauren Lawson. And Lindsay McGinnis and Brandi Jordan. When you got to play softball for Kern in the spring and summer, you got close to Lesley Kelley. The first boyfriend you seemed to like quite a bit and who gave you your first kiss (I think) was Bret Hudson. Before him, Trey McDonald was the boy of choice. I remember when you were in nursery school, you said your boyfriend was Nathan. You called him "Nafan" though because you couldn't say Nathan then.

You liked older people too. Mr. Edmond next door taught you a lot about nature. You liked Granny's little lady friends too. You liked your dad's friends, especially Baxter Underwood. When you were little you called Baxter "Friend" like that was his name. And you liked James Powers. When Steve came into our lives, you grew to really care for him. He would have been your step-dad.

Casey, you are always in my heart and in my thoughts. I love you. I miss you. – Love and Hugs and Kisses and Tears, Mom

❦

March 4, 1997
Dear Casey, Last night while I was cooking supper, a story about the Oak Ridge Lady Wildcats basketball team came on. Coach Prudden was interviewed, as well as players, and footage was shown of several games and practices. I could feel hot tears rolling down my cheeks. You should be there! You would have been there! Why, God, why? Why did this happen? Why were you taken away? Was it a terrible tragic accident that just happened, that even God grieves for? Or was it predestined that you would be here 14 years and that on July 25, 1996, you would be taken back home to God? I don't understand. I don't know. I only hurt. There are no words that express the sadness of my heart. I want you back so much. I want to see you grow up. I want you in my life. I wanted to die before you. Maybe I am selfish, but I don't care. I want you back. I hope God understands the anguish I feel when I say I don't care what His plan is – I only want you back. My mind knows that can't be, but in my heart I will cry till the day I die that I want my Casey back. – I will love you forever, Mom

❦

March 4, 1997
*Dear Casey, I closed my eyes today and a picture of you crawling
around pretending you were a dog popped into my mind. "Spike" was
your dog name, and your best friend Jessica's dog name was "Fudge."
The two of you did that all the time for about a year. I remember we
lived in Cookeville at the time, so you were probably seven or eight. You
even told people you wanted to be called "Spike." You wrote that name
on papers and even painted a visor with that on it as your name. The
knees of your little blue jeans were worn from your crawling around
acting like Spike the dog.*

Casey, you were really funny. I loved that about you. – ❤*Mom*

March 6, 1997
*Dear Casey, This morning I awoke from a dream about you. You were
wearing your hair in braids and you had on your Lady Wildcats softball
uniform. You looked exactly as you do in one of my favorite pictures of
you taken on your last birthday. You were showing me a removable,
wash-off tattoo you had on your hand above your thumb. You had to
leave though. That was the feeling I got from the dream. You were
showing me the tattoo but you had to go. I was kissing you and hugging
you. I awoke from the dream and cried. It was about three-thirty a.m.*

*I couldn't go back to sleep for a long time, but I must have dozed off
because I dreamed about you again. This time I walked into the living
room and you were lying on the couch watching TV. There were two
dalmatians there beside you on the floor. They were lying on quilts and
they were big dogs. I walked to the doorway and said, "Steve, look at
this." I then asked you where you got the dogs. You said they were just
there. You got up and the dogs got up and started walking around. Until
they started walking, I thought they were stuffed animals.*

*I was thinking just yesterday about how it seems like I'm just biding my
time until I can die. I guess I am depressed. I want to be around for
Steve and Nikki and Erin, but at the same time I feel like I'm just waiting
to die, and that's really OK with me. I can laugh sometimes and joke
sometimes, but life just doesn't feel the same anymore. It used to be easy
to say life is for living and we should try to be happy. I don't feel much
like that anymore. A couple of days ago someone at work told me that I*

show a lot of strength. I don't feel strong. I feel sometimes like I could just break in two and dissolve, and I really wouldn't care.

This morning while I was taking a shower getting ready for work, I was thinking about when you were little and I had laid out your little red shorts and the white top with red polka dots, a flower on the collar and a ruffle around it. I'll never forget how you brought the shirt to me in the kitchen where I was, threw it on the floor, and said to me, "I have told you many times. I do not wear spots, ruffles and flowers!" That was so funny. You were so cute.

Oh, Casey, my little Casey. You brought such joy to my life. I miss you so. – Love always, Mom

❦

March 10, 1997
The feelings I have, trying to understand how this accident happened, just get worse as they sit there. It's been almost eight months, and I'm no closer to understanding how. Maybe if I could understand how, I'd get a better grasp on why. More time passes. No contact. Waiting for the State Trooper or the County Deputy to do their investigation into the rumors I hear from my mother and sister. Rumors or truth? Was Jennifer run off the road? What do I believe? I DON'T KNOW! This bothers me so. If I could only know. However it happened, the result is the same. Casey is gone. But this part of the puzzle could be laid in its place. Dear God, please let me know. I know I lost Casey. I know that. May I please know how it happened? I lost Casey. I lost my home. I lost the life I had known. I lost my daily job of mothering. I lost the desire to live. I lost the relationship I had had with my mother and sister. Can I please have this much? Please help me.

❦

March 11, 1997
Dear Casey, Last night right before I went to sleep I thought of you, and it almost literally took my breath away. I cannot believe you are gone from my sight. On Sunday at Compassionate Friends a mother said it would not surprise her at all to see her son walk right through the door. I understand that feeling. I have it too. In spite of "accepting" some facts, I still would not be surprised to see you walk right in the door too. How I wish! How I can almost believe that might happen. The memory of you that flashed before me was of you standing in the hallway outside

your bedroom, wearing your t-shirt and shorts, long hair not pulled back this time in your familiar ponytail but instead just loose. (You must have just washed it.) Casey, I can see you. I can feel you near.

Last summer when I was meeting weekly with our pastor, I told him about watching and listening to you sleep at night during the ball tournament just days before the accident. He said maybe you're now watching and listening as I sleep. What a beautiful thought. It made me cry when he said it, just as it does now as I recall it.

Casey, I want to tell you that I am so sorry for every cross word or hateful thing I ever said to you. I am so sorry if I ever hurt your feelings. I always <u>always</u> loved you with all my heart, and I will never stop loving you. Yesterday I was reading a newspaper article in which the writer described her frustration in not knowing <u>how</u> to respond to her 16-year-old daughter who could be so sweet at times but so moody and hateful at other times. Should she ignore her? Let her know her behavior was unacceptable? Argue back? Have a heart-to-heart? Suggest she talk to someone else? She said she did all of these things at various times, and sometimes <u>all</u> of them within the course of an hour. She didn't know what the right thing was. She said a wise person told her to keep doing what she was doing – <u>all</u> the things she was doing. It showed she cared, I guess was the bottom line.

I guess I too felt the same way sometimes with you, especially since you hit that 12-to-14-year-old phase. I did all of those things too, wondering all along if what I was doing was right. I remember on our last Sunday together, you were sort of cranky for awhile and my response was to ignore you, that you'd get over it. Was that the right response? I don't know. It doesn't feel right now. I only hope you knew I loved you. I know you loved me. How can I tell you how much I love you? I will close my eyes right now and send some of my love to you. I believe you'll feel it. –
❤Love forever, Mom

March 12, 1997
The best way I can think of to describe how I feel is that sometimes I go down and touch bottom. I will rise to the surface again, my head will emerge that is, but the biggest part of me will still be underwater. That's the way I imagine it will always be. The only thing that would allow me

to get out of this horrible pool is for time to go back and for this not to have happened. Right now I feel like I'm on the bottom and struggling for air.

❦

March 18, 1997
Holidays. In February, we exchanged Valentines. You made Valentines for me when you were little, then when you got older you selected a special one for me from the box you bought to give to your friends. I still have, on my desk, the Valentine with the little lion (from the Lion King collection) on the front, and on the back you wrote, "I love you very much. Casey Shelton." I laugh when I think about how you signed your full name, like I wouldn't know which Casey. I always gave you a "Daughter" Valentine and a little gift. The last gift was an angel Mud Pie ceramic box that you kept your earrings in. Now I just dread Valentine's Day. It's not special anymore.

In March or April, we celebrated Easter – our favorite. You were my little nature girl. I guess that's why we loved Easter so. You decorated the trees with Easter eggs. One year you slept in your sleeping bag in front of the sliding glass door that opened onto the deck, hoping to catch the Easter bunny. One year you threw your hat, purse and gloves down on the ground because you didn't care for such finery. You were not even two years old yet. So many memories. How can I make it through Easter without <u>you</u>? Erica Casey Shelton. Casey. Casey. Casey.

❦

March 21, 1997
Dear Casey, I just read: "What is a friend? A single soul dwelling in two bodies." It's attributed to Aristotle. You are my friend, my little girl. I feel in many ways our souls are one. I miss you, Casey. I love you. You have part of our soul; I have the other part. Maybe that helps explain why I feel a part of me is missing. – Forever, Mom

❦

March 24, 1997
Dear Casey, Erin has painted a beautiful, beautiful birdhouse for you. She painted ladybugs all over it and hot-glued some others. It is so cute. I hope you know about it. We also have a flower pot that sits in a watering can arrangement. We're going to take it to the park for you.

Casey, I miss you so much. It has been eight months today since I have seen you. I miss you more and more every day. Today I was just walking down the hall at work, and I thought about the time you ate so many chicken legs at your birthday party. Memories like that make me chuckle inside, then feel like I have been punched in the stomach. The sadness that washes over me so many times every day is unreal. It would be good if no other person had to experience this feeling. It would be the most wonderful miracle I could even imagine if I could wake up from this horrible nightmare and you would be with me – that this didn't happen.

I thought a lot about you this weekend. Mostly I was thinking about just what a special person you were. I hope you know how special you were to me. I wish I'd done more to make you know just how much I really loved you and just how much I really <u>liked</u> you too. I would have liked you even if you hadn't been my own kid. You had a wonderful personality. Oh, Casey, why did you have to go? You had so much life ahead of you. Of all the people in the world, why you? Why Casey, God? I love you, Casey. – Mom

❦

March 25, 1997
Dear Casey, Eight months ago today. The saddest night of my life. The beginning of many sad days and nights.

Casey, I was thinking today of the time you and I went into our yard one night last year and saw the comet – I can't think of its name right now – that was blazing through the sky and only visible for a short time. We saw that together. That was special. Now I look at the beautiful nighttime sky and say, "Hi, K-K." Are you seeing it from the other side? Do you see comets and stars? Do you see me? I love you my precious, precious little girl. – Mom

❦

March 31, 1997
My dear little Casey, Easter came yesterday. I'm glad it's over. I miss you so much. It's not the same anymore. Nothing is the same without you. I miss you so much, Casey. Sometimes it hurts so much. I wish I could just say, "Please come back," and you'd come. I'd be so happy. I love you with all my heart. – Mom

P.S. We had two Easter lilies for you in church yesterday. Erin had gotten one for you too. The church bulletin read that it was for "Casey, my beautiful sister" from Erin. That really touched me. She had a hard time in church yesterday. So did Nikki. Her face was splotched and stained with tears. Your sisters and I – how we love you and miss you.

April 1, 1997
Dear Casey, Today is April. It seems like April of last year is when life began to unravel. Kathy, my best friend since we were freshmen in high school, died on April 27th. Little was I to know how much more horrible life would become. Little did I know I'd lose you too a little less than three months later. I sometimes look at a picture of Steve and me that was made on April 26th. I looked happy in that picture. I have a picture of the last time I'd ever be really happy.

I think back to how you were so very good and caring to me while I dealt with Kathy's death. Right beside me. Thank you so much, Casey, for the comfort you brought me. Isn't it ironic that we visited Kathy's grave on July 23rd, two days before you died? You put your arms around me as I cried. I will never forget that.

Casey, I hope you and Kathy are spending time together. You and Kathy are two of the most special people to me. Kathy's sister Karen told me Kathy would be your mom until I get there to you. She'll be a great one, the one I'd chosen for you if something had ever happened to me here on earth. I wish you and Kathy could be here, and I could have been the one who died. You had so much life ahead of you. And Kathy had sons to raise and things to do for herself that she had missed out on. You would have been fine without me. You would have loved me always, but you had the capacity to go on and become someone I would have been so proud of. I'm not so sure I can make it without you.

For some reason this morning inside my head I could hear the answering machine message we used to have: "Hello. You've reached the Sheltons. Please leave your message at the beep." Sometimes, right after you died, I'd call our phone number just to hear that message. It was our home when it was a home. It was my voice when I was happy. I miss our life. I really miss you. – Love forever, Mom

April 4, 1997
Dear Casey, I am sorry I never took you horseback riding. I know you
wanted to do that. I wish so much that I had taken you. I hope there are
horses in heaven and that you're getting to ride. When I get there, I hope
you will take me riding with you. I love you. I miss you so. – Love, Mom

April 9, 1997
Dear Casey, Steve and I met with the Highway Patrolman who
conducted a follow-up investigation into the car wreck. I know now <u>how</u>
and <u>why</u> *it happened. I am so angry.*

I pray that God's angels came to you immediately and helped you on
your journey. I pray that you did not suffer. I believe with all my heart
that God was there or perhaps watching over the whole thing and that
He lovingly took you home without letting you feel pain. Casey, I am so
saddened now, but someday, my little girl, I will see you again and I'll
be so happy.

Casey, stay with me. I love you, my littlest ladybug. – Love, Mom

April 15, 1997
Dear K-K, This morning before work Steve and I took Jordan (our
Camry that you named "Jordan" and that I will never sell because I can
glance over at the passenger seat and just see you) to be tuned up. That
meant driving past Robertsville Middle School as students and buses
and cars were arriving. I was overcome with such sadness that I felt like
I wanted to scream. But at the same time it's hard to breathe, so where
would my scream come from? Tears flow as I remember so many times
dropping you off at school. Casey, I cannot believe this happened. I have
such a strong urge to go somewhere where I can scream and scream and
scream. I miss you so much, Casey. I LOVE YOU! – Love, Mom

April 18, 1997
Dear K-K, I will always remember your precious face – the cute little
face you had as a baby with the huge blue eyes, and the slender face that
your 14-year-old structure took on. The eyes never changed, and the
sprinkling of freckles across your nose never changed. When I picture
you in my mind, I feel a smile inside my soul, and then I feel the smile
replaced by pain and the tears just happen. Casey, how can I get

through this? I know you're OK, you're with God, but I want you with me so bad. I still sometimes get caught up in wondering how I can undo this – knowing I <u>can't</u> undo it but nonetheless trying to think of something, anything, that would take the last nine months back.

Do you know why I call you "K-K" sometimes? I know you do, because we talked about it numerous times, but I'll tell you again. You were just a little girl, still in a stroller, and we were at a ball game. I remember Debbie and Jodi Morrow had stooped down, talking to you. One of them asked you, "What's your name?" and you said, "K-K." It stuck.

For some reason, I used to call you "Casey Lou" and "Casey Louise." I don't know where that came from, just rhythmical I guess. You would answer to those names. Today if you were here, I could go out in the yard and yell, "Casey Lou," or just "Louise" or "Louie" – and you'd respond. I wish we could do that. I love you, my little girl. – ❤Mom

❧

April 21, 1997
Dear Casey, It's raining today. I kind of like rain; sometimes I think I prefer rainy days to sunshiny ones. I think now of the rain as something to water your plants at the park and keep them looking good.

If I looked up the weather records for the first weeks after you died, I'm sure I would find that it rained every day. The rain began on the night we drove away from the hospital, leaving you there. It rained the next day and the next and the next and the next. . . . I just know it did. I remember thinking, as I sat at the kitchen table and looked out the window a few days after your memorial service, that nature itself was crying. I remember the day your body was taken to be cremated. That was such a dreary, rainy, depressing day – but it matched my spirit and I thought it was a fitting way for the day to pass its time.

We – you and I – liked to watch it rain. I remember us sitting together on the porch. You were never afraid of storms either. You thought lightning and thunder were neat. Then after Granny's house was struck by lightning and burned, I remember after the first storm that happened, you and I talked about how we didn't feel the same way about lightning and thunder. I remember that storm came during the night, and the next day you and I talked about how we had both lain awake and thought of the storm that had destroyed Granny's house and hurt her. Storms for us didn't seem to hold the same magic anymore.

I guess now I like storms again, and rain. I think of you as seeing them from the other side. I'll bet it's exciting. I'll watch them with you someday. I LOVE YOU! – Love, Mom

April 25, 1997
Dear Casey, I've dreamed about you the last two nights, and both times you were a little girl about four or five years old. I wish I could dream about you every night because I get to spend time with you that way. Not bad dreams though. The theme of my dreams sometimes is that I can't find you. Those dreams make me so upset. But now most of my dreams just have you <u>with</u> me. Just normal. You're just <u>there</u>. I love those. I love having you with me like normal. – Love you, baby. Mom

April 25, 1997
Dear Casey, Nine months. Can it really be that long? I haven't seen you in nine months. It seems like just yesterday that this nightmare began. It's still so fresh. I can even remember more details now than I could months back. But, on the other hand, it seems like a long, long time since I've seen you. I really miss you, Casey. You were such a wonderful good person, and I wasn't even aware when you were with me just what a role you played in determining the kind of <u>me</u> that I was. You were literally and figuratively a part of me. Part of me went with you. That's OK, because part of you stayed with me. I just wish <u>all</u> of you was here with me. I wish I could have taken your place. I would gladly, gladly have given my life for you. You should be here playing fast-pitch at high school and slow-pitch for Kern. You should be here, a teenager with so much living to do. You should have gotten to drive and date and go to college and be the vet you wanted to be. Remember your and Brittney's slogan? "Casey and Brittney – The Vets for Your Pets." And you should have grown up and given me grandchildren. Remember I told you that coming from a family of only girls, you'd probably have boys?

I was just looking at the picture of Clifford the dog that you drew. You were really a good artist. I haven't been able to go through all the drawings I saved from your room. Too many painful memories to deal with. Maybe I can do that soon. I want to look at and cherish each picture you drew, each word you wrote.

In art class last year when you were in the eighth grade, you drew a picture (and painted it) of Granny's house that had just burned. You really did a good job. We framed it and you gave it to Granny. It hangs on her bedroom wall. You put "ECS 96" in the concrete walk that was poured at Granny's house just right before the accident.

I really liked you. And I really loved you. I will always like and love you. – ❤Love, Mom

April 28, 1997
Dear Little Ladybug, I look at your pictures and still cannot believe you're not here. I cannot believe this happened. It is still so unreal. Losing one of my children was the one thing I was most afraid of, but I never spent a lot of time dwelling on that fear because I never thought it would happen. How could it have happened, Casey? My precious little girl. How could you be gone?

I look at life, life now. It's so different. It's like it's not my life. I feel like I'm living someone else's life. I was a mom. That was my job, and that's what I loved. I was happy cooking and cleaning and driving you and your sisters to ballfields and gyms and doing all those things that moms of active children do. When I lost you, I lost my job – who I was. I don't know who I am anymore.

When I'm around people I don't know, I don't talk about my children anymore, which is what I used to talk about. I'm so scared someone will ask me if I have children and how many. How can I say I have a daughter at Vanderbilt, a daughter who's married and at UT – and a daughter who is in heaven? How can I say that? It breaks my heart to even think it. Yet I would not and will not ever leave you out. I HAVE THREE DAUGHTERS.

What if they ask about you? How can I say I lost you in an automobile accident? I can't say that. I can't say I lost you. I can't stand that. I can't believe I lost you. I can't believe it.

God blessed me with a cheerful disposition and a positive outlook. People who meet me for the first time now probably have no idea of the pain I feel. People who know me don't know the depth of sadness in my heart and soul. But I am so wounded. My little girl is gone. My little girl I love so very much. I will be so happy to see you again. I can imagine being happy again in heaven with you. Someday we'll all be together again. That will be so great. Life on earth was great, even in spite of some rough times through the years, but it doesn't seem that great anymore even in spite of all the good things that do happen and the wonderful and good husband and daughters I have left. I would not want Steve and Nikki and Erin to think they're not important to me. They are very important to me. But I just feel like I need to be with you.

My mind tells me you're fine. My faith tells me you're with God. But my heart tells me I want to be with you. I should have died first, Casey. Not you. I was thinking driving home from work the other day that I should have been there for you as you crossed from earthly life to heavenly life. I should be there waiting for you, instead of you waiting for me. I would never have let you go to a new place without me with you. I have to tell myself that my dad and Kathy were there to meet you. And of course God treated you lovingly on your journey. But I just needed to be there for you. With you. I have to leave this all up to God. I just can't understand how everything works. Thank God for God. You're probably telling Him to help me. I need that.

Yesterday morning as I was preparing to leave home to take a real estate licensing test, I felt so sad because used to when I'd get ready to go take a test, you'd give me "Baby Luck." When I was in school, you'd give me your rabbit's foot to carry with me for luck. I miss my Baby Luck. I miss you, little girl. I love you! – Love, Mom

❧

April 28, 1997
Dearest K-K, I was thinking this afternoon of when you were little and went with me to the Tech Library where I'd have to study or watch a film or look up a reference or whatever. I can still see you sitting there beside me in the library with your drawing paper or coloring book. You were such a good, well-behaved little girl. You were a little trooper those years I was in school. Remember when you and I and Erin would be walking on campus and we had a certain spot where you and Erin

pretended it was an alligator pit and you chased each other? Remember the walks around the track at the football field? I can actually sit here and smile as I write this. Most of my letters to you are through tears – and here they come now. My little girl. So many wonderful memories you left me with. How I miss you! God! I miss you! You made me laugh. You made me so happy, Casey. I can still see you in those days with your little jeans and Tennessee Tech t-shirts on. You went to school, you went to college – with me. Thank you for being such a wonderful part of that. I love you, my little girl. I love you so much. – Love, Mom

❧

April 30, 1997
Dear Casey, Today I was thinking about the times I would be home during the weekday for whatever reason (a work holiday or vacation day or sick day or whatever) and I'd pick you up from school (if it wasn't during basketball season) when school dismissed. There weren't many of those days, but they stick in my mind because that pleased you so. I'd be parked in the church parking lot at the back of the school. I can still see you coming across the grassy area between the school and church. You were always happy that I was there to pick you up. It meant you didn't have to ride the school bus. (Plus I'd like to think you were happy to see me.)

Sometimes I wish I could have stayed home and not worked so that I could have been home for you all the time. I would probably have gotten bored staying home and goodness knows I could not have afforded not to work – but yet it would have been great if you'd never had to go home to an empty house. You would always call me to let me know you were home. I feel so sad to think now that I wasn't there for you. You weren't home long by yourself, and through the years Nikki or Erin or both were there with you, but that's a real regret I have. I'm sorry I wasn't home standing at the door when you got off the school bus, or parked in the parking lot waiting on you when school dismissed. I am sorry, Casey. When I see you again, I will hug you and tell you I'm sorry and that I will always be with you from then on.

I miss dropping you off at school. That's one thing, regardless of where we were or what school, I always dropped you off at school. When you were in kindergarten through fifth grade you always stayed at school in the After-School Program until I got off work and picked you up. The last few months of fifth grade, you went to Brittney's grandmother's house after school. You girls had a ball there – riding go-carts, jumping on the trampoline, playing with the dogs. Sixth grade, though, you didn't want to do anything except go home after school. Too old for day-care anymore, and Brittney had moved and was going to a different school. I was glad when you were the manager of the basketball team in seventh grade because that meant you stayed after school and I picked you up. That was the routine from November through the end of the season anyway. Then last year in eighth grade, you were of course on the team and then even after the season you stayed after school to help Coach Petrie with spring tryouts. And other afternoons you were practicing or trying out for the high school basketball and fast-pitch teams.

Oh, Casey, you had so much fun and life ahead of you. I cannot bear to read or see pictures of the high school teams. You should be there. The fast-pitch team is wearing a #21 patch in memory of you, and the Kern softball team is going to have your number on their uniforms. The basketball team honored you by retiring your jersey. Everyone loved and respected you, Casey. No one more than I. I miss you, my little girl. I love you so much. Stay close to me.

I used to worry that I would forget things, but as time goes by, I find my mind flooded with memories of different things about you. You will never be away from my heart and the vision I have of you forever in my mind. I don't worry anymore about forgetting things. During the first months after the accident, my mind wasn't as clear and I was scared to death I'd lose images of you. But I won't. Not ever. Will you still be 14 when I see you again? I wonder about that. It doesn't matter though. I'll know you and you'll know me. That's what the Bible says. We will see each other. I'll be so happy to see you. I will never let you go or leave me again. I love you! – Forever, Mom

May 7, 1997
Dear Casey, I was thinking this morning about how glad I am that you were alive. I am so unhappy and sad that I had you with me for so <u>short</u> a time. But I want to dwell on your <u>life</u> and how very thankful I am that you were here, not on the horrible accident that took you away.

At Weatherford's and at your memorial service, what I wanted to do was celebrate your life. I was dying inside, but it mattered to me that you be remembered for your life. The pictures your sisters chose to surround us showed your life and what an active happy life it was. Casey, I am so glad you were alive. It is important to me that others remember you and that when they think of you, they think of the lively, fun-loving, kind person you were. Occasionally I imagine what you must have looked like <u>after</u> July 25th, but I can't let those thoughts linger for long. I must replace them with a memory of you <u>before</u> that day. And I have so many of those wonderful memories. You were truly a wonderful, precious child, Casey.

Sometimes I feel like I can't bear the sorrow I feel. Sometimes I wish I could die. But always I am thankful for you and for what you mean to me. You will always be a part of me. I know I will always miss you. I know I will always grieve for you. I know I will always cry. But how else could it be when a person loses someone so very precious to them? That is life now. My little girl, I miss you. – Love forever and ever, Mom

❦

May 8, 1997
Dear Casey, There are very few things in my life that do not have a memory of you associated with them. Today when I changed stations on the radio in the car, I thought of how stations #3 and #4 were yours. I had my stations tuned in on #1, #2 and #5; your two were in the middle. I had to get a new battery for the car a couple of months ago. After the battery was taken out, the stations were no longer tuned in and I had to reset them. I reset my three; I left yours empty. I don't think I'll ever let anybody tune a station in on your two channels. Those are yours. It's like Jordan is yours too. You named "him" that. We traveled a lot of miles together in that car – just you and I. I feel lost sometimes without you. I cannot stand to think about it. More and more as time goes on I have to stop (or try to stop anyway) <u>thinking</u>. There are so many good memories of you, but so many that make me so sad I tell myself, "I can't go there." It gets harder as time goes on, not better. There's a difference in now and one month ago and three months ago and nine months ago. I can't describe it. I can only feel it. It's worse. It's still unreal. But I'm not sure I could ever deal with real.

I love you, baby. Little Ladybug. I'm getting ready to go by your niche and kiss the little image of you that I see in the granite. I love you. – Love, Mom

May 9, 1997
Dear Casey, I was thinking about this time last year when you were at Robertsville Middle School. The teachers you really liked at Robertsville were Coach Burkey, Coach Carson, Coach Bell, Coach Petrie and Mrs. Beeler. All athletes. The teachers you didn't like, well, actually I didn't care for those teachers either, but I couldn't tell you that.

I think in many ways you were the class clown, especially when you were in the eighth grade. That year you blossomed and became much more self-confident. I remember having to meet with several of your teachers that year because they were concerned that you were goofing off a little too much. The message was always that they really liked you a lot, that you were a pleasure to be around, that even they thought you were funny – but you were not turning in homework all the time (on time) and you needed to buckle down. Of course I never heard anything but praise from your coaches because you <u>always</u> buckled down for them. You know something, Casey? That was OK with me. I got after you and really tried to be stern because I expected you to do your best – I knew you were capable of making A's in everything – and I was really tough on you especially if you brought home a bad grade or I got a call from one of your teachers. But I really did like the way you were. Maybe I didn't let you know that. I hope I let you know that. I really did LIKE you. I hope I got that through to you. I know I told you. I hope you understood. I hope you knew some of my toughness with you was what I thought was the right kind of mother to be. I just hope it was right. You really were a good child. I really <u>like</u> you, besides <u>love</u> you with all my heart.

Some days <u>all</u> I can think about is <u>you</u>. Today is one of those days. The thoughts fill my heart with such happiness that then becomes a sorrow like I have never known. Oh, I miss you. What a horrible waste that you are not here. Gone. I am having so much trouble dealing with that.

Yesterday someone asked me how old my daughters are. I told them 21, 18 and 14. They just don't know that the 14-year-old will always be 14 years old.

Casey, you are always with me. I love you, little girl. – Love, Mom

❧

May 14, 1997
Dear Casey, When I close my eyes, I see you around the age of 10, glancing at me as you turn the corner into what I think is your room. I think this is part of a dream I was having a few days ago. The picture is just burned into my mind and pops before me if I shut my eyes. It's so real. How I wish it were really real. How I want to see you! I am struggling, Casey. Some times are worse than others. I'm in one of the hard times. How can life ever be good or happy again?

Sometimes I almost feel torn between two worlds, the "world" where you are and the "world" where Steve and Nikki and Erin are. I want to be both places. I didn't know how happy I was or how very thankful I should have been when we were all together. Just this time last year we were all together. What I would give! How I long to have you here!

One of my friends said something one time to the effect that she wished sometimes she could just go to sleep and not wake up. I was so alarmed when she said that and I fussed at her. Now I understand. I can't say that to anybody – but I can share it with you. Sometimes I wish that too. The sorrow would be gone for me – I would be with you! – but that would cause more sorrow for Nikki and Erin and Steve. I know if you were here, you'd fuss at me like I did at my friend. But if you were here, I wouldn't be having these thoughts. Oh, God, Casey – and I don't mean "God" in a swearing sense. It's just a cry of sorrow; I am hurting so. No one even knows how much, not even Steve. Losing you has broken my heart, my spirit. I love you so, my little girl, my little Casey. – Love, Mom

❧

May 15, 1997
Dear K-K, Yesterday as I drove home from work, I stopped at the park and tidied up your flowers and birdhouse and softball on top of your niche. I know you're not there – you're always with me – but going by and kissing your name and checking on your things is good for me. I

always do our special knock before I leave the park. I close my eyes and imagine how it used to sound when we did it. I can hear your knock, my response, then my knock and your response. That was the last thing you did the last time I saw you. Twice because you were going to be gone for two nights. I hugged you and kissed you and told you I loved you that night. I wish I'd hugged you harder and kissed you a thousand times and told you a million times I love you. I wish I'd never let you stay at Granny's with Jennifer. How can I ever ever forgive myself? I wish you'd gone home with me. Then this wouldn't have happened.

Casey, do you know how much I love you? I ask God to tell you. I don't know how this heaven and spirit thing works – but I believe with all my heart that they're real. I <u>know</u> they are, and they're even better and more wonderful than what I could even imagine, so I have to believe you are receiving all of the love I am sending you.

I love you, Ladybug! I miss you. – Love forever and ever, Mom

P.S. I thought about you and my dad celebrating his birthday yesterday. I wondered if you celebrate birthdays in heaven. Then I thought, well, if you do, I'm sure <u>you're</u> making your Papaw's special. What a special day for him.

❦

May 19, 1997
Dear Little K-K, Yesterday was a day of talking about snakes and reminiscing about your interest and knowledge of the creatures that most of the rest of us were only scared of. You knew so much about snakes. It was unreal. And you certainly weren't afraid of them. On our way back from church yesterday, Erin and I were talking about your fondness for Monroe, Felicia and Elvis (the king snake). [These were snakes her teacher kept in her classroom.] *I told Erin I was going to write a story someday. It would star you (of course), Debbie the monkey that I made up tales about, and Monroe, Felicia and Elvis. Wouldn't that be neat? I also told Erin that someday I was going to write a story about you, so that her children and Nikki's children could know you better.*

You were a real person, a person who left us too soon and took big chunks of our hearts. You were such a wonderful, wonderful person. It makes me sad to think that I didn't fully appreciate just what it meant to have <u>you</u> for a daughter. I loved you and Nikki and Erin with all my heart – but I guess I just took you (and probably still your sisters) for granted. I just thought I'd always have you.

I think back to the months right after I lost you. I don't remember much. What did I eat? Did I go to the grocery store? Did I cook? What happened to those days? I don't remember. Yesterday in church I thought about the songs I really always liked – "Sweet, Sweet Spirit" and "The Spirit Song." I would have had those songs sung at your memorial service if I had been thinking. But I couldn't think then. I remember expressing that I did not want you buried, but I don't remember a whole lot else. I remember bits and pieces of walking through stores in the mall to get you underwear and socks. What a daze. I guess, though, I should be grateful for the daze that set in because I could not have done what I needed to do otherwise.

There are many days that I still feel that the stunned daze still surrounds me, but many days I feel the raw pain of reality. I have to keep myself sometimes from just pretending. I think, "I'll just pretend this didn't happen. I'll turn around in the front seat of the car and she'll be sitting there in the back." I don't know if how I cope is healthy or not. Some days I am so down. Some days I wish I could die. Some days I think, "I can't do this!" I don't know what I look like on the outside. I probably look maybe normal. But I know inside I don't feel normal. I can't imagine being happy again. Normal is gone. Normal was when you were here. Happy was when you were here. Life was when you were here.

I thought I hurt so much when Kathy died and when my dad died. Those feelings don't even compare to the despair of losing you. Whoever coined the word "heartbreak" must have glimpsed the despair. I understand the word "heartbreak." That's how it really feels. My heart broke and the air and the life escaped – escaped except for some that's still in there that keeps me going whether I want to or not. If I described how I envision me, it would be like a helium balloon that doesn't have enough helium in it to float or rise, but enough in it that kind of keeps it from lying totally flat – not quite bobbing, but not totally flat.

Thank you for hearing me. You are my outlet. Isn't that strange? I tell you what I feel. You know, I did use to tell you how I felt about some *stuff. Not everything, of course, because that wouldn't have been right or even fair to you. But I told you as much as I probably told anyone. Casey, I wanted you to grow up and be my pal. You were that already in many ways, but I can only imagine how wonderful it would have been to have my baby daughter, my youngest daughter, always close to me. Remember how we were going to live on the beach together? We'll be on the beach together someday, just not the way we dreamed.*

I love to look at your pictures, to stare at your pictures. Other times I can't. I love you, Casey. I want to undo the past 10 months. I want you back. I want to erase this. God, how can we erase this? What happened!!!?? Stay with me, Casey. – I love you, Mom

❦

May 23, 1997
Dear Casey, I was spending time with you today. That's what it is when I dream about you. How I wish those dreams didn't have to end. How I wish I was spending time with you in "awake" hours, instead of "asleep" hours. When I awoke this morning, it was from a dream where you and I were in the kitchen of our home in Oak Ridge and then in the part of our yard that was between our house and the Tittsworths' house. You were unloading the dishwasher. I was telling you that we were going somewhere at two o'clock and then the rest of the day would be a "Casey Day" – that's what I said to you in my dream – and that we'd do anything you wanted to do. You were about eight or nine years old. In the outdoor portion of the dream, the lawn was not grass but like lamb's wool. It kind of reminded me of Dennis Rodman's hair. Don't you think that's funny? I can hear you now laughing as I tell you this. Then I was in a store – I don't think you were with me in this part – looking for a doll for you.

When I woke up, for a few seconds everything felt so good. The world felt right again. Then I remembered. Then I had to revert back to "get up, go on, don't think."

Later this morning, I was conducting an interview at work and I was thinking about the dream. For some reason, it occurred to me that I still have my body and the self that everybody sees, but my heart is with you. That's OK. I love you, baby. – Love forever and ever, Mom

❦

May 24, 1997
Dear Casey, It's Saturday morning, May 24. Ten months since I last saw
you. I'm sitting at the kitchen table just thinking about you. When I woke
up this morning, I just thought for awhile about our Saturday mornings
in Oak Ridge. You would be sleeping late unless you had ball practice.
You'd watch some TV, do stuff in the yard, maybe we'd plant some
flowers, you'd visit with Mr. Edmond in either his garden or yard, play
with Devin his grandson. Maybe Brittney or Elizabeth would come over
today, or maybe you'd want to go to their house. Casey, I miss you and
our life so much!

I'm going to study all day today for my real estate test that I take next
Saturday. I'm going to move into another career. I don't have enough to
do anymore. When I lost you, I lost my main job, my job of being a
mother. I'm still Nikki's and Erin's mother, but they're "adults" and
don't live at home anymore. I miss being your mother. I mean I'm
always going to be your mother, but I guess I mean I miss mothering
you, doing all those things that being your mother meant.

I cannot look at newspaper articles or news stories on TV about girls'
ball teams. Casey, we should be there! I love you, my little precious girl.
I miss you so much. – Love forever and ever, Mom

May 30, 1997
Hi, baby. Last weekend I watched a show on TV I'd never before seen. It
was "Touched by an Angel." This episode dealt with the death of a little
girl named "Katie," whose father was having a terrible time coping. He
had about lost his faith in everything, including life. The angels were
sent to help him. One angel told him that when children die, they are
always special to God and He sends angels to be with them every step of
the way. I thought of you. I remember Marilyn Stanley telling me last
summer that Dr. Stanley truly believes from his experience in situations
where he has lost patients that angels are all around them. That was
comforting to me. I guess I think that if I could have been with you that
nothing could have happened to you. I wish so that I had been with you.
To think that God's angels were with you, well, I know you weren't
alone, that they helped you.

Last summer I remember telling Erin that you seemed like a dream to me. You were with me for such a short time. Yesterday you were born, then today you were gone. It was so fleeting – like a dream. And you were unique. A dream child. Not quite like anyone else I've ever known. Different. Better. Only in my memory now.

Erin wondered if you were an angel.

I told Odessa Stewart about that at work the other day. She said maybe you were an angel. I like talking to Odessa. She told me that sometimes some of the black kids say bad stuff about the white kids (just like some white kids do black kids) but that none of the black kids ever said anything bad about you. She said they all liked you. She told me her daughter Kim had told her that she had seen you with your hair all grown long and you were looking so pretty and she said something to you like, "Casey, look at you!" She said you got all embarrassed and said, "Oh, Kim!" (I can just hear you, embarrassed when anyone commented on how pretty you were and how you were becoming more beautiful all the time.)

You were beautiful, Casey, inside and out. I love you, my little girl. Have fun in heaven. I can't wait to see you again. – Love you with all my heart, forever, Mom

❦

June 1, 1997
Dear K-K, Today I opened the closet and moved around some clothes. Your bridesmaid's dress slipped off the hanger. I put it back and put it in a plastic bag with Nikki's dress. I felt like I couldn't look at it long. (That's how I'm dealing with lots of things.) The thought occurred to me as I put it back in the closet that in many ways I act like you're coming back. But now I'm crying. I love you, baby girl. This is our birthday month. – Love you always and always, Mom

❦

June 2, 1997
Dear K-K, How am I going to get through your birthday? I can't think. I can't look at your pictures. I can't think about this for long. I went to the store during lunch today and got balloons for you. I have a pretty flower to put at your niche. I called the church and requested that a sunflower be in the arrangement of flowers on the altar next Sunday in memory of

you. I'm doing things. But I can't let myself think for long. It hurts too much. I can't stand this. How can I do this, Casey? Your <u>birthday</u> is tomorrow. I love you. – Love, Mom

❦

June 11, 1997
Dear Casey, Odessa told me the funniest story about you today. It just tugs at my heart, making me cry because it was so "Casey."

She said a girl who had been on the Robertsville basketball team when you were in seventh grade and were the manager of the team came to visit Kim yesterday. (The girl had moved away that year.) Odessa said she was asking Kim about you. Kim called her mom into the room and Odessa told her what had happened. Odessa said she just fell to the floor and could not believe it. She was very upset. Odessa said Kim and her friend then started telling how they had always kidded around with you and that you were so quiet but then managed to get back at them. They remember you as being little, with freckles across your nose.

They told her one time they had been ragging you all week and that you just quietly took it. Then in the basketball game – they thought the game was in Cookeville where they were getting trounced – you rearranged their water bottles so they couldn't find them. They said you always kept the bottles arranged orderly and they could get their own bottle hardly looking. This game, though, you "rearranged" the bottles. She said Kim said they'd run over to get a drink but couldn't find their bottle, so they'd run back on the court without ever getting a drink. She said they were afraid to look for their bottles too long because Coach Carson would have yelled at them. Then she said Coach Carson noticed they were having trouble finding their bottles and he yelled, "Shelton!" She said you just held your arms out to your sides, as if to say, "I don't know what's going on." Then, with your back to Coach Carson, you just grinned.

That was so Casey!! I love this story. Odessa said you paid them back. She said you all got a big laugh on the way home from the game. And Kim and the girl (whose name Odessa couldn't recall) laugh and laugh telling it. Odessa and I laughed today too. Thanks for your Casey stories. It feels good to laugh. I love you, baby. I miss you so. – Love forever and ever, Mom

❦

June 18, 1997

Dear Casey, I haven't been able to write you for some time. It started with your birthday. I felt like I talked to you a lot that day, yet I haven't been able to put things down on paper since then (except for one time when it just flowed). I have been in a strange frame of mind since your birthday. Many sweet and wonderful things happened on and since that day, many tears have flowed, many sad thoughts have filled my mind, many precious precious memories have played themselves for me, many times have been spent just thinking about you, many screams have filled my soul until I think I can't keep them in.

On your birthday, I awoke from a dream of you. I heard your voice in my dream. I've dreamed of you often, but never recalled hearing your voice. But I did this time. Your voice. I dreamed I was at Granny's. The phone rang and Pat answered it. It was for me. Pat said it was Margaret. When I answered, it was you! You said you were ready to come home but that you and Brittney were watching cartoons while Brittney's mom washed your clothes, so I could come get you then. This dream was so typical of times and conversations we really shared. How I wish this could be!

Steve, Erin and I went to Clingman's Dome in the Smokies and released balloons to celebrate your birthday. Steve said Clingman's Dome would be as close to heaven as we could get without being in an airplane. I can imagine you lying on a cloud, with your head dangling over the side, and catching the balloons as they got to you. I had gone to the store on June 2nd and got a balloon that said "We Love You" plus six other bright shiny ones to go around it. I put them in the living room, but when I came downstairs on your birthday morning, all but the balloon that said "We Love You" had lost its helium. So Ko-Ko (or Co-Co; I'm not sure how <u>you</u> spelled his name) is holding those balloons. Steve, Erin and I got some more.

The balloon I chose for you was a big smiley face. Steve's balloon had dalmatians on it. Erin's said "Miss You." Nikki's said "Happy Birthday" and had a basket of flowers. Brad's said "Happy Birthday" and had a cartoon character with a basketball on it. Nikki and Brad weren't with us, but their hearts were, I'm sure. We hiked up to the dome. It was a cloudy, overcast day. The actual length of the hike was only a half-mile, but I really had a hard time making it. People passed *us, and several commented on the balloons and asked if we were going to release them at the top. (They had no idea <u>why</u>.)*

Erin released her balloon first, and it literally shot into the heavens. It was so appropriate for Erin's balloon to behave that way. I know if she could, she'd run to you. I wasn't surprised at all that her balloon reflected what she would do. It was so touching. We lost sight of it very quickly as it rocketed to you. The other balloons lifted quickly too and sailed on their way to you – except for mine. I was last to release mine, and it dropped and hovered around the tree tops (we were above the trees) for what seemed like a few minutes. Then the smiley face turned in my direction, bounced a second, and then shot off and joined the others. The way I interpreted the behavior of my balloon was that it didn't want to leave me – as I believe you didn't want to leave me. Then it smiled as if to say it's OK. There was a silence that was very noticeable as we released the balloons. Probably people figured out what – and why – we were doing this and were very respectful. That was a nice touch.

After we left the mountains, we took Erin home and then Steve and I came home. Casey, you won't believe what happened when we got there. Steve stopped at the entrance of the driveway to get the mail out of the mailbox. I was just sitting there, looking down, when Steve called, "June, look!" Casey, there was a dalmatian running through our yard. It was real playful and just going back and forth between our yard and the neighbor's. We stood there in amazement. Then the young neighbors next door came out and watched. Greg, the neighbor, called to one of the boys up the street and asked if he knew who the dog belonged to. He didn't. After the dalmatian frolicked for awhile, it ran off down Westin Place and onto Ebenezer Road and disappeared.

That was so truly amazing. I feel like it was a sign to us from you.

Casey, you were born at 8:27 p.m. So at 8:27 p.m. on your 15th birthday, I went outside and walked in the rain. Remember how we did that? Remember the time we played tennis in the rain and laughed and had such a good time? Well, I walked in the rain in honor of you, and I turned my face to the heavens and let the rain mix with my tears as I said "Happy Birthday" to you.

Casey, I cannot believe you are not here. I know your spirit is very much alive and will be as long as your sisters and I are alive. But I just miss you. I miss you so. I love you, my little girl. You were my birthday present – the best present anyone could ever ever receive. I love you! – Love, Mom

The dalmatian seemed to be a sign because before Steve had asked me to marry him, he had talked to each of my daughters and got her blessing. Casey told Steve it would be OK with her if he married her mom IF she could have a dog. And she wanted the dog to be a dalmatian which she planned to name "Jake." Steve agreed to that, and she agreed to the marriage. But Casey died before we got married and before Steve could make good on his deal to get her a dalmatian.

June 21, 1997
My dear little Casey, I think of you so often. You are always with me. I know you will be forever. I miss you so much.

I am getting ready to pack for a trip to New Mexico. I talked to Erin last night, and she's going to come by after while. I just wrote Nikki to tell her bye. I tried to call her last night but she wasn't home. I feel like I need to say something to you too. Can't leave my little K-K out. But really I'm not saying bye to you cause you're always with me. I wish you were <u>here</u> though so I could say bye to you and tell you to behave and be careful and take care of yourself. Oh, Casey, I miss you so much. There is <u>nothing</u>, <u>nothing</u> I wouldn't give to have you physically here. I know you are with God, and I know you're OK. I just want you with me. I love you, my little girl. – ❤*Mom*

June 30, 1997
Dearest Casey, I feel so down. July begins tomorrow. I've dreaded July. July is full of so many memories – and memory dates. The most horrible thing of my whole life happened in July. Yet some of July's memories are good. Like Erin's birth in July. Like your softball tournament last year and the year before. But now, Casey, I dread July. I wish I could sleep through it.

I dreamed two dreams of you early Saturday morning. I woke up so depressed and have pretty much stayed that way. You were eight or nine years old, and I lost you. You were there one minute, and then I couldn't find you.

I feel this huge scream inside me. I am so – what is the word? I don't know a word for how I feel. I just want to scream "NO!!!"

Yesterday afternoon I went for a walk. I always think of you. I cried almost all the way to the lake. The scream rings in my ears – the scream that no one hears but me. On my way back, it started to rain. It rained really hard for a few minutes. Steve brought the car out to look for me and took me home. But not before I got drenched. I liked getting drenched. I needed that. It made me feel better. Remember when you and I played tennis in the rain one Saturday afternoon? We loved it. What a wonderful memory.

Stay with me, Casey. I love you. I asked Nikki this weekend if she thought you knew how much I loved you. She said, "Oh, yes." Please know. – ❤Mom

❧

July 2, 1997
Dear K-K, Your baby picture . . . I can't look at it for long. It hurts too much. The memories of you at that age when I held you and rocked you and hugged you and kissed you and smelled your sweet little baby smell and had my face touched by your pudgy little baby fingers – those are just memories that take my breath. My little baby. My little daughter. My youngest daughter.

Yesterday I went to the cemetery. No one was around so I practiced screaming "No." It seemed to help. It seemed to release some of the boiling screams I feel inside. I wish I could go somewhere all alone so that I could yell and yell as loudly as I possibly could. But those screams won't bring you back. I wish I could do something to bring you back. I miss you so badly. I love you so much, Casey! – Love, Mom

❧

July 14, 1997
Dear K-K, Yesterday at Compassionate Friends, I said aloud that we do not send our children or let our children go to places we haven't checked out first. That's how I feel about your going first in our family to heaven. I should have gone first. I also said that I try to be a good

person because I want to go to heaven to see <u>you</u>, not God. That's how I feel. This morning I talked to God about that on my way to work. It will be wonderful to see Him, and I meant no disrespect to Him. I know He understands how I feel. I don't feel guilty about making that statement. I know God knows my heart. And it's OK.

I loved you so deeply, Casey. I love you so deeply. I always will. I know there will never be a day in my life that I don't think about you and feel an intense love for you. You're my little girl.

Yesterday at Compassionate Friends, someone spoke of a child being a gift, not a possession. You were a gift. I just wish I'd got to keep you longer. Do you know I love you? I miss you, Casey. I miss you so much. – Love forever and ever, Mom

July 15, 1997
Dear Casey, Last night your friend Lesley Kelley called me. She had been to your niche yesterday. She goes there fairly often. She said her new boyfriend took her. Sometimes her dad does. Back when your softball season was starting, she took a softball and placed it on top of the niche, with messages to you written on it. Lesley said she and Liz Polfus, who had been one of your best friends, have become friends. Liz spent the night with Lesley, and Lesley said they cried and laughed and talked about you for hours. She said Liz played shortstop for Kern this year – your position – and sometimes she looked and sounded like you. Lesley played in the field behind her, and she said it was like playing behind you. You and Liz do look so much alike. Even I would mistake you for each other on the basketball court. Lesley said something that I had forgotten. She said you used to say you were going to "hit the ball to Nicaragua!" I can hear you say that.

Casey, when this first happened, I was so scared I'd forget something about you. But you are stronger all the time in my memory. I remember exactly how you looked, felt, smelled. I remember exactly looking into your eyes and fixing your braids and combing your long hair after you'd washed it. You had skinny hands, long fingers, really pretty nails. Your face was freckled and so cute, changing shape just in the last year, getting longer and more oval. You were a beautiful person, inside and out. I miss you, little girl. I will see you again some day. I can't wait for that. – Love forever, Mom

☙

July 16, 1997
Dear K-K, Last night I dreamed you and Erin were little girls. You were about two, and she was about six. You were walking down a street together, holding hands. You were walking to me, and I was walking to you. I got to you and you were both so dirty from playing. I said I'd have to give you two a bath. You were both so cute. It was just like a memory, not a dream. I dreamed I saw you, as I really had. It was a happy, happy dream.

You and Erin were real buddies when you were little. Nikki was more like a little mother to you. They both loved you dearly. That never changed, and will never change. You loved them too. I was such a lucky mother. The best little girls there ever could be. It's hard to imagine that anyone could love their children as much as I love you three. Love to my little girl, my baby. – Mom

☙

July 17, 1997
Dear Casey, For the last few days I've been thinking about how this time last year these were your last days on earth. I woke up this morning around four a.m. and thought about how these were your last eight days; July 15ᵗʰ had marked your last 10 days; etc. Thank goodness we didn't know. But then if only I hadn't let you spend the night at Granny's!

Casey, I think so much about you. I wonder what you're doing. I believe you're in heaven – no, I <u>know</u> you're in heaven – but I wonder what it's like and what you're doing. I just finished a book about heaven. The author said something I really liked. Talking about how we can't even imagine what heaven will be like, he said it would be like trying to explain to his twin before birth that they were going to leave their mother's womb and go to another kind of world. He said how would he explain that in this other world they would no longer be in water and would not be confined, that they would breathe air. How could his twin imagine such a thing or ever think that it would be better than their mother's womb? He would explain there would be a tunnel they would pass through to this new world and there would be pain – but they *wouldn't remember that. He said dying is like this. We pass through to another world that we can't even imagine.*

Is your soul already with God in heaven, or is it at rest until the resurrection? Whichever way is great. I know your spirit is with me too.

I love you, little girl. You are so very precious to me. I miss you so much that sometimes I can't stand it. I go on, but with my deepest thoughts being that I'm just going on until I can die too and be with you. Life is not what it used to be, and it doesn't have the meaning it did before you left.

Sometimes I try to trick myself and think, "I'll pretend I'm June before I had Casey and Erin and Nikki." But I can't do that. Not even for a minute. You three girls define who I am, and I can't even remember what it was like before I had you. I can't pretend I'm 22 years old or younger and that I never knew you or Erin or Nikki. I guess a brief respite from pain is what I'm looking for, but that's not going to happen. I can't pretend. Really, I don't know that I even want to (even for a minute), because somehow that would be disloyal to you girls. I couldn't miss you if I didn't know you. Can't pretend though. I did know you. You are a part of me. I thank God you are a part of me. I will take the pain. The 14 years I had you with me are worth a zillion years of pain because those 14 years were filled with you.

I wish I could have died first, Casey, and that I could have had you with me all my life. I will just have to wait till I get to heaven for that. We will have eternity together. I'm just anxious. I don't mean to sound like I'm not being fair to Nikki and Erin by wanting to leave them, but they would be OK without me. I know they love me and would never forget me, but they will be fine without me. Mothers are supposed to die before their children. They're supposed to. Why didn't it work that way? You would have been fine without me. But I'm not fine without you. I love you, Casey. – Mom

❦

July 18, 1997
Dear Casey, How do I live without you? Driving in to work this morning, a song came on the radio with those words, and I cried and cried. I started not to go on to the office; I thought about just going to

Oak Ridge Memorial Park and sitting at your niche. I thought I wish I could just take your urn out and at least hold it. How do I live without you, Casey? Life is not life anymore. I don't know why I have to be here. As I drove on in to Y-12, I thought about how I wish there was a place for people like me to go. A place for mothers and fathers who don't feel a part of the "regular" world anymore. Everything is so messed up. I don't want to be here, but where is there to go? I cannot get away from the fact that you were in an automobile accident and I've lost you. I can't stand that!

God! I can't stand this! I've been at work five minutes. How am I going to get through this day? Casey – God – be with me. I love you, Casey. I miss you. – Mom

July 18, 1997
Until July 25, 1996, I was so involved with living that death was not an issue. Now it's the biggest issue in my life. How to live with death. Casey's. I hate this. It will be one year ago next week. This was Casey's last week last year.

On July 18, 1996, we were packing to leave for her state tournament games in Hendersonville. On July 19th, we drove to the motel where we stayed in Gallatin (the Shoney's Inn Motel). It was a beautiful day. We had fun driving there together, just the two of us. We looked at clouds and said what different shapes we saw in them. We saw what each other saw, always, every time. Casey listened to her tapes some, we liked seeing horse farms we passed, she helped me look for streets so I'd take the right one to the motel. When we got to the motel we ate some stuff we had picked up from Wendy's, and she chummed around with the girls on the team until it got time to drive into Hendersonville for the game that night. She and Jill Broughton and Erin Hinton and Lesley Kelley were especially chummy and excited and running in and out of rooms and up and down the steps and flirting with some boys who were in town for a tournament too. That was the first time I saw Casey kind of flirt. It was cute, and I guess it kind of struck me that she was acting like a teenager.

We went to the game that night and Casey played really well. Her team, Kern, won. I remember seeing her – it's a powerful picture – playing shortstop. She was so good. A natural athlete. The pastor of Kern was there. Ron Ingram. It was the first time he'd seen the girls play. He was sitting behind me and Judy Keiser, and I kept hearing him make comments about how good Casey was. The ball would go to her and he'd say,"Watch her step into the ball, pick up, step, throw. Just like you're supposed to do!" I was bursting with pride to hear people comment on the way she played. Casey said our pastor Ron had been the team's good luck charm. He came that night and they won. I told him later that she said that. He was touched. He said he remembered thinking that if his daughter who had died at birth had lived, he'd want her to be just like Casey.

During the game she got her finger jammed and it also bled. The game had to be stopped to put a band-aid on her. After the game, I remember seeing her sitting on the steps, drinking her Gatorade, while the coaches talked to the team. We had taken one of every flavor of Gatorade in a cooler. I think she had chosen the purple one to drink after the first game. I was trying to maneuver around to make pictures of the team, and she tried to ignore or avoid me as she always did when I had my camera. But I think I got a side and back shot of her.

The team had to play only one game that night, so we returned to the motel and the girls did their thing. Casey went to the pool but didn't go swimming. The girls made a zillion trips up and down the steps and to the pool and to each other's rooms. Casey really had a good time. She was right in there, one of the most talkative, fun ones. There was a Dairy Queen across the street, and Jim Eaton took the girls there for ice cream. I remember Casey asked me if she could bring me anything, because she knew I liked Dairy Queen. I said no because I didn't want her to have to fool around with anything for me, but that's a real sweet memory for me, that she asked. When they got back, the girls sat on the railing on the landing between the first and second floors of the motel, right outside our rooms. I checked on her several times, and she was having a ball cutting up and acting silly like the rest of the girls.

I went to Jim and Karen Eaton's room to get directions to Hendersonville from Nashville for Nikki since she was going to come from Nashville and watch Casey play the next day. Jim called his dad who lives in the area and got directions. I stayed and talked with them awhile. I told them about Erin's wedding and how Casey had been so upset the night before the ceremony because she didn't want Erin to leave. (Jim told me later he would always remember that conversation. He and Karen provided a reading called "A Parable of Immortality" for Casey's memorial service and then gave me a framed copy of it.) When I called Nikki to relay the directions to her, she couldn't believe it was so late and I was still letting Casey be outside. I remember I told her I could see her and she was with the other girls.

That night the opening ceremonies of the Summer Olympics were on TV and I watched that while Casey was out. When I eventually made her come in to bed, she wasn't ready but that sort of broke the party up and everybody else went to bed too. By the time Casey brushed her teeth and washed up, I had turned off the TV and was half asleep. She laid down on top of her bed, not turning it down, and used her stuffed dog pillow as a pillow, covering up with a little quilt that she carried. She did that at home a lot too, rarely turning her bed down unless I made her. The next morning I woke up around seven, but I lay there a long time because I didn't want to get up and disturb Casey. I thought she'd need all the rest she could get for who knew how many games she'd be playing that day. It was a double elimination tournament. I just lay there listening to her breathe and looking at her occasionally. Lesley Kelley came to our room and asked Casey if she'd go to Shoney's and eat with her. Shoney's was attached to our motel. So that worked out fine. Casey got a decent breakfast.

While Casey and Lesley ate, I decided Casey and I were not staying Saturday night at the motel, regardless of how late we had to drive home. When she found out we weren't staying there Saturday night too, Casey wasn't happy. But as it turned out, not a single family stayed. Everybody in our group left, so that made it better for Casey. So while they ate, I checked us out and got the car packed. I noticed everybody else was leaving for the game – and Casey and Lesley were still eating. By the time they got to our room, we really had to hurry to get Casey's hair braided. Lesley laughs now when she recalls that Casey was going to wear the dirty socks she'd worn the night before and I made her change. Lesley gave a computer-made poster to Casey that had something about "the JIGS" on it. I forget what the acronym means, but "the JIGS" were Casey, Lesley, Erin and Jill. Lesley rode to the ball game with us.

Nikki and Kurt came to the game and stayed for the duration. That was the first time we'd met Kurt. It rained terribly off and on all day. We played two games and lost two games so got eliminated. I made pictures of Casey playing that day but lost them, or rather destroyed them, as I ripped film from the camera, not thinking, just a week later because I forgot what I knew about exposing film in my haste to get the film from the camera. I regret that so. I know I had made a wonderful picture of Casey sliding into home in the last game.

That Saturday after the game, Casey and I headed home. I got lost and we ended up driving a lot of unnecessary miles. I told her that would be our secret. We stopped in Cookeville and ate supper at the Cracker Barrel. I remember sitting across the table from Casey and telling her how good a ballplayer I thought she was. I'm really glad I told her how I felt. We ate pie that day, the first time I remember us ever ordering pie. She had lemon. I remember her clothes were damp from sweat and rain and she changed there. I also remember she wanted me to let her drive in the Cracker Barrel parking lot. She just wanted to pull the car out, go around the restaurant and to the exit. I didn't let her of course. But last fall one day that memory pasted itself to the front of my mind. It was during the time when I still didn't know <u>why</u> Jennifer had wrecked. I thought, "What if Casey was driving?" That thought drove me crazy for hours until I told Steve and he assured me there was evidence that no, Casey had not been driving. She was in the passenger seat, and she was wearing her seatbelt. I don't know why that scared me so, but for a few hours that day it did.

The next day was Sunday and Casey and I went to church. She tried on the dress she and Erin (and maybe Nikki too) had given me for my birthday. It was a little tight and short for me, but Casey looked good in it. She ended up not wearing it because she wanted to put a shirt under it that spoiled the effect. I haven't worn it either. I think there must be something of Casey in that dress so I'll keep it just as it is, always. At church, Ron commented that Kern should be proud of its team and he said something to Casey. That afternoon Casey went with Steve and me to the movie ("Phenomenon"), and then we went to Erin's and helped move some more stuff into her and Brad's apartment. Casey was grouchy that day. She sat in the hot truck instead of coming inside the apartment for a long time. I was just ignoring her (which now I regret)

*and figuring she'd come inside when she got hot enough – which she
did. We laughed later as we recalled how she rang the doorbell and
asked if anybody was going to help her. She had a drawer or something
she was carrying. On Monday I don't recall anything out of the
ordinary, but it seems like Casey was kind of moody that day. She was
like that occasionally, especially since becoming a teenager. I just
ignored it for the most part. But I did stop on my way home and pick up
her Alanis Morissette cassette. That made her happy and the mood
changed. She loved that tape.*

*On Tuesday when I got home from work I told Casey we'd eat a chili
bun before I took her to Granny's to spend the night. I don't remember
how it came about that Casey was going to spend the night there. I don't
know if she asked or if I asked or if Granny invited her since Jennifer
was staying there while Gail and David were out of town or just how it
came about. We ate and Casey packed clothes for one night in her little
bag that looked like a baseball. It was providential that while I fixed our
chili buns, her dad called her. Casey came into the kitchen later and
said her dad wanted to spend more time with her. That pleased her. I'm
so thankful for that phone call. She had a smile on her face about that
phone call. We drove on to Granny's and Casey played her silly
harmonica while we traveled. She'd pass it to me and tell me to play
something. There was a part in one of Alanis Morissette's songs where
she played the harmonica and Casey could imitate that real well.*

❧

*July 1997. It has almost been one year since we lost Casey in a car
accident. Casey was really something. She had the best, kindest heart of
anyone I have ever known. She was so funny too. She was funny and
sweet and mischievous all wrapped up into one beautiful child. She
loved her family, and she loved her friends dearly. Casey loved God and
it showed in the way she loved her family and friends. Although it has
been almost one year since we lost Casey, it seems like the accident
happened yesterday. To borrow a description from Ted Wampler, a dear
person I met at Compassionate Friends: "It has seemed like one real
long day."*

*Casey's teammates and coaches haven't forgotten her. Her schools
haven't forgotten her. Her church hasn't forgotten her. Last winter a
plaque, her picture and her #22 basketball jersey were placed in the*

trophy case at Robertsville Middle School, the school she attended her last year. Just before her death, Casey had made both the Oak Ridge High School girls fast-pitch team and the girls basketball team. This spring, an award was presented in her name by the high school fast-pitch team that she was to be part of the year she died. And when the basketball team, again a team she was to be part of the year she died, received state championship rings, Casey got one too. Her Kern slow-pitch teammates, coached by Jim Keiser, wear patches with her number this year. On June 6, 1997, Girls Incorporated of Oak Ridge established the "Casey Shelton Sportsmanship Award" to be presented annually to the Girls Inc member who has demonstrated outstanding attitude, team spirit, effort and commitment. Casey's schools, church and Girls Inc have shown so much care for Casey and our family. They have no way of knowing what their kind gestures mean to us.

A few years later, I learned that Rusty Sampson, who coached girls fast-pitch at the high school, set up three things after Casey died. (1) The jersey she would have had (#21) was put out of service. Nobody would have that number until she would have graduated. (2) Team members wore a #21 shoe decal the four years she would have been in high school. And, (3) the best newcomer each year, whether a freshman or not, was given the "Casey Shelton Award." Rusty also told me that the players had ID tags on their bags, which were basically the players numbers. He and Coach Mary Ann Johnson carried Casey's.

I also learned that a planting bed in front of the main entrance to Kern Memorial Church was placed as a memorial to Casey. In a church bulletin it was noted that a unique maple tree, the Bloodgood Japanese Maple, surrounded by Mondo Grass and Helleri Holly, were to remind people of "the beautiful young lady who left us all too soon."

Like many parents who have lost children, I search for something positive – a message, something I could tell someone to help them, something I could do to keep others from traveling down the road I'm on. I don't know what my role will be in the future. I feel like there must be something. I just don't know yet what it is, but I feel like I should do something.

I want to say: Parents, please cherish your children. We often hear of how teenagers think nothing can happen to them, but it's not just teenagers who think like that. During the course of raising three daughters, the scary thought occasionally crossed my mind: What would I <u>do</u> if anything happened to my children? But I never thought anything really would. Then it did. So parents, please tell your children what they mean to you. Hug them, squeeze them, tell them how much you dearly love them. And enjoy every precious minute you spend with them.

July 23, 1997
Dear K-K, I am having so much trouble getting through this time. The memories overwhelm me. Your Uncle Bill made a tape of you and gave to me. It's a collection of videos shot by him and Dustin, your cousin, through the years. I love watching. You are so alive, so real, having fun, laughing, being funny. The first one, you were just a few days short of being three years old. The last one, you were 13 years old. They're wonderful. So wonderful.

Yesterday I drove to Oak Ridge and picked up Elizabeth Polfus and took her to my house, and then back home. We talked about you the whole time. She had called the night before and wanted to know if she could come see me. She loved you so, Casey. I asked her who her best friend is now, and she said nobody. She told me about Brandi Jordan calling her and telling her about the accident. Her mom was not home, but found out, and came home crying, to be with Liz. She said the night the accident happened that a strange feeling had just come over her and she brushed it off, not knowing what made her feel that way.

She also told me that you and she were with her mother at the Piece Goods Shop and that's where you saw the penguin pins you gave Erin and Brad. She said you told her you had to get them for Erin and Brad. She said you left the bag and your change in her mother's van, and she has the bag with the money inside hanging in her room. She told me something funny too. She said you and she each wore one of the penguin pins on your ball socks that night for luck (but she said you both got skinned up that night – some luck!). She said you then took the pins off to give to Erin and Brad. I can't wait to tell Erin that. She'll love it.

Liz also told me that you told her one time that something happened, that you were thinking about. That Steve talked to you about giving your mom a ring. She said you said that you had to protect your mom. But she said you said you thought Steve would be good to me and not hurt me – and Steve said he'd get you a dog. She also told me that she remembers when you were so upset about Granny's house burning. She said you were real quiet that day and you said you could just see your grandmother trying to put it out.

I loved spending time with Liz. You and she look so much alike. Several times I caught myself trying to pretend she was you. That's probably not good, but I couldn't help it.

We took new blue flowers to your niche, and I let her put them on it. She wanted to go there; she hadn't been and didn't know where it was. She had so much fun with you. You were her best friend. I told her I would never forget her, that even when she's 40 years old I'll always remember her as 13 and your friend. And that's true. You made her a part of my life's experience, a person I will always remember because of you.

Casey, my little girl, I love you so. I went for a real long walk yesterday and cried for you, cried for me. I will see you again some day. I will see you again. I miss you so much. – With all my love, Mom

❧

July 24, 1997
Dear K-K, Brittney called me last night and we talked about you for a long time. I can hear the sadness in Brittney's voice. I've heard it every time we've talked since we lost you. She was your "bestest best friend" as you called her. After we talked, I was looking through some of your things. You had a little photo album you kept special pictures in. You had pictures of me, your dad, Nikki, Erin, Brad and Brittney. Brittney said you and she never argued or disagreed even once the whole time you were together – which was since fourth grade. Your best friend status even survived her moving out of Oak Ridge and changing schools several times. I asked Brittney if she thought you knew how much I loved you, and she said you did. That made me feel good. I don't know what I would have done if she'd said no. Brittney said you told her if I was in a bad mood, you could start talking to me about the sky and that would make me happy. Brittney said one day when she was at our house, I

seemed in a bad mood and you said, "Let's go start pointing out clouds to Mom and that'll make her happy." Brittney said you two talked about everything.

Brittney had just returned home from vacation when she called me. She said she always took your picture everywhere she goes and that one night your picture somehow was wherever her mom was, instead of where Brittney was. She said she discovered she didn't have it when she went to bed. But her mom promised her that she had taken care of it. She said her mom tried to get her to ride the sky dive at Six Flags with her and her brother, but she wouldn't because of the memory of riding it with you. That was your ride. Brittney's a sweet girl, and there's no doubt in my mind she grieves tremendously for you.

Casey, I love you. It has now been one year since I saw your precious face. Stay with me. I miss you so. – Love to my little baby girl, Mom

❧

On July 25, 1997, the one-year anniversary of Casey's death, our family spent the day and night together at Marilyn and David Stanley's lake house. We talked about Casey and watched home movies of her. We each wrote a letter to her, then got into the boat together and one-by-one burned each letter and let its ashes fall into the water. Marilyn was such a good friend to me. She was so thoughtful and supportive. She had left a copy of Richard Dew's book *Rachel's Cry* at the lake house for me. I read it that day and copied four poems that just seemed to speak to me, on a pad of paper. With Richard's permission, I am sharing the poems with you:

<u>Looking Back</u>
When the
Future seems gone
We look to the past, preferring sweet dreams
of them
To the nightmare
of now.

Painful Pleasure
It hurts so much to remember,
But to relive those moments again
Is the closest I come to pleasure,
Yet it's not very different from pain.

Then why hold so hard to memories
That are painful and make me upset?
If I let myself stop hurting,
I'm afraid that I will forget.

Come Away
Come, my child, and go with me,
We'll do all the things that we planned.
Things will be like they used to be,
We'll run and we'll play hand-in-hand.
Hurry, my child, I'll go with you
To places that we've never been,
Many new things we'll see and do,
We'll laugh and be happy again.
Oh, no, my child, don't stay behind,
And leave me to live all alone.
I think that I'll go out of my mind
With nothing to touch but a stone.

An Ordinary Day
It was just another day.
No one special came.
Nothing unusual happened.
The evening was the same.
Just an ordinary day
And then the telephone rang.
From that moment on forever
Everything was changed.

July 28, 1997

Dearest Casey, All day I have relived July 28th of last year, the date of your memorial service. I tried to stay so busy cleaning the lake house. I dreaded two o'clock coming. Your memorial service last year had begun at two o'clock. But then when the time approached, I went outside on the deck and called your name and told you I love you. As I did that, the sky began to rumble. So I sat down on the screened-in porch and watched and listened. It was beautiful. The wind blew, the temperature dropped, the thunder sounded like a bowling alley. It did my heart so much good. You and I both love storms. We communicate with each other. I know that's what it is. And I thank God for making that happen. I feel silly sometimes telling God to take care of you (like I could do better than God!), but I know He understands.

I so dreaded July 25th this year. Steve and I came to the lake house on the 24th after we got off work and spent the night. I spent all day the 25th thinking of you. It was a difficult day for me.

That evening, something happened that was almost breathtaking, something probably not just everyone would believe really took place, but I know it did and that's all that matters. Again, I felt you communicating with me. I was alone because Steve and Chris had gone to the store. I was sitting down at the dock and at eight o'clock my heart really hurt. (The best I can figure, the accident happened between eight-thirty and nine o'clock p.m. last year.) I literally had stabbing pains in my heart. After awhile, I walked to the house and got a drink and ate some strawberry Twizzlers, and then I walked back to the dock. I sat on the deck over the boathouse and watched the sun set. I completely forgot about my heart hurting because the clouds and the setting sun put on a spectacular show. I felt this was your presence and God's way of letting us be together in spirit. What happened was that I saw a cloud and at first I thought, "Oh, that looks like an angel." But the longer and more closely I looked, it was your profile. Your face. Your hair. Your arms. It was you. I saw you. You were the angel in the shape made by the cloud. Your arm reached toward the sun which was going down in the sky and which was a blazing red. Then I turned to look at something else and when I looked back I saw a cloud shaped like Shay, your dog, running toward the angel. It was the most beautiful display. I know you and God did that. And you did it for me. I cry and feel like my heart will break, but it is you and God who comfort me. Your presence in my heart. God's presence.

Nikki, Erin, Brad and Kurt arrived at the lake house later that night. How your sisters miss you! How they loved you so! On Saturday night, we all wrote a note to you. We went out in the boat and one by one lit our notes with a match and sent a special message to you. There were seven of us: Steve, Erin, Brad, Nikki, Kurt, Chris and me. It was a special time and our way of honoring you. Kurt said he saw shooting stars in the sky. Did you like that?

My little precious girl, I miss you so much! I love you so very very much. I don't need certain dates or times to remember you, because I have you always in my thoughts. I've spent the last four days sort of stepping out of the everyday world, and in a place that is becoming more and more familiar to me. You're with me all the time wherever I am, but the solitude and the time I have to write to you and about you and to read books and poems that deal with losing your child and just the alone time with my thoughts have been good for me. I would give anything to feel at home again in the world we once knew where it was fun because you were there and this nightmare didn't happen, but that world doesn't exist for me anymore. It's just a memory.

Steve will be here in about an hour to pick me up and take me back "home," and I'll get up and go back to work tomorrow. I wish I could just stay here. Here in this little world where I see reminders that you are very much with me. It doesn't surprise me that I see those reminders in clouds and storms. That was our thing – yours and mine.

I love you, Casey. I really, really love you. I miss you. You are precious. – Love, Mom

❧

July 30, 1997
Dear Casey, Mr. Edmond called me today to say hello. Someone at work had told me yesterday that they saw Mr. and Mrs. Edmond at church and they talked about remembering that we had lost you at this time last year. Mr. Edmond told me that you had gotten real close to his heart and that he would always remember you and that he loved you and our family and misses you. He said he would always ask you if you wanted a

cookie, and you'd say, "That's OK." He said that meant you wanted one, and he'd get some for you.

I told Mr. Edmond that you had learned so much about nature and animals from him. You used to follow him around outside, and he told you about how to tell it was deer eating his plants because of the height they stood. And he showed you the baby bunnies hidden under a carpet of rabbit fur in the ground. And he showed you the baby birds in the pot of flowers hanging on his porch. He taught you about snakes and groundhogs and who knows what else. He pumped up your bicycle tires and gave you lumber to build me a flower box. He was the "grandfather" you missed out on. And you knew that.

I remember the time Mrs. Edmond fell and broke her ankle and the ambulance came for her. You were so upset to think that something might have happened to Mr. Edmond. We stood in the yard together and were so relieved to see Mrs. Edmond <u>sitting up</u> on the stretcher as they carried her out of the house. You were so upset you were shaking.

It's amazing how many people you touched. One of the things I remember Dr. Ingram saying at your memorial service was, "Everybody loved Casey." Everybody did. Everybody. – Love, Mom

❧

We made it, somehow, through the first year. I don't remember having any expectations for what the second year would be like. People continued to say it would get easier with time, but I couldn't even imagine that yet. For me, it didn't get better, only worse. There was so much more to go through.

❧

August 1, 1997
Dear Casey, It's August now. I hate July. Remember when it was a rule in our house that the first words out of your mouth on the first day of every month had to be "Rabbit, Rabbit," and then you made a wish? Do you still do that? You always did. Your sisters always did. I always did. It was one of our things. I think about it every month now, but I don't do it anymore. It's lost some of its meaning.

This afternoon I was thinking about how you had names for people. Do you remember how you always called Baxter Underwood "Friend"?

Never "Baxter" – always "Friend." That's what you started calling him as a little girl, and it stuck. That was another special, unique thing about you – you liked nicknames and gave them away freely. You had a way of seeing humor in lots of things, even names. I was "June-e-o" (pronounced with an "H," like "Hoon-e-o"), Erin was "Air Head," Rachel Harris was "Ray's Child," Elizabeth Polfus was "Lizard," Sara Keiser was "Sara-B." Your Kern coaches were "Buford" (Jim Eaton), "Loafy" (Harold Harder) and "Hubert" (Randy Cantrell). You didn't give your head coach, Jim Keiser, a nickname. You always called him "Mr. Keiser."

You had laughter in your eyes, your beautiful eyes that were like pools of clear blue water. When you were a baby, one of your tear ducts had not opened up. Tears, or just eye moisture, would overflow (like spill out onto your cheek). I had to be careful about people taking their Kleenexes or whatever and dabbing the tears from your little cheek or from your eye. I took you to Dr. Francis Reid, whom Dr. Preston had referred us to. While you screamed bloody murder, I held you down and Dr. Reid examined you. He said if the duct was going to open, it should do so by the time you were nine months old, so we'd watch and wait. If it didn't open, he had a procedure he could do. Well, fortunately, a few days short of turning nine months old, the duct opened. I was really glad of that. I couldn't stand the thought of you having to have any sort of procedure done.

The only other time you came close to having to be hospitalized was in March of your first year. You had a cold and were close to being dehydrated. Luckily, you got better and Dr. Preston didn't have to put you in the hospital. That was always scary for me – trying to take care of my little girls when you were sick, and being so scared something would happen to you. None of you were sick very often. You would get the normal colds and ear infections, and you had chickenpox. When you had chickenpox was when I gave you your journal. I glanced over your journal when I gathered up your things to move. Someday I'll read it closely and relish every word your little hand wrote. I still can't look at your things. But someday I will. Someday.

I love you, little girl. You sure gave me a lot of memories. I wish you were here so I could tell you about them and about how cute you were. I love you so much. I miss you. Love forever, blue eyes. – Mom

❦

August 4, 1997
Dear Casey, Where are you? The answer doesn't stop the grief in my heart. I know you are with God. I want you with me. I miss you. I love you. – ❤Mom

❦

August 6, 1997
Dear Casey, I was in a daze this time last year. A world so unfamiliar. So sad. So literally breathtaking – not in a good sense, but in the sense that I felt like I was holding my breath all the time. Losing you caused me to stop breathing. I really <u>wanted</u> to stop breathing. I wanted to die too. I remember Marilyn Stanley coming to see me, and she told me that every mother in Oak Ridge was grieving with me. I know when other mothers lost children, I'd think, "How do they stand that?" I truly don't know how I am surviving this. I would never have thought I could. It's God and Steve and Nikki and Erin who keep me going. For them I'm grateful. But, sometimes, I still wish I could just die too. The pain of losing you will only end when I die. I miss you so much. – Love, Mom

❦

August 7, 1997
Dear Casey, Last night I was thinking about the letters I write to you. They flow so easily. I wondered if I would run out of things to tell you someday, but I quickly thought no, that won't happen. And it won't. As long as my life goes on, I'll have things to tell you. I'm looking forward to someday listening to all the things <u>you'll</u> have to tell me. You have passed me in wisdom and understanding and will have glorious things to tell me. Little girl, I miss you so much.

This morning I was thinking about how you liked to fish. A couple of years (when you were around 11 or 12 years old) you went to the Trout Fishing Tournament at Frozen Head State Park with David and Max. You liked that. We always laughed because Max called it "The Tourney." Erin has your fishing poles and tackle box now. When she opened your tackle box, it had the remnants of a Subway sandwich in it. You never threw away anything. That was one of those things about you. You had wrappers and papers and all sorts of stuff stashed all over your room and in your drawers and in your backpack. Why does that seem so precious to me now? Your garbage would be precious to me.

Sunday afternoon Erin and I were at the mall and as we walked, we talked about how neither of us can bear to wear the dresses we wore to Weatherford's Funeral Home and to your memorial service at church. I thought only I felt that way, but Erin said she does too. I purposely didn't buy a new dress, because I didn't want a "funeral" dress. And I purposely didn't wear black. So I wore the yellow dress I had worn to Erin's wedding, to Weatherford's. And the pink dress I had worn to your baptism, to your memorial service. Now I can't look at those dresses. They had been associated with happiness; now it's sadness. I can't bear to wear the dress I was wearing when I found out about you and went to the hospital. I had worn it all the time. It was a blue dress. Now I can't stand it. It's associated with pain. Erin told me she had been ironing when she found out about you. Now she won't iron anymore. That is associated with pain. Nikki had told me that a phone ringing in the night upsets her, because she associates that with being told about you. Her friends at school last year unplugged the phone in her room at night. They told me that.

We love you so much, Casey. Your leaving has changed our family so. You left a huge gap that will forever be there. You will always be missed. In many ways you embodied the best parts of all of us. Your personality from the time you were an infant was charming. Your heart was huge. Your kindness was low-key and almost an embarrassment to you. That's what made it so special. You really were a special person. I love you. – ❤*Mom*

❧

August 13, 1997
Hi, Little Girl. Do you know I tell you hello when I walk in my office in the morning and see your picture? I tell you and Nikki and Erin hello. Of course by the time I arrive at work, I've had you on my mind for a while. It's sort of a little ritual though to tell your picture hello. Another ritual I do is blow a kiss when I pass your niche. As many times in the past year as I have driven on the highway in front of the memorial park, I have never forgotten to blow you a kiss. I will always do that. I promise.

I've been worried about Erin. For the past several weeks she has seemed very down. I know she hurts so. I wish I could help her. I feel so down myself that I'm not sure how I can lift her up, but talking about you seems to help both of us. We are lost without you, Casey. You sure were a big part of us.

Nikki is home this week. She's getting ready to move to Louisiana. I can hardly let myself think about that. I'm happy for her and always want her to never be afraid to <u>live</u>, but that will be a long way from home. You'll be thought about in Louisiana now.

Nikki and I took a walk Sunday night and then sat on the deck till 11 o'clock. The whole time, we talked about you. She said she feels cheated to have lost you. I do too. We talked about how you endeared yourself to everyone, without even trying. All her friends just loved you. I remember in particular how Brandy Barton loved you. You called her "Rock-N-Roll," and you two had this little special sign you made to each other. I can remember how distressed she was when I saw her at the receiving of friends. And Ben Witt and Darren Stewart and Brad Teague were there and Yvette Roberts and Jennifer Morris. Those kids spent a lot of time at our house and loved you.

Erin's friends loved you too. The whole ball team was there. Plus tons of your friends. You had such a way, Casey. You really had a special way that drew people to you. I sure admire that. You were a heck of a kid, little girl. I know you would have grown up to be a heck of an adult. I feel so sad to know that won't be. Like Nikki said: I feel cheated.

I saw a Family Circus cartoon this weekend. It showed the grandmother being stopped by a friend who told her she was so sorry she had lost her husband. The grandmother replied that she hadn't lost her husband, she knew where he was (it showed him in heaven) – it was she who was lost. I feel that way too.

I really miss you, Casey. I really do. More and more every day, not less. I love you, baby. – ❤ Mom

August 14, 1997
Dear K-K, Schools are starting today. I can't stand to listen to news reports about "the first day of school" now, so I avoid that. You should be here, starting school.

I remember last August I would actually almost lose my breath, or have something that's probably akin to a panic attack, in stores when I came across school supplies. I would think, "I have to get out of here." I have learned to avoid certain things: the school supplies aisles, the toy sections, pet stores and supplies.

One of the biggest changes or journeys I've made from last August to this August is last August my emotions were so raw, literally raw. I felt like I was about to jump out of my skin. It's like I wanted to run and run and run and collapse and never wake up again. Sometimes I still have those feelings, but mostly what I feel now is just an intense sense of sadness. I remember the absolute misery I felt in the first month or so when I would awaken. It's like my brain would wake up and I'd be OK for just a second . . . and then I would remember that you died. Everything inside me cried out, silently. I don't know if I actually breathed a sound, but I felt a cry and groan inside me. A misery beyond my ability to describe.

I miss you so much. I feel so sad. I feel like my head is full of tears (as in teardrops that flow from my eyes) and my heart is full of tears (as in openings made by being pulled apart). Tears and tears – two different pronunciations for a word that has such meaning for me now.

I wasn't ready to quit being your mother. I wasn't ready to stop attending all the basketball and softball games that had played such a huge role in my life since the day your oldest sister played her first t-ball game and blazed the trail that you were still following. I wasn't finished being your mother. At the time you died, I had been baking birthday cakes and having slumber parties and dropping kids off at school and transporting kids to basketball, softball and fast-pitch games for a long time. But I had four more years to go with those kind of "mom" things, because you had four more years of school before you would head off to college. Those were four years I looked forward to. But with your death, those "mom" things ended abruptly for me. I no longer have anyone to chauffeur. The other girls drive themselves, and they no longer live at home. All those million and one activities you should have been participating in as a teenager ended for me too. I heard someone say that she looked up the word "mother" in the dictionary, and its first definition is as a verb. It's something you "do" before you become one. I wasn't finished doing. Nikki and Erin didn't need for me to "do" much anymore, but you did.

I can no longer even imagine attending a high school or college sporting event . . . because you should be there. There is no longer a child with me, daily, to cook for or wash clothes for or just be with. There is no one to tap out "Shave and a Haircut" on the wall. It may seem like a small thing, but along with my anger that you have been cheated of these things, I feel cheated too. I wasn't finished being your mom.

It's been said that a mother is never out of a job. And in a sense, that's even true for the mother of a deceased child. We often spend more time thinking about our deceased children than we do our surviving children.

I don't understand why <u>you</u> of all the people in the world had to die. I don't understand. I can't believe this. Why was it <u>you</u>? I should have died first. I had lived 44 years. You had just begun. I can't stand this. How I miss you! How I miss our life together! I love you, Casey. I always will. – ❤Mom

I don't know when I wrote the following; it's undated.

I used to think I would like to write a book. I never got to the point of choosing <u>what</u> I would write about. Now, it's been chosen for me. I have become a member of a minority (although I'm learning all the time just how many there are of us in this minority) that I would give my heart and soul not to be a member of. I never wanted to be like everybody else. But now it seems like those "everybody elses" – at least in my circle of friends and acquaintances – have something I desperately long for. They have their children, all of them. Their lives are normal, not torn apart because they lost a child so precious to them. I want to be like everybody else.

What will the name of my future book be? "Casey"? "My Littlest Ladybug"? "Heaven Is Much Closer to Me Now"? "Tears and Tears"? "Just Like A Hollow Easter Bunny"?

August 20, 1997

My Precious Little Girl, I have returned home from Louisiana where I spent the last five days with Nikki, helping her get moved and settled in. Yesterday when I left her, it hurt probably more than it would have had I not experienced the loss of you. On the drive to the airport, a huge lump developed in my throat as I recalled the last time I hugged you. What if that was the last time I hugged <u>her</u>? So many times every day I have to tell myself, "Stop! Don't think that! Don't go there! Don't remember! Stop that thought! Think of something else! DO NOT GO THERE!" . . . I'm becoming the master of escape.

Sometimes I even worry about what I'm doing, because I think most of the time you must deal with life head-on. But I can't anymore. I'm at my most confused period. Outside, I go on and try to be somebody that's good for Nikki, Erin and Steve. But, inside, I am so confused. It's like my insides are screaming and crying. I <u>wanted</u> my plane to crash on my way home. But that's unfair to Steve and your sisters. I wanted to say to them before I left that if anything happened to me, it would really be OK because I'd be dancing with you. But I can't say that kind of thing to them. It would hurt them. I don't love them less than you, or want to be with them less than with you. It's that I want to be with you all – ALL OF YOU. My <u>three</u> girls and my husband. But now it's two girls, and I am so torn between where do I go so I can be with you <u>all</u> and be happy? What can I do? How can I be with you and with them? Oh, Casey, no one knows except God and me (and maybe you?) how I feel.

Last Friday as Nikki and I were driving to Baton Rouge, the sky was full of those fluffy white clouds like it was on that last Friday that you and I had looked at them on our drive to Gallatin for your ball tournament. I found myself thinking of things their shapes reminded me of, and the thought occurred to me that I had not done that since you and I had done it that day on our drive (except for the one-year-anniversary date of your death when I saw you and Shay in the clouds, but I wasn't really "looking" then). That was <u>our</u> thing to do. So I had to stop. I can't do it *by myself. That was our thing. Clouds aren't the same without you. Nothing is the same.*

I hate Oak Ridge and everything in it. Although I love Steve dearly, I hate Knoxville. I hate going to Kern Church. I hate those kids I see going to school every morning. I hate the kids I see at the mall. I hate the kids I see at the movies. I hate life that just goes on. I would not have one single mother lose one single child, but why do I keep having to see them? I don't want anything to happen to any of the kids I see who look so much like you, but why do I keep having to see them?

Casey, I miss you so much. It gets worse as the days go on, not better. I miss you so much! God, how I miss your sweet little face and the <u>life</u> you put in my life. You were such a good little kid. You had a way like nobody else ever had or ever will have. You were so CASEY, and that was so good. I love you. I always will. – ❤Mom

August 20, 1997
Dear K-K, This afternoon I was looking up a word in the "L" section of the dictionary when I came across the word "llama." It reminds me of the time when you were little and just learning your ABCs. You were reciting a word that started with every letter . . . A, apple; B, boy; etc. When you came to L, you said, "L, llama bean." That was so cute. When you got older, I'd tell you about that and you'd just laugh. I can just see you and hear you laughing. I love you, baby. – ❤Mom

August 21, 1997
Dear Casey, Why did you put the dot in the C when you signed your name? I don't remember you ever telling me why, only that that was your signature C. I like that. You signed your name with your very unique C for probably a couple of years. I know the Valentine I have hanging in my office that is dated Valentine's Day 1995 has the C on it. When did you start doing that, and why? Like I say, I like that. Nice touch.

When you were in third grade at Sycamore Elementary in Cookeville, there was a little boy in your class who was deaf. You had a really neat teacher (Brenda Vickers), and she thought it would be good for the class to learn sign language to communicate with the little boy. The aide was very skilled in signing and taught the whole class. You picked it up real quickly. I remember telling you that maybe you should do something when you grew up that involved signing because you were so good at it. At the end of the school year, your class put on a nighttime program at Sycamore and a daytime program at Tennessee Tech where your class signed the words to the songs "From a Distance" by Bette Midler and "Love Can Build a Bridge" by the Judds. All of the class wore tie-dyed shirts (blue and pink) and black shorts. I can just see you on stage doing that. You were really good, Casey. The other day I was driving to work and "From a Distance" came on the radio. That memory just burst into my head. It's a wonderful, wonderful memory, but now it hurts too much to hear the song, so I turned the station. Maybe someday. Maybe.

You're very special to me, Casey. Very special. I miss you so much. I love you. – ❤ Mom

🍃

September 8, 1997
Dear K-K, There are times when I feel like you are sending messages to me. And those occasions have always, without exception, been comforting. The last "message" was two weeks ago. As Steve and I drove back from visiting Ginger and Harry in Germantown, we passed over Rockwood Mountain. The memories of you always <u>always</u> asking, "Where are we?" on the hundreds of trips we made over that mountain together always get to me now that your precious voice is not here to ask me that question that was our little ritual. I was thinking so deeply about you that I could hear your voice ask, "Where are we?" And in my mind, I would answer you, "Rockwood Mountain." Then you'd ask it again, and I'd answer again. And then you'd say, "Just one more time" or "This will be the last time . . . where are we?" I imagined you sitting in the back seat asking me, and I literally turned around to see if you were there. I knew you wouldn't be, but the need to just turn around and make sure was strong, very strong. So I turned around to look. When I didn't see you, I started crying. I cried for miles, and then just as my tears ebbed, I looked out my car window and there, right there on the side of the interstate, was a patch of sunflowers. (The girls told me that it was a blanket of sunflowers that covered your casket, so since that time I have associated sunflowers with you.) Thank you, Casey. Thank you, God. I know you're OK. You're with God. And you're both helping me. I love you. Both of you. – ❤ Love forever and ever, Mom

🍃

September 10, 1997
Dear Casey, Last night I dreamed of you. You were just a little girl. We were in a swimming pool. I remember the sensation of carrying you on my left hip, with your right arm around my neck – just like I always carried you. Then I saw you in the water. The water was crystal clear, and you were on the floor of the pool. You were smiling at me, even though you were underwater, and I was walking toward you. I know I reached down to lift you up, and I know I got you. But that's all I can remember. Maybe that's all I dreamed.

Today that dream has crossed my mind several times. I saved you. It wasn't like you were drowning or anything. You were just standing there, maybe even walking, but you weren't panicked. Just standing there smiling at me. You knew I would pick you up. You were waiting for me.

I saved you in my dream, Casey. I am so sorry I didn't save you in real life. I am sorry, Casey. So very, very sorry.

I love you, my little girl. – Love forever, Mom

☙

September 11, 1997
Dear Casey, For some reason, I was thinking today of how I am glad that I don't have to think about your little body buried in a grave. I could not stand the thought of that. During the past 13½ months, my mind has skimmed the surface of imagining your cremation, but I will not let my mind linger there. That is truly too painful. So I just think about how cremation was better. I can deal with that better. I will be cremated too. Just like you. Oh, Casey, <u>why</u> <u>why</u> did it have to be you first? It should have been me. There is nothing I wouldn't give to trade places with you. <u>You</u> should be alive. You were so young. You had so much living to do.

When we took Granny home last Sunday from spending the weekend with us, we passed by the tree where the accident happened. Even as I write this, I feel such a wave of anger. How could that have happened? I am so angry. So very angry. And I only feel angrier as time goes by.

Casey, I miss you so much. – ❤*Love forever, Mom*

☙

September 15, 1997
Dear Casey, Boy, am I having a hard time. Yesterday at Compassionate Friends a lot of the discussion was about the anger parents feel toward the person responsible for their child's death. Although I didn't speak at the meeting, I was thinking, "How would you deal with it if the person was your sister's daughter, your niece?"

I protected you from activities (or the ones I knew about, anyway) where I thought there was a possibility you could get hurt. Why did I not protect you this time? Casey, I am so sorry. I am so very, very sorry.

I love you with all my heart. I feel like my heart is going to break. I miss you so much! – Mom

❧

September 19, 1997
Dear Casey, Sometimes I don't have the words to describe how I feel. Then I'll read something another parent who's lost a child has written and I'll think, "Yes. That's how I feel too." People who see me probably think I'm coping well. And I am. Coping. But it's so hard. It's so hard to "cope." Today I read something to the effect of, "How dare you go on with your lives as if nothing has happened!" And, "Don't tell me your troubles, I've got troubles of my own." Sometimes that's how I feel toward other people. Life goes on, but I don't care. I'm sorry.

You, Casey, are always with me. I love you, Casey! – Love, Mom

❧

September 25, 1997
Dear Casey, September 25. Fourteen months since you were taken away. Fourteen months. I still cannot believe this happened.

It does not get better. It does not get easier. I cannot see you. I want to see you so much! I want to hear you. I cannot believe this happened. I cannot believe it.

I can't think about it, but can't not think about it. I like to think about you. I remember so many things about you every day. The nights are so hard. Remember how I used to sleep? I dropped off as soon as my head hit the pillow and didn't wake up till the alarm went off. That doesn't happen anymore unless I've taken something to help me sleep. I wake up and get so depressed. I try to not think about it, but that is so hard. So very hard. I get so angry that I feel my heart pound. Sometimes I wish I didn't have to stay here and endure life. I hate living with this. There are so many wonderful things about life, but how can anything be wonderful anymore? There's an intense sadness and hurt that make up who I am now. Who I will always be. Casey, I was happy until you were taken. Life was getting better and easier for us. Then this happened. You were hurt. It hurts me so to imagine that you were frightened, then hurt. I can't stand that. And I really can't stand that you didn't come back. I cannot stand this! I cannot stand this!

Casey, I miss you so much. You were so precious to me. – Love forever and ever, Mom

The following is undated, but it's with the letters and notes I wrote in September 1997. It's a poem that just seemed to write itself with my pen.

"I"

I think I tried to deny it.
I would not participate in choosing her casket.
I would not participate in choosing her urn.
I would not wear black. I wore the yellow dress I had worn for Erin's
     wedding, to the receiving of friends. Then I wore the pink dress I
     had worn to her baptism, to her funeral. I would not wear black.
I would celebrate her life.
I would stay in a room filled with pictures of her life. I would not go in a
     room where her lifeless body rested.
I would not look at her that way.
I would tell her friends "Thank you" for being her friends and being a
     part of her life.
I would tell them to never forget her.
I would comfort them.
I would pretend she'd be back.
I would pretend this didn't happen.
I would pretend, because I could not take what seemed to be happening.
I would go from store to store to buy underwear and socks for her to
     wear for the last time.
I would not look at her. I would not – not ever – say goodbye.

But now I cannot deny it.

*And although I didn't help choose the casket or urn or even see them, I
    do see them. I see them in my mind.*

*And maybe I should have worn black. I hate those yellow and pink
    dresses now.*

*I do celebrate her life. I thank God for who and what she was. But I
    wanted her longer.*

*Pictures of her. Sometimes I stare at them. Sometimes I talk to them. But
    sometimes now I can't look at them.*

*I never saw her "dead." But my tortured mind does sometimes imagine
    how she looked. After all, I saw her asleep almost every day of
    her life. (There's that word again: life. How I loved life! How I
    hate it sometimes now.)*

Did her friends think I was strange?

Sometimes I still pretend she'll be back. I like to.

*Too many things say this <u>did</u> happen to allow me to pretend it didn't. I
    haven't seen her now for almost 14 months. 14. She was just 14.
    God, she was just 14.*

September 28, 1997

*Dear K-K, Today Erin and I visited a new church. I haven't been to
Kern for two months now. It's too painful. Too many memories. Too
hard to see the girls your age who are changing and growing up.*

*Today when we recited the Lord's Prayer, I thought of when you were
learning it. You said it over and over and over and over and over. What
a precious memory. What a precious child. How I miss you, my little
girl! –* ❤*Love forever and ever, Mom*

September 29, 1997

*Dear Casey, Today is my last day of work at Y-12. I know it serves no
purpose to think about – but I can't help but think if I hadn't worked at
Y-12 I'd still have you. If I'd gone somewhere else to work, somewhere
not in the vicinity of Granny's home, you would not have been at her
house. You would not have been with Jennifer. We would be together.
This would not have happened. I didn't want to work at Y-12. If only I
had gone with my gut feeling. If only I'd worked somewhere else, this
would not have happened. You would have been somewhere else on
July 25th. I feel so incredibly sad when I think of how you lost your life*

and that maybe I could have prevented it. We could have stayed in Cookeville. We could have gone somewhere else. I know my promise was that we would come back to Oak Ridge – that's where you and Nikki and Erin wanted to be. Maybe we couldn't have gone somewhere else to live – but I could have worked somewhere else. Somewhere else would have changed the circumstances. If I'd been a school teacher, you would have been home with me because I would have been home in the summertime. I screwed things up so badly. I lost you. I lost you! I was supposed to be a teacher. I would have been off in the summer. You would have been home. I hate myself so much.

But I love you. I love you so much. I miss you so much. – Love forever, Mom

September 30, 1997
Dear Casey, I'm sitting here at home looking out the window and thinking, "What am I going to do now?" I'm only hours into being unemployed. I know I won't stay unemployed for long. I have nothing to do. Nothing to do. I want to go home. But home is not there anymore. You are gone, Nikki now lives in Baton Rouge and Erin now lives in Seymour. I could have taken Nikki and Erin growing up and moving away – that was what was supposed to happen. But you are gone. Not moved away. Not grown up. Gone. Gone from me. Home was you, Nikki, Erin and me. And then home was going to be you, me and Steve until <u>you</u> grew up and moved away. Where is home now? It does not exist. It ended July 25th. I am a visitor wherever I go now. Right now I feel sorry for myself. I hate that. I am so lucky to have Steve and the home he has given me. I would not hurt him for anything in the world. No one has ever been as nice to me as he is. I love him dearly. He has saved me. But I want home. I want my girls. I want what WAS, not IS. I want my girls and Steve. <u>All</u> of you.

I stopped by your niche this morning. I had not been there before at that time of day. Your niche sparkled with the sunlight on it. It was very beautiful. It should sparkle. It has the urn that contains the most precious remains (I don't like that word, but what else do you use) of the most precious child. Remains. I don't like that word.

Casey, my heart is gone. It is with you. I do have so much love for Nikki and Erin and Steve. That will never change. That will never leave. But my heart, my spirit, for everything else is – where is it??

I look at your picture and it takes my breath away. Remains. I don't like that word. I won't use it again. That reminds me of when you were going to be taken to be cremated. Erin said you were "going on a little trip." Then I remember telling her that you were back. That breaks my heart to remember. My heart feels like it will break. I miss you. I love you so much. – Mom

October 1, 1997
Dear K-K, I scribbled this down from a magazine I was looking through while waiting in Dr. Griffith's office today. I thought of you. Always. – Love, Mom

"When you have a baby, you'll know a secret no man can ever know. You may forget it later, but for a little while you will know that within yourself you hold another's life.

"If you ever lose a child, you'll know the other side of the truth. You'll understand what it means to be destroyed and still get up every day and fill the kettle with water. You will see steam from the kettle and weep. Insist nothing is wrong. A piece of dirt flew up and lodged beneath your eyelid. If you show your grief, it won't go away. If you keep it secret, it won't go away. But there may be an hour when you don't remember. An evening when the sky is blue as ink. Whisper your child's name. Then be quiet. If you're lucky, you'll hear the name said back to you every time you close your eyes." ["What Grandma Knows," advice from Lillie Lulkin, 1903-1987]

October 8, 1997
Dear Little Casey, You are so very dear to me. This past week I have been almost obsessed with organizing and storing all the thousands of pictures I've made over the past 20+ years. I've looked at your sweet little face countless times and smiled inside, but died inside over and over. This week has been very, very hard. But I have that job done, and I feel glad about that.

I have been so very troubled. I have a really hard time dealing with losing you, and it seems to only get worse, not better. Sometimes I wish I could go too. But that would hurt Steve and Nikki and Erin, and I could never do that. You'd be disappointed too if I gave up. I know that. I'm just looking for relief from how I feel. One night I was thinking about giving Nikki and Erin their baby books and photo albums, but then I thought about how people sometimes start giving their things away in preparation for taking their life – and I didn't. I'm not going to. Whenever it's my time, I'll go, just like you.

I hope I'll be as prepared as you were in the sense that there is absolutely no doubt where you are. I've done so many wrong things in my life that it's hard for me sometimes to hear or read of God punishing people. Am I being punished? But then I think of you, and I know God wasn't punishing you by taking your life, because you had done nothing to be punished for. Doug Manning in his book "Don't Take My Grief Away" said, "To think He took another person's life to teach you a lesson or to punish you is arrogance. This says your life is more important than the one He took."

No, God is not punishing. He's loving. I've seen God's love in helping me the past 14½ months. I believe you're incredibly happy and peaceful. I just miss you.

Today I got a letter from the doctor saying I need more surgery for a basal cell carcinoma. I'm really upset. I guess seeing the word "cancer" checked on my pathology report and then reacting as I am is not in line with someone who thinks they'd like to die. The only reason I'd want to is to see you again. But God promises me – us! – eternity. Casey, you be with me and keep me fit for being with you and God for eternity.

I'm probably rambling, but putting some of my feelings on paper to you helps me. As I said, I've had a rough week. Now that I'm on a respite from work, I feel guilty because the time I should have been staying home was when you and Erin and Nikki were growing up. There's no reason for me to be home now, although my emotional frame of mind is not the best. I just wish you were here. I'd have a reason to be here. I miss being your mother. I really miss you and what you added to my life.

My life doesn't even resemble what it used to. I miss you. I miss Erin. I miss Nikki. I miss me.

Little Louise. K-K. Casey Lou. You were something else. I loved you dearly. I always will. – Love forever, Mom

❧

October 9, 1997
Dear K-K, I was reading the newspaper and saw a picture of Chipper Jones of the Atlanta Braves. You really liked Chipper Jones. You really liked the Braves. You went to see games in Atlanta several times with Gail and David. I'm so glad you got to go. You also liked Steve Avery of the Braves. We'd look through your baseball cards, and you insisted I pick my favorite player. I picked the shortstop. His name was Jeff Blauser, I think. You loved those Braves. You liked to watch games on TV with Granny. You liked all sports.

I love you, my little girl. I miss you very much. I loved the way you were, the way you loved sports. I often think of the dream you had where you were playing ball with your papaw. I can imagine you doing that. I know that thrills my dad.

I love you. I miss you. – Love always and always, Mom

❧

October 14, 1997
Dear Casey, Last night I dreamed I had you in my arms and I was washing your hair. I dreamed you pulled me to you and hugged me. I can still feel that hug. Thank you for coming to me in my dreams. I can feel your hug. You were a little girl, probably three or four. I was washing your hair. It was so real, a little routine we went through hundreds, probably thousands, of times. But the hug you gave me was deeper and longer and stronger. It meant the world to me. I hope the remembrance of that hug never ever leaves me.

I love you, my precious Casey. Come to me again. Please. – Love forever, Mom

❧

October 18, 1997
My Little Girl, How I miss you! As I was packing to go away for Steve's and my anniversary weekend, I was thinking about how we used to sing

the "Kookaburra" song. I could hear your laughter. How I used to pretend to get upset when you girls would purposely call the bird in the song a "Kookaburry," and you would just laugh and laugh. I miss your laughter so much. I can still hear it inside my head. I pray that I will never lose that sound. Casey, I miss you so much. Only God knows how it hurts.

Until we meet again, my heart will hurt. I love you, my little girl. You are precious to me, so very precious. – Love forever, Mom

❧

October 28, 1997
My Dear, Dear, Casey, I know you are with me, but I miss seeing you and hearing you and being able to hug you so much. I have been off work for the past month, taking care of projects and doing stuff around the house and just sort of trying to get a hold on this different life that happened when I lost you. I don't know that I will ever think of life as normal again. It's all still strange and foreign to me. I cannot explain that feeling to anyone, and don't even try. I think the only person who would understand would be someone in the same situation.

I visited with Kathy's mother one day last week. While we didn't discuss this in particular, I think she might come as close as anyone to understanding how I feel. I really love her. You know I really loved Kathy. It gives me a feeling of peace (along with sadness and wanting to be there too) when I think of you and Kathy together. Kathy was my best friend, and I'll never have another like her. You know something? You were my friend too. I would have liked you and wanted to be around you even if you hadn't been born my daughter. I think that's neat. I really LIKED you – as well as LOVED you, with all my heart.

I often think of how I just took it for granted that I would always have you. I wish I had been a better mother. There was never ever a second that I didn't love you or want you; I just wish I'd been more loving and made absolutely positively sure that you knew how crazy I was about you. Please know that, Casey. Please feel my love for you even now. My love will always always be there for you. You were so precious to me. I cannot believe this happened. It will hurt until I die.

Yesterday I took Granny and our Aunt Mozell for a ride to Kentucky to see the beautiful leaves. I thought of you so often. When I was driving back home by myself, I especially missed seeing you sitting there beside me. I still look over and expect to see you. We were always together in the car. The passenger seat was your seat. Your seat. Nobody else's. I miss you being there, little girl.

I did something yesterday that I could not keep from doing. As I was driving on Illinois Avenue in Oak Ridge, a car pulled alongside me at the traffic light where Illinois Avenue and Outer Drive intersect. The driver looked so much like you, except she was an older version of what you had looked like when you were 12 and 13. She had a pony tail exactly the color and length of yours, and she was wearing glasses. When we pulled out from the traffic light, she drove off faster than I did (and I felt myself get irritated because I thought she [YOU] were driving too fast.) I sped up and followed her and even ran through a caution light at Illinois and Robertsville Road so she wouldn't get away. The next traffic light caught us, and I pulled alongside her so I could see her face. Looking at her straight on, she didn't look so much like you. But she sure did from the side, so that's the angle I looked at her from. We were stopped at two more traffic lights, and I was so happy just to sit there and look at her. Then she turned left at the street that runs alongside the Comfort Inn. When I saw her change lanes and signal to turn left, I felt so disappointed because I would have loved to keep following her to Knoxville. I'm not sure I would have stopped in Knoxville if she had driven on. I was that caught up in looking at her. But when she turned, and I went on, I asked God to bless that girl and I cried.

I love you, my Casey. I miss you so. – Love, Mom

❧

November 1, 1997
Dear Casey, Today is November 1. I don't say "Rabbit, Rabbit" anymore. That was yours and Nikki's and Erin's and mine. Without you, it's not the same. The meaning is not the same. I know Nikki still says it first thing every time the month changes, because she has called me before and said, "Rabbit, Rabbit." I haven't told her that I can't do that anymore. I believe Erin still says it too. It's still ours – yours and your sisters' and mine.

Today I read an article in the paper about the second coming of Christ. Many, many people believe it will happen in the year 2000. The article I read listed specific reasons why so many people believe it will happen then. It's a very convincing article. Once upon a time that would have sort of frightened me. While not exactly being afraid, at the same time I didn't exactly want that to happen in my lifetime. Now I hope with all my heart that it does. The year 2000 would be wonderful. Actually, today would be wonderful. I could be with you again. Your sisters and Steve and my mom and the people we love could go together to be with you and to see God and live in the wonderful new world that awaits us that you have already experienced. You can be our guide. I really want to see you, Casey. I cannot wait. I wish God would come today. I am ready.

As I read the article I thought if 2000 is right, that means I only have to endure this grief a little over two more years. Casey, I will be so happy to see you again. So happy!! I can't even imagine how happy I will be. It will be glorious. When I think about it, I get so emotional. To see my little Casey again!! I could not stand the sadness if there was no hope that I would ever see you again. I know I will see you again.

Yesterday I took Aunt Hazel to breakfast and spent the morning with her. She told me about an experience she had had a long time ago that proved to her that God exists. She said she had not shared it with many people but felt moved to tell me about it. I appreciated that. I believe with all my heart, more strongly even since I lost you. I have not lost my faith in God; I feel His presence in my life even more. I could not have gotten through this without His love and care for me. I know you are with God and that He loves you very much. And He loves me too. Someday my life on earth will be over and I'll get to share in the wonderful life that you already have. Until then I will miss you every day as long as I live, and I will love you with a love that is so very very strong. You are very precious to me. If God had told me before you were born that I could just have you for 14 years, I would have taken those 14 years. I am thankful you were born and that I had 14 years with you. I just wish it had been longer. I love you, my baby girl. – Love forever, Mom

❦

November 8, 1997
Dear K-K,
This past week I worked in my new job as a librarian. I feel sure you would make fun of that. You'd have some funny remarks to make for sure. But, remember when you went to the library with me at Tech and you colored or drew while I studied? That's a very sweet memory for me.

This week was very emotional at times for me because I came across so many children's books that <u>you</u> had read. It hurt every time I saw and touched one. They brought back so many memories. The book "All About Dogs" was the book that had gotten "misplaced" when you were in seventh grade at Robertsville. The very day I went in with you to pay for it, the librarian said it had been found. Remember that? The other books that made me feel so sad were the little books about Frances and Curious George and the books by Shel Silverstein. I remember the little poem on page 12 in "Light in the Attic" by Shel Silverstein that you had memorized. It was your favorite. I can just hear you reciting "How Not To Have To Dry The Dishes." I can see you as you said it. How I miss you, Casey! Do you have any idea how much I love you? I ask God often to tell you and let you know. I hope with all my heart that when you left this world, you left knowing you were very loved. I miss you so, my little girl. I hope I will see you soon.

You are my sweet and precious child. I miss you so much. – Love forever and ever, Mom

November 8, 1997
Dear Casey, For some reason I was thinking about the time when we read some of "Charlotte's Web" before you went to sleep each night. I would sit on your waterbed and read to you.

But we didn't finish the book. Why didn't we? I don't know. I don't remember. I wish we'd finished it. I'm sorry we didn't finish it.

I love you. I miss you. – Love, Mom

November 20, 1997
Dear Casey, I didn't last long in my job as a librarian. I resigned. Quit.
What has happened to my strength and desire? I could have dealt with
learning the job and dealing with the frustrations at any other point in
my life prior to the horrible accident that took you away and in many
ways took me away too. I just don't care anymore. I have flashes of
inspiration and desire to do something productive, but those feelings
don't last very long. I know I'm fighting depression.

I worked on putting together a photo album of you all day and night
yesterday. It saddens me, but at the same time I'm spending time with
you. I'm reliving the moments those pictures captured. Sometimes I want
to be with you so badly. Even more than that, I want you to be with me,
because I know life; I don't know what it's like in your world. I have
faith that you are OK, better than we are. But it's a mystery I can only
imagine and not <u>see</u> yet. I must have faith. And I do. But it's just hard.

I listened to Barbara Walters interview a person on TV who says we are
surrounded by those who have died. She literally <u>sees</u> those people. That
made me feel good. I want you right here beside me. Are you really
here? I hope so. I wish I could see you.

I love you so much, my little girl. I miss you so. I will always have a
huge empty place in my heart that only you could fill. I will see you
again someday. Till then, please stay with me and don't ever leave my
dreams. I love you. – Mom

❧

November 21, 1997
Sometimes I think about how I grew up in a family where you didn't talk
about the deep stuff. You kept a stiff upper lip and went on about your
life, about your business. I used to pride myself on being strong, on
being able to carry on. I'm not so sure about that anymore. Maybe I
appear strong in dealing with Casey's death. But I'm not. I hurt with an
ache that I have no way to describe.

❧

January 16, 1998
Dear Little Ladybug, It has been a few months since I wrote. I know you
are with me always, that a "letter" alone doesn't connect us. But
somehow I feel like I'm almost letting you down by not writing. Silly,

huh? You are on my mind very often; I don't think you're ever really totally out of my mind, even when I am engaged in some activity that requires my attention. You are so much a part of me.

I've been staying home for awhile. I didn't think it would turn into this long, but I guess in some ways it's been good for me. I know I can't NOT work. Being alone most of the time and not really having much to do are not good. I think that's why I haven't written for awhile. I have been way down there. Very depressed. I feel better now, though, than I did during November and December. Those were very bad months for me. You know that, though, don't you?

I had an experience a few weeks ago that troubled me. I had been unable to sleep. I seem to have fallen into a pattern of sleeping every other night. I had gotten up around three or four a.m., my usual waking time on my off nights, and gone downstairs to read. I was reading "Hello from Heaven" and thinking how I wish I would have one of the experiences like those described in the book where a loved one comes back and is either seen or heard or smelled or sensed. Later in the morning, I went back to bed and drifted off to sleep. I was awakened by your voice. It was your voice. You were saying "Mom!" in the tone of voice you used when Erin and Nikki were bothering you – like "Mom, make them leave me alone!" It was distinctly your voice, your tone, the way I heard you say "Mom" many times. I think I heard it about three times, but didn't fully wake up until the third time. I would love to hear your voice – how I would love to hear your voice and see your beautiful face!! – but I was so sad after this happened. I could not shake my sadness that day.

I hope you will come back to me and show me that you are OK. I know you are OK. I know you are with God. I would like to see you or hear you or feel you though. Come back to me and give me the peace that others speak of who have had such experiences. OK?

I miss you so much. It does not get better. In some ways I guess the past few months have been my time for facing facts. I sure miss the shock and disbelief.

Casey, what am I to do with the bad, angry feelings I have? Yesterday I was out driving in the pouring rain to fax some resumes and drop off applications for jobs. I thought, "What am I doing here? Why am I in Blount County looking for a job?" I lost you. I also lost control of my life. I lost the life I had, the life I loved. Those don't even compare to the devastation of losing you – I would gladly, gladly give up my life for you – but I lost you and my life. I am so angry. God really has a lot of work to do with me. Never in my wildest imagination would life have turned out like this.

Erin and I went to the Lady Vols game on New Year's Day. That's the first basketball game I've been to or even watched. It was so hard. When the music began to play – the very music you had bought Christmas 1995 and played every time we got in the car – I began to cry. When the players came on court, I thought of how you might have been doing that someday. I hated being at that game. I don't know when I'll ever try that again.

Thanksgiving was yucky. Christmas was yucky. New Year's was yucky. I don't like holidays anymore. Your Christmas arrangement was stolen from your niche again this year. I can't believe people do that. Erin said there should be a hot place in hell for people who steal flowers from cemeteries.

I took your Christmas basket to the cemetery on a day when snow was coming down like crazy. I felt you were with me and watching. I talked to you the whole time and didn't even cry that day. I felt like I was making you happy somehow. I put a silly little red bird in your arrangement.

We decorated your Christmas tree in the foyer and added new ornaments. I chose a set of picture frames and put some special pictures in them. Steve chose a little lamb. Nikki chose a picture frame with a dog on it, and Erin chose a dalmatian. Someday we'll have to get a huge tree to hold all the ornaments that we will add every year. I found some really neat fiber optic lights for your tree this year, too, Casey. I'll bet you approved of that tree, didn't you?

Steve's Aunt Hazel said something to me that I've thought quite a bit about. She said she believes I can't find "peace" or whatever the word is, because I did not look at you. I told her I couldn't do that, that I didn't want to see you that way. I still believe that I made the right decision for me. Casey, I could not see you any other way but alive. But sometimes in my lowest times I feel so bad that I was not with you. I was not there with you when God took you to heaven. I was not there to hold you and kiss you and let you know how very very much I loved you. I cannot stand to think about you being all alone in the ambulance. I know you were already with the angels, but I wish I had been with you. I didn't even know until hours later. I didn't even know. I should have been there. I should have been with you. I couldn't look at you at the hospital. I couldn't. But should I have made myself do that? Would you have felt my love and my anguish? Would you have known? Casey, I was not rejecting you. I was rejecting that this had happened. I look back at the first days and months after this all began, and everything I did was such a rejection. Such a denial. I just pray that you know that however I acted and whatever I did and said were from somewhere outside myself.

I think back to the memorial service. I asked Rev. Ingram to select the songs. But I wish I had selected them. I would have stood in line outside the church and been open to the hugs and tears of all the people who came to honor you. I would have worn black. I was trying to just get through. Actually, I wasn't trying anything. I was just functioning. Just being swept along. Not really in the world anymore. Not really me anymore. I hope I did nothing to dishonor you. I just wish I had done something special for you. Something to say to the world how special you were to me. But I couldn't do anything. You know how special you were to me. That's what really matters. You will always be special to me. I will never be OK with losing you. The hurt will end when I die. I only pray that you knew how much I loved you. I wish I had been a better mother. I could not have loved you more, but I could have loved you better. I could have been more patient. I could have been more understanding when you hated certain subjects in school and made bad grades. I could have helped you more. I could have talked to you more. So many things I'd give my life to do over. Did you know how much I loved you? Did you know how special you were to me?

I am sitting here crying my heart out. No one knows how horrible it feels to lose your child. No one but someone who has been there. I cannot imagine anything more awful. I am so thankful though that you did not suffer, that you weren't tortured or murdered or kidnaped. I don't know how parents bear that. So I thank God that if this had to happen, that He took you the way He did.

I've worked on your pictures and got them in a special book. I work so hard on something, and then I can't look at it after I finish it.

I got the condolence cards out of the closet one day last week and thought I'd re-read them. But I couldn't.

I hope someday I can do something really special to honor you.

You, Casey, were one of the joys of my life, along with your sisters. I loved you. I loved your personality. I loved the way you were. I loved your outer beauty and your inner beauty. You were such a good person. I am so glad you are my daughter. I will never ever forget you or forget how very special you are. Stay with me. I will love you always and always. I will be so happy to see you again. – Love forever, Mom

In retrospect, I see that I was physically sick during the first holidays – actually the first few years – after Casey's death. The first Thanksgiving, the first Christmas, I was so heartsick. I was so down. Then the second Thanksgiving I had the most horrible pain in my abdomen and legs. At Christmastime we went to a lot of movies just for the distraction. I was so sick I napped through most of them. I was, I guess, depressed. I couldn't sleep at night, but couldn't stay awake in the day.

January 20, 1998
In a few days it will be 18 months, one-and-a-half years, since that horrible night that Casey died. It's still so hard to even say that. It took a lot of time right now for me to type that word "died." I am not at peace with that. Life has become more "normal" – or what is normal now – but I'm still lost. Still confused. Still a stranger in what has become my life. I look at Casey's pictures and search them sometimes for insight or <u>something</u>. Other times I can't bear to look at them. Sometimes I wake up at night and think about how I have her pictures

beside me on the night stand and the love chest that holds her things just two feet away from me. Then I have to try to paralyze my mind. To stop my thoughts. To get up and do something because I can't stand to lie awake and think.

I miss Casey so much. I am mad that she did not get a chance to live. I am mad because it all seems so unfair. She had so much going for her. She was just coming into her own. Life was good, and it was even getting better. She was such a great little girl. Such a wonderful, wonderful person. She was kind and caring and loving, and she had such a way about her. It is true that everyone loved her. Everyone. Little kids liked her, her own age kids liked her, grownups liked her. How could you not like Casey? She was truly great. The best person I have ever known. And I wish I had known to express that to her before I lost my chance. I wish I had told her how very, very much I loved her and admired her. I know I told her many, many times that I loved her. I was good to her. But sometimes I get lost in remembering times I yelled at her and fussed at her. I wish I'd never done that. I wish I had taken more time just to sit beside her or have her just put her head in my lap while I stroked her hair. Those were such good times. No words were even necessary. If there had been friction between us, it dissolved during those times. I just had to sit beside her on the couch or put my arms around her or stroke her hair and watch TV with her – and everything was OK. For both of us. Nikki says Casey and I had something special. We did. I miss that. I miss my little friend. My little shadow. My little passenger in the car. My little corny jokes partner. Casey was so special to me. I miss her. And I miss the "me" I was when she was alive.

Besides struggling with losing Casey and the feelings of grief and sadness that are sometimes overwhelming, I struggle with the fact that I don't know how to deal with the feelings I have toward Jennifer and Gail and my mom. Their lives go on – and I wouldn't have it any other way – but I am at such a loss to even understand what I would be willing to do differently to make things better. I am angry. Absolutely no doubt about that. I know Jennifer would never have chosen this to happen. She loved Casey, and Casey loved her. Of course Jennifer and Gail and my mom hurt deeply. I know that. I never forget that. But I'm angry. How am I supposed to go on and just pick up the pieces? What is there for us to talk about? I would never say the angry words I hear inside my head.

I know they hurt, and I wouldn't want to hurt them any more. But I don't feel like acting. Will time make things better? What if I don't have time? Everything seems to just reinforce to me that Casey is dead.

I remember all the things I know about how you're really hurting no one but yourself when you carry around anger and resentment and unspoken rage. I do wish I could set the story straight. I've just got to let go of my resentment and focus on my life and Casey's sisters' lives. Letting go will be quite a challenge. I'm not doing well with that so far. But I know I need to, for me. I will never say it's OK. It will never be all right. It's sad, but people I have met at Compassionate Friends who have similar situations say the same thing. It's like, for the survivors, well, life must go on. And they go on. But we don't.

Writing helps me. Maybe with the help of my word processor, I'll find some relief.

I want to scream.

☙

February 17, 1998
Dear K-K, Today I've thought often of the dream I had of you last night. In the last two dreams I've had of you, I've known in my dream that you had died. That's a big change.

Last night's dream was not a sad dream though. You were three or four years old, as you are so many times in my dreams, and I was watching you play and telling someone that you were already dead but didn't know it, and wasn't it wonderful that you would never have to die again, because you already had – but you were alive. I know there is a message there. You are alive. I just wish I could see you and watch you play as I did in my dream.

Did you see the balloons I got you for Valentine's Day? I know you did. They said "I Love You" and "Happy Valentine's Day." I miss you, my little girl. You made Valentine's Day a special day always.

I miss you so much, Casey. I cannot stand to think about it. God! How I miss you! I want to see you and talk with you. I love you. – Mom

☙

February 18, 1998
Dear Casey, Last night I dreamed I was cleaning out my office at Rural
Legal Services, getting ready to move. Darlene Bradley was there, and I
was just going through all sorts of stuff. I dreamed I had just stacks and
stacks of your spelling tests. They were strips of paper – exactly like the
strips of paper you really did use for spelling tests. I would have
forgotten about those strips of paper you and your classmates used, if
not for my dream. Remember them? In my dream, I had apparently taken
your spelling tests and kept them in my office.

When I woke up from this dream around four a.m., I got very down
because the longer I lay there awake, the sadder I felt. Why, oh, why did
you have to leave? I never in my wildest nightmare would have believed
you would be in a car wreck and go away. Die.

I started thinking about all those times we went round and round about
your spelling. You really had problems with spelling. I wish I had been
more patient and found a way to help you with spelling. Occasionally I
could help you – like the times I'd make up a tune to help you remember
letters for words – but most of the time we ended up fussing at each
other when I tried to help you. I regret that so much. I was never any
good at helping you or your sisters with homework. We always ended up
fighting. I could never have taught any of you in school because all three
of you got mad at me and I got frustrated with you. There must have
been a better way. Maybe it's that way with most parents and children.
Maybe that's normal. But it still doesn't help erase the guilt I feel for not
being able to help you more. I'm sorry, Casey. I'm sorry for not finding
a way. I'm sorry for getting mad at you or for making you mad at me for
the way I was trying to help you. I'm almost sorry for the times I insisted
you spell words over and over, but I thought you'd remember them that
way. I'm sorry for anything I did wrong. I didn't mean to make you mad
or sad or make you feel bad about yourself or me.

I asked Steve this morning what happened with the balloons he cut loose
from your niche. He said the one that said "Happy Valentine's Day"
went toward Y-12. The one that said "I Love You" went toward Oak
Ridge, our house. I'm not surprised. That's what I would have expected.

I love you, little girl. My little girl. I miss you so. – Love forever and ever, Mom

❧

February 25, 1998
Dear Casey, It has been 19 months today. When the 25ᵗʰ of each month comes, I always feel an extra sense of sadness.

I'm still working a temporary job at St. Mary's. It's the job where I met the lady who was declared dead and then returned to life. She tells me heaven was wonderful. God's voice was wonderful – not big and booming, but gentle and comforting, as though soothing a child. Oh, Casey, you're there. You are there!

Erin and I talked a long time on the phone night before last about you and about how wonderful it must be for you. We miss you so much, Casey. You really made us better people. I know I'm more in touch with God because of you, and I sense that Erin is too. She is becoming more and more spiritual. We want to see you again desperately. There's no doubt <u>you</u> are in heaven. We're working to get there too. I know God knows I want to see Him, but I feel in my heart that He knows I want to see you – and that's OK with Him. He knows how I feel about you.

I wonder about you all the time. What are you doing? Can you see me? Can you feel my love for you? Do you know I miss you? Do you feel sad to know I hurt so much over what happened to you? Will you be the first person – soul – to meet me when I die? What will you look like? Do you see my tears? Do you know when we do special things in your memory? What was it like for you? Did God plan for you to be with us only 14 years? Or was it unplanned? An accident?

I wish I had answers for all my questions. My mind is sometimes consumed with questions. I cannot turn my mind off. It's terrible to wake up during the night, or hours before I want to wake up. I'm so vulnerable then. That's why I must take Tylenol PM to keep me asleep. I tried to do without it beginning last fall, but I was in such a state from being unable to stay asleep or go back to sleep when I'd wake up that I decided to go ahead and use that crutch. I took an antidepressant for a couple of weeks – I think maybe it was 10 days – but I couldn't stand the zombie feeling it gave me. It got me through the memorial service at

Compassionate Friends though. I felt like some of the edge was taken off for those few days I took it. But I didn't like the other feelings I had. I think nothing will help, because nothing will undo that you are gone.

On Sunday I sent my first letter to the Governor. He is backing a bill to place more limitations on young drivers, and I wrote to thank him for his support. Anything to reduce the number of deaths caused by young drivers. With more restrictions, more training, more experience, maybe you'd still be here. Casey, I feel so responsible for what happened to you. Why did I not protect you? I am so sorry. I am so sorry.

My little precious girl, I love you so. I would give my life, gladly, to have you live. I am so sorry I failed to protect you. I think sometimes of the future when Nikki and Erin have children. I'll be so afraid to babysit them. I failed to protect you. I failed as your mother. What if I was responsible for their children dying? I will be afraid of my own grandchildren. I will be afraid I will fail them. I failed you, Casey. I am so very, very sorry. I cannot stand the thought that I failed you. Casey, I am so sorry!

I love you. I love you. I love you. – Forever and ever, Mom

March 4, 1998
Dear Casey, Today is Steve's birthday. Do you remember his birthday in 1996 when you gave him some socks and made him a birthday card? On his card you wrote that now nobody could make fun of him for having holes in his socks. He kept that homemade card and has it hanging on his side of our dresser mirror.

I really wish you were here for his birthday this year. (I wish with all my heart and soul, my very being, that you were here everyday.) Tonight Steve, Erin, Brad, Chris and I will go out to eat to celebrate Steve's birthday. We will miss you. We will miss you so much. Everything – everything! – was better and more fun when you were here. You are always in our hearts. Always. I wish you were alive though and that "in my heart" was a phrase I never had to use, a phrase that never even crossed my mind.

Yesterday afternoon I wrote down the names of 20 or so of your friends and I'm thinking about asking them to write down a remembrance of you and give to me. I want to make a memory book about you. It will be something I can make as a loving memorial to you, and something I can look at when my heart can take it, and even something to show your future nieces and nephews so they will know you. The only reservation I have about asking your friends to do this is that I know all of them took your death very hard. I saw and heard their grief. I don't want to upset them. I'm going to try to think of a positive way to make my request of them.

Steve told me something last night that really touched my heart. We knew that your Kern softball team wore patches with your number last summer, but Jim Eaton told him that at the beginning of every game they put their gloves together and yelled, "Casey!" That breaks my heart. They loved you so, Casey. You were so much fun.

I cannot believe this happened. I cannot believe you were taken. Of millions of people, why you? I love you, my little girl. My precious little girl. – Love Mom

March 5, 1998
Dear Miss K-K, Just felt like calling you that today. I had a funny remembrance of you on my way to work this morning. I met a Red Dog truck, and it reminded me of the long-sleeved t-shirt that your younger cousin Max gave you. He apparently was with his grandmother when he saw the shirt and wanted it for you. I don't know if Mrs. Newman bought it or if Max had the money, but at any rate he got the shirt for you.

What's memorable about that shirt to me is that you came out of the dressing room after your first basketball game in eighth grade dressed in that t-shirt with the Red Dog beer logo on it. I didn't know you had taken it to school. I about fell off the bleachers. I probably should have taken you home and made you change, but I'm glad now I didn't. The beer part of it meant nothing; you liked the red dog. It was as simple as that. But you didn't wear it to school anymore, at least that I knew of.

I saw in the newspaper a couple of months ago that Coach Petrie had a baby girl on New Year's Eve. You always liked Coach Petrie. And she liked you. I remember when she and her husband Roger took you, Liz Polfus and Gina Grubb (an Oak Ridge police officer who helped with the basketball program) to the Regas to thank the three of you for your help. You and Liz had helped Coach Petrie with spring tryouts for the kids coming along behind you at Robertsville.

I can still see your little red face when I'd pick you up from the gym. You put your all into basketball. You were good too. Your team was the first team that got to play in the new gym. I remember that your face got especially red and splotched those first few games. I knew it was because of the "Shelton Girls Curse" that you, your sisters and I all have – we get red splotches in any situation that pumps us with adrenaline – but one of the mothers in the stands (I think it was Lindsay McGinnis's mom) said maybe you were allergic to the sealant on the new gym floor. Don't think so. You, my dear, were just like us – you got those darn red splotches.

You got the Coach's Award at the Basketball Banquet. That was so neat. You were collecting quite a few trophies. When you were little, you would count Nikki's and Erin's trophies, just waiting for the day you had more.

Little girl, I love you so much. I would give my life if I could only hug you. – I love you. Mom

❧

March 6, 1998
accident
1) an event occurring by chance or arising from unknown causes

It wasn't an "accident." The cause is not unknown. It was not a "car accident." In January 1998 using the word "accident" seemed incorrect, wrong. At Compassionate Friends when it was my turn to introduce myself and tell about Casey, I said she was killed in a car <u>wreck</u> *on July 25, 1996. I noticed that every parent who followed me who had lost a child in a car wreck said "wreck" – not "accident" as we normally said. I don't know if they just followed my lead or whether using the word "accident" didn't seem right to them either. I didn't discuss it with anyone.*

accident
2a) an unfortunate event resulting from carelessness, unawareness,
ignorance, or a combination of causes
2b) an unexpected happening causing loss or injury which is not due to
any fault or misconduct on the part of the person injured

I wasn't aware of this second definition until today. This definition is
accurate. It describes the event that happened to Casey. She was in a car
accident.

accidental
1) arising from extrinsic causes
2a) occurring unexpectedly or by chance
2b) happening without intent or through carelessness and often with
unfortunate results

2b is accurate. Very accurate. I know the car wreck was accidental.

There's so much I don't understand. My intellect says fairness and
justice aren't absolutes. So much about life is not fair or just. But my
heart cries out that life should be fair and just. If it were, Casey would
be here. Why can life not be fair and just? Casey was innocent. She
should not have died. I don't understand. My head says that's the way it
is, but my heart says that's wrong.

I know I've got to let this go. It serves absolutely no purpose. Maybe
someday I'll be able to. Maybe I've just got to think and think about it,
till someday I stop.

❧

March 17, 1998
Dear Casey, This last week has been terrible. My grief comes in waves,
and right now I feel like I'm drowning. Saturday we went to Granny's.
For reasons I don't quite understand myself, I hate to be there. I know it
has to do with losing you and associating my mother's house and town
with losing you. I can't stand to be there anymore. I think it would
sadden you to know that, but it's how I feel. I was so sad by the time I
got back home to Knoxville that I cried myself to sleep.

Sunday wasn't any better. I felt like I was choking on tears all day. I literally spent two hours in Michael's looking for flowers for you. I can't even make decisions sometimes. I chose some real pretty hanging flowers in cardinal red – to show you that I haven't forgotten the cardinal red uniform you would have been wearing last week at the State Basketball Tournament.

It was hard last week to avoid the news about Oak Ridge girls back at the State Tournament. An Oak Ridge girl won "Miss Basketball" for the second year in a row. She would have been your teammate. You should have been there!

I love you. I miss you. – Love, Mom

❧

March 20, 1998
Dear Casey, I wish I lived somewhere where it didn't get springtime and kids didn't start practicing ball. For the last week or so, I've seen so many children out, beginning the season. I have to just look away when I drive by this scene. When I'm out walking and pass by the kids, I can look away but I can't put the sounds I hear on mute. They're <u>happy</u> and <u>alive</u> kids out playing.

Spring begins today. I used to like spring, but now I don't. It's depressing. I've thought several times the last few days about how I'd like to live where it's just cold and rainy or snowy. I'm envious of those children – or, rather, I'm envious of the parents of those children – who are welcoming springtime. <u>You</u> should be here getting ready for the fast-pitch season to start. <u>You</u> should be alive. I would be so happy then. I miss being happy. I cannot imagine ever being happy again. I miss you so much. I want you back so bad. I love you, my precious, precious Casey. – Love, Mom

❧

March 23, 1998
I read something that helps me. I have times when all I can think about are the times I fussed at my girls. Because of what happened to Casey, I think in particular of her. Was I too hard on her? Did I expect too much? How I wish I had never raised my voice or yelled at her. How I wish that all I had shown her was love and understanding and patience. There was never a second that I didn't love her. My expectations and

discipline were part of my love for her. I wanted to make her <u>future</u> better by making her ready for it. And that's where my guilt now has a life of its own. Her future was taken away. So I was preparing her for something that wasn't to be. If I had known that, there would have been no point in expecting her to do her best in school. No point in trying to shape her into a responsible adult. She wasn't going to be an adult. How I wish now I'd just let her be a kid for all it was worth.

I read, though, that the guilt I feel is to be expected when you lose the future you thought you were getting your child ready for. You were doing what you thought was right – and it would have been, if she hadn't died.

I can't take credit for the great people my girls turned out to be, but I tried to encourage them to be their best. To be responsible. I expected that. And they have never disappointed me. Why, though, was I not better and kinder to them? Why did I ever yell and fuss? It seems all so unnecessary now. My life was not easy. No one except me knew how hard it was. Sometimes that stress caused me to explode. But why did I explode at them? They were the very people I love most in this world and in my whole life. I wish I'd never been anything but sweet and gentle with them. I could have been such a better mother. I wish with all my heart I could do it over.

"Groovy" was always one of my favorite words, mostly because it caused my girls to roll their eyes when I said it. When they'd get out of the car at school, I'd tell them, "Have a groovy day!" They hated it. It was a word my generation used in the '70s. It dated me. But now I'm thinking that "groovy" might be a word I could use when people ask, "How are you?" I could say, "Groovy," and they'd think that meant I was doing OK. And I would let them think that. But, really, I knew it meant "groovy" in the sense that I felt like I had ups and downs, ins and outs. I was groovy. I wasn't being dishonest. I felt groovy.

❦

March 24, 1998
"A persistent ache buried beneath the surface of my daily life" = a phrase in a book I'm reading.

It describes what I feel. But sometimes that ache isn't buried, or if it is buried, it's not very deep.

On the surface, I look fine. The ache is always there though. And it always will be. That's OK though. I lost my Casey. I have every reason to ache. And I do. Oh, how I do.

Last night I went to bed thinking about how I could not bear it if Casey was in the ground. I could not bear to think of her precious little body underground, decaying. I could not stand that. I think I would have to throw myself on top of that ground. I could not bear it if she were there. That's what I went to sleep thinking about.

Dear God, I don't understand. Why Casey?

April 2, 1998
Hello, My Little Girl. I see your sweet little face in every flower and tree that are blooming this spring. I looked up at the beautiful sky last night just before dark and saw your face in the little crescent moon that was shining in that deep deep blue color that the sky sometimes is – that deep deep blue color that was your favorite. I don't ever <u>not</u> want to remember you – I know I will as long as I live – but those memories hurt and it's like I can't stay with them for long. A memory of you sometimes literally takes my breath away. It hurts. My throat chokes up.

Sometimes even now I get caught up in trying to think of a way I could undo what happened. I think that's what Dr. Friedman had referred to all those times I met with him as "magical thinking." If only I had said you couldn't stay one more night at Granny's. If only I had taken you home with me that Wednesday night. Oh, Casey, I wish I had! If only I had done that.

You called a crescent moon a "cookie moon." I don't know where you got that. I remember the first time you said it though. I was washing your hair in the sink in our bathroom on Ithaca Lane. The way you were lying on the sink counter top, your sight would have been focused on the window. You were looking out the window and seeing the moon. You called it a "cookie moon." I love that name for it. Just think, it's the very same moon I now look at. Do you see it too? Do you see me? All those

*times I ask God to tell you hello and that I love you, do you hear me?
Does God tell you?*

*I really, really love you, Casey. I really, really miss you so much. I want
you back so bad. – Love forever and ever, Mom*

☙

April 14, 1998
*Hi, My Precious Little Girl. I woke up the last two mornings dreaming of
you. It was wonderful. I feel so thankful that I get to spend time with you
in my dreams. We were so happy and having so much fun. I LOVE those
dreams. Don't ever leave me.*

*Easter was hard. I've had a heavy heart and a lump in my throat for
days. Yesterday (Monday) it all caught up with me, and all I could do
was just give in to my sick feeling and go to bed. One more holiday
behind me. Thank goodness. I miss you every day. Somehow holidays
are even worse.*

*I love you, my little girl. I took an Easter lily to the cemetery for you, but
it was taken again. I hope you know I try. I have to believe you do.*

*I miss you so. I will be so happy to see you again someday. Stay in my
heart, my memory and my dreams. I love you. – Love, Mom*

☙

April 28, 1998
*Dear Casey, I miss you so much. This weekend Steve and I went to see
Ginger and Harry. On the way home yesterday I could think of nothing
but you. Driving through Nashville – driving the road from Cookeville
that you and I traveled so many times together – hearing your voice
inside my head as we crossed Rockwood Mountain – remembering the
way you always gave truck drivers the signal to blow at you – my throat
squeezes up and my head feels like it will burst. Casey, I want you back!
I want all those precious times we had together back. I want you here
with me. How can this be life anymore? It cannot without you. When we
got home I read in the newspaper that the mother of a 16-year-old who
was killed three months after you in a car wreck, had died of cancer. She
was 44 years old. I could only think, "Why couldn't that be me?" She is
with God and she is with her daughter again. She must be so happy. I
would be. I pray that God knows my heart and will do what is His will.*

Sometimes I so want to die so I can see you again. Then I think of Nikki and Erin and Steve, and I wouldn't want to cause them pain. I guess I feel like everybody could get over losing me, but I can't get over losing you.

I try so hard. I think I probably appear OK. But I hurt so much inside. I cannot recover. I want to undo what happened. I sometimes daydream of how I could undo what happened. I feel so weak. I can't do anything to make everything OK. It will never be OK. You are gone. My Casey. My precious, precious Casey. I miss you so much. No one knows how much. Casey, I love you. I will miss you forever. Someday I will see you again. I will. – Love, Mom

May 9, 1998
Dearest Casey, Your big sister Nikki graduated from Vanderbilt yesterday. You would have been so proud of her, just as I am. How I missed you. My memories of the time at Vanderbilt always include you. It was you and I most of the time visiting Nikki there. I felt your presence and at times almost felt like I could see you there watching the commencement and giving Nikki that little look that was yours alone that meant "Good job. Way to go." I imagined you watching the whole time from the edge of a cloud. You were there, Casey, I know you were there. Nikki told us that when she reached her seat, there sat a ladybug. But of course!

My heart aches for you. I love you so. – Mom

June 7, 1998
This is something I read today from "I Will Not Leave You Desolate: Some Thoughts for Grieving Parents" by Martha Whitmore Hickman:

> *Someone has said that children who have died are with us in a constant way that living children can never be. We also know the pain of the reverse of that statement, that the child who is dead cannot be with us in ways we yearn for, to put our arms around and hold close. But in our hearts, after a while, we come to know the truth of the child's presence, close as our own skin, as integral to our life as the beating of our heart. It is not what we would have wished, but it is a gift, a gracious presence, as*

are the memories we have, the reflections of the child's personality we may discover in ourselves now, as in others who are close.

Casey, you are always with me – as close as my own skin, as integral to my life as the beating of my heart. I love you, my little girl. – Mom

❧

June 7, 1998
Dear K-K, You would be 16 years old. I dreaded for a month June 3rd. But it came. I didn't know how I could make it through the day that marked your 16th birthday. I dreaded the day. It's not for a second that I wanted to forget or ignore the day – not for a second would I ever forget or ignore a day that was one of the happiest days of my life because that was the day you made your appearance in the world – but I thought I could not bear the sorrow I feel every day heightened when the calendar moves to June 3 – your <u>birth</u>day. Your <u>birth</u> day. I can imagine you being 16. Erin and I talked about what we think you'd look like. I asked Erin how she thought you'd be wearing your hair. We both think long, with bangs. You'd be beautiful, that's for sure. Probably tall. Long-legged. Long slender fingers. Gorgeous eyes. Beautiful on the outside. Beautiful on the inside.

Your birthday was always special. We had a birthday celebration every year. Casey, I am very glad you were born. The pain and sorrow of losing you is so hard, but yet I had 14 years with you. I would not trade having you those 14 years for anything. I can't imagine a sorrow more deep, but still if the choice had been given to me I would choose to have you 14 years than not at all. I just wish with all my heart that you were still here with me. Fourteen years was not long enough.

On Wednesday, June 3rd, Erin, Steve and I drove to Clingman's Dome and took balloons for you (as we did last year). I got the same kind of smiley-face balloon that I got you last year. Erin got a balloon that said "Love You Today . . . Tomorrow . . . and Forever," and Steve got a balloon with dalmatians. We also got one for Nikki and Brad – a "Sweet 16" from Nikki and a "Happy Birthday" with a ladybug on it from Brad. It was cold and very windy at the top of Clingman's Dome. Erin released her balloon first, and it got hung up in a treetop, where we had to leave it. My balloon felt like it was almost pulled from my hands and rushed up heavenward. Was that you, pulling that balloon? I think so.

As I took a shower before we left for our trip to the mountains, I thought, "I wonder what signs we'll get today." Well, we did get signs of your presence. This year butterflies. There were butterflies everywhere on the seven-mile road to Clingman's Dome. It was like they were leading the way, saying, "Come on. Follow us. This way to the top of the mountain for Casey's party." Mostly yellow butterflies. They're very, very special to me now. I have bought a big yellow butterfly to hang in the house now – in honor of you.

My precious Casey, I miss you so. I want to see you so much. I still turn around in the truck and think maybe, just maybe, you'll be sitting in the backseat. And when I'm driving Jordan, I still glance over at your seat and think maybe you'll be sitting there. How I wish! I love you, my precious child.

I sat outside on your birthday until one of the moonplants opened up, as I knew it would. The moonplant is a part of our family's history. Our first moonplants came from Mr. Edmond. Their first bloom always seemed to appear on your birthday. For this reason, we associated them with you.

The moonplants are like the evening primrose or nine o'clock flower or the Nicodemus plant. Their flowers open up around nine o'clock each evening from the first of June until well into July. The blooms are full and beautiful until the next morning's sun wilts them. It's ironic – again that word "ironic" – that the evening primrose (or moonplant) stands for eternal love, memory, youth, hope and sadness according to *Stories in Stone – A Field Guide to Cemetery Symbolism and Iconography* by Douglas Keister.

While I sat there, six flowers opened up, three flowers on each of two plants. Three plus three equals six – 6/3 – June 3rd. Your birthday. A very special day. I am so glad you were born. I am truly grateful I knew you. You were a wonderful, wonderful person. You made us all better people. I know you will be there, waiting for me. I cannot wait to see you again. And I will. Casey, I love you so! – Love, Mom

July 18, 1998
Dear K-K, I am writing this at Frozen Head State Park. I have come hiking today, and I've stopped now to catch my breath and write a little. I've been composing a letter in my head to you the whole time I've been walking. You liked it here. That's why I've come here. I did something. I defaced some property. I wrote "Casey was here!" on the wooden rail of the bridge over the creek.

It's peaceful here, except for an occasional person or two passing by. I hear jar flies, leaves dropping from branches, bugs buzzing near my ears. I see butterflies. It seems there are so many of them this year. More than I'd ever noticed before.

I really miss you, Casey. Two years ago today we were getting ready to leave the next day for your ball tournament in Hendersonville. Our last trip together. I will never forget that trip. It was really special.

Awhile ago as I walked I remembered the time – in 1987, I think it was – when we came to Frozen Head for a picnic. When we got home, you were sitting in my lap watching TV and I found a tick behind your ear. Glad I found it. What a sweet memory of even finding a tick on you is.

You came to Frozen Head for the trout fishing tournament with Max and David. That was neat. You loved doing it. Where, my little girl, did you get your love for fishing?

How you loved the rocks here and "accidentally" falling into the creek. And you loved the water life you found. And I think one of your turtles came from here. Yes, I'm sure it did. We took it home to Cookeville and I think you took it to school – yes – and then we turned it loose in the woods.

I like to think of you as being so happy. I will be so happy to see you again, Casey. I cannot imagine the joy. I can't even imagine the thrill of seeing you again.

Will there be peace in my life again, Casey? I work hard at functioning, but I am so sad in my heart. I can't imagine not being sad though. You

are not here. I want you here. I love you, precious child of mine. – Love, Mom

July 29, 1998
Dear Casey, We are now past the two-year mark. I cannot believe it has been two years since I have seen you. I do see you in my dreams, and I am so thankful for that. You are so real and alive in my thoughts. I think about you all the time.

Today as I drove to work, "From a Distance" came on the radio. That song reminds me so much of you. I can just see you wearing your little tie-dyed shirt and black shorts and <u>signing</u> that song with your third grade class in Cookeville. Mrs. Vickers was your teacher. You liked her, and she liked you. You were so good at signing. You caught on so quickly and your fingers were so graceful as you signed. I can remember how you looked as you did that. You were very talented, Casey.

As my mind goes back to 1991 and those days, I remember for some reason the silly goldfish you got at the school carnival when you were in second grade. That must have been the heartiest, healthiest goldfish in the history of carnival fish. It lived forever, even when we ran out of fish food and fed it oatmeal. Remember that? Oh, Casey, how those memories make me laugh, but hurt.

I love you, my little girl. I miss you more every day, not less. I cannot wait to see you and hug you and be so happy to be with you again. I will love you forever. Love, Mom

August 3, 1998
Dear Casey, Tonight I got my hair cut. The way the mirrors at the hairstylists' stations were positioned, I could see the back of my head at another stylist's station across the floor. The first time I caught a glimpse of my head (the back), I didn't recognize it as mine. I thought it was you. My heart raced because I saw what looked like the back of <u>your</u> head. Once I realized what was happening, I just sat there staring, kind of pretending it <u>was</u> your head. It made me feel good to recognize the resemblance of our heads. Very good. But sad too. I want it to be <u>you</u> I see. I love you, Casey. – Forever and ever, Love, Mom

September 10, 1998
Dear Little K-K, I awoke with such a sad feeling this morning as I realized I was only in a dream. For whatever time my dream lasted, though, I was happy because I was with you. You were a little girl, about four years old, and you were wearing your little blue undershirt – the one I remember so very well. We were at Dr. Preston's. You were pulling a red wagon, and I was sitting in his office talking with Dr. Preston. I heard water running and I got up to check on you. You were under a sink and you had taken the pipe out and water was running out. I reached under the sink and got you and asked you what you were doing. You said, "I don't know." You started crying, and I was holding you. Then I woke up.

I miss you so much, my precious Casey. I awoke and asked God to help you feel how much I love you. I will love you forever. – Love, Mom

❦

September 24, 1998
I feel so nervous about attending the Girls Inc banquet. It will be hard to see so many people that were a part of our life in Oak Ridge and even harder to hear and see an award presented in your memory. Your memory.

This is what I would say if asked to speak:

We thank you so much for honoring Casey's memory by awarding the Casey Shelton Sportsmanship Award. It matters very much to us that Casey always be remembered. She was a remarkable person – a young girl who was very much her own person and on her own chose to be just the type of daughter and sister and friend and representative of Girls Inc that you would hope for. When it came to playing sports, her attitude was always upbeat, she gave all she had, and she seemed to never forget that whatever she was playing was a team sport. She loved playing sports, and she loved her teammates and coaches. I am very glad that Girls Inc was there to provide the avenue for Casey to develop her skills and to provide a place where she had so much fun. Casey literally cut her teeth at Girls Club games watching her big sisters Nikki and Erin play. She couldn't wait till it was her turn.

We are still grieving because we miss Casey. Casey left us much too soon. But it helps to remember, when we can, the quote that it's not the number of years that a man has lived, but the number of people who are glad he did. Thank you for honoring Casey and remembering her and being glad that she lived.

– June Gibbs, Casey's mom

I never delivered this speech. I attended the dinner, but just sat there and cried. At least I attended this year. When the award was established and awarded for the first time in 1997, I couldn't bring myself to attend. Erin did, and she told me about it.

September 26, 1998
Dear Casey, It's kind of strange but I used to think when I was young that I would die in a car wreck. I never thought I'd live to have children. I think the only person I ever told that to was Kathy. I was thinking this morning that, while I didn't literally die in a wreck, I <u>did</u> die in a wreck, because the "I" I was died with you. How I wish it <u>could</u> have been me instead of you. You were much more ready for heaven than I, without a doubt, but how I wish you had been given more years of life on earth. Of course God will tell me all about it some day, and I will understand. For now, I don't. I only wish.

I wish you were here. I miss you so much. I'm going to go get you some new flowers for your niche. I love you with all my heart. – Forever, Mom

I knew I needed to talk to someone, a professional, about the torment I was going through. I penned the following letter in order to get my thoughts together, but then I just put it away. I probably should have sought professional help, but instead I tried to work through it myself, with only my husband witnessing how distraught with grief I was.

Dear Professional (Doctor? Minister?) – My emotions get the best of me sometimes, and I probably will not be able to say to you all the things I need to. I am writing this in preparation so that you will have the background for my situation. On July 25, 1996, I received a call from my brother that my 14-year-old daughter Casey and my 17-year-old niece had been in a car wreck and that I should go to the hospital.

I remember when I ran out the door to go to the hospital, I fell on my knees on the porch and prayed that God would let Casey be OK. I didn't know that she was already dead. On the drive to UT Hospital, David, Gail and I never mentioned the possibility of death. And on the drive to Oak Ridge Hospital, Butch, Linda and I never mentioned that possibility either. I would only allow myself to think and say out loud that it must be a good sign that Casey was at the hospital in Oak Ridge. That had to mean she wasn't hurt as badly.

I have a mental image of myself running into the emergency room and being ushered to the chapel. In my heart I knew that was not a good sign. There I was told that my daughter Casey was dead. I've always been a walker. It's been my way of dealing with bad stuff. So, the night of the accident, that's what I did at the hospital. I walked and walked around the outside of the hospital. A nurse insisted on going with me. Then Steve got to the hospital and joined me. Then our pastor joined us. It was our pastor who gently told me that we needed to go back inside, that there were things to take care of. I think I might still be walking if someone hadn't stopped me. When I walked away from the hospital that night, I walked away a different person. Casey died, and I died too – except I'm still here.

God gave me a strength that other people see, because I give the appearance of being OK. But I am not OK. I have so many questions. Please, please help me. I respect you as a wise, learned person and look to you as the person most capable of helping me find an answer to questions that consume me.

Before Casey died, I had been in control (for the most part). I had three daughters. My daughters' father and I divorced when Casey was 4 years old and her sisters were 8 and 10. For almost 10 years it was us girls, and I think they turned out very well. They were good students, they played all kinds of sports, and they were really good kids. Nikki was a junior at Vanderbilt University; Erin had just gotten married and was getting ready to attend UT; and Casey had just completed the eighth grade and was getting ready for high school. Steve and I were engaged to be married on April 12, 1997. The girls all approved of Steve, and life was looking good for us.

On July 19th and 20th, Casey and I were in Hendersonville where her church-sponsored softball team was playing in the state tournament. She was the shortstop. She was good, really good, and really happy and full of life like only a 14-year-old can be. And five days later she was dead.

On July 23rd, I took her to my mother's (30 minutes away) where she was going to spend the night and visit her granny. She asked to spend the next night as well because her 17-year-old cousin, Jennifer, was also going to be there. So I said OK and went back the next evening after work and took her another change of clothes. I had no idea when I pulled out that evening to return home that I would not see her again.

What happened was that her 17-year-old cousin had just been given her own car (a Toyota Tercel) a few months earlier. On that Thursday night, Casey and her cousin ate dinner at their granny's, then went to play ball with other kids in the town.

On the way back to my mother's, only about a mile from her house, Jennifer ran off the road and hit a tree. I was told the girls had been airlifted to UT Hospital.

My sister Gail and brother-in-law David and I went to UT Hospital together as soon as we were notified. In retrospect, I'm thankful that David took charge and insisted I go with them. Although my first instinct had been to jump in my car and go to the hospital where Casey was, the truth was that I had never driven to UT Hospital and I didn't even know exactly how to get there. I can't imagine what might have happened if I had insisted on driving myself.

On our trip to UT Hospital, David drove and my sister rode lying down in the backseat because she was ill. I sat up front with David. None of us knew what had happened, and we didn't let ourselves even broach the topic of what could be. I remember David saying, "June, you know we both always taught the girls to wear their seatbelts." Of course the three of us knew in our hearts it had to be serious – my brother, after all, had said LIFESTAR had been called – but we didn't talk about that. We certainly didn't talk about the possibility of death. I can with all truthfulness say that the thought never crossed my mind that Casey *could be dead. I thought I would get to the hospital and she might be scratched up.*

When we got to UT Hospital, David let me out at the entrance to the emergency room while he and Gail parked. I ran inside to the counter and asked to see my daughter, Casey Shelton. I said she had been brought in by LIFESTAR. They said they would try to find out something for me. Casey's father had gotten to the hospital before I did, and when he saw me he said, "June, I saw LIFESTAR bring in someone but it wasn't Casey. I haven't seen Jennifer in a long time, and I don't know if it was her." It seemed like forever before the emergency room people could tell us anything. I remember pacing and Casey's dad saying the girl LIFESTAR had brought in looked bad . . . and it could be bad . . . but I closed my ears and didn't want to hear anything bad. Finally, someone told us that we needed to go to Oak Ridge Hospital, that Casey had been taken to Oak Ridge Hospital. They couldn't (or wouldn't) tell us anything else. Just that Casey was at Oak Ridge Hospital. I remember the relief I felt. Casey was at Oak Ridge Hospital. That was good! Wasn't it good?

So I got in the car with Casey's dad and his girlfriend. It was a two-seater sports car, but somehow it didn't matter. We left UT Hospital in Knoxville to go back to Oak Ridge. On the drive there, Casey's dad and I kept saying what a good sign it was that Casey had only been taken to Oak Ridge Hospital, not UT Hospital. That meant she hadn't been hurt as badly and didn't need to be in a trauma hospital. Again, in all truthfulness, I can say the thought that she could be dead never entered my mind. I fully expected to see her sitting up on a hospital bed with maybe some scratches or a little blood. And I think her dad did too. Jennifer was the girl who had been airlifted to UT, so Gail and David remained there. I hoped Jennifer would be alright, but all I could think of was Casey.

When we got to Oak Ridge Hospital, again I ran into the emergency room, while her dad parked, and asked to see my daughter, Casey Shelton. The woman at the counter, in retrospect, did get a look on her face that's difficult to describe. She said she would be right back, and she walked away. While I waited for her to return, Casey's dad walked up from parking the car and I relayed the information to him. Then a nurse came out another door and asked us to come with her. We followed her down a hall, and I recognized that she was walking us toward the chapel. I looked at Casey's dad and said, "This can't be good." We were ushered into a small room, and then a doctor walked in. The doctor told us that Casey was dead. That she was dead when she arrived at the hospital. He told us that the force of the crash had caused her heart to go into an arrhythmia. The dashboard had crushed into her chest. She was dead. He was sorry.

I don't know exactly what I did. I felt like my life left my body. All I could do was stare at the doctor and try to comprehend what he was saying. I remember Casey's dad fell to his knees and cried. I couldn't cry though. I couldn't do anything. I remember someone asked if they could call my minister and I said yes. And I said I wanted to go outside. A nurse said she would go with me. I told her no, but she said yes, that she wasn't leaving me. So a nurse and I (I don't even know what her name was) walked around the hospital perimeter. I don't know how many times we walked before she said we needed to go inside for a minute. When we got inside, my daughter Erin, my fiancé Steve, and my minister Ron had gotten there. This was in the days before we all carried cell phones, so Steve and Erin had been on their own odyssey between hospitals. Erin stayed with her dad, and Steve and Ron went back outside with me to walk. Again, I don't know how many times we walked around the hospital before Ron suggested gently that we go inside, that there were things to be done and decisions to be made. Things to talk about . . . like organ donation . . . which funeral home to call. Things to talk about that I could not imagine talking about.

I remember thinking and even saying, "I don't know what to do." I was stunned. I was bewildered. Looking back, I must have appeared so strange. Stunned is the only way I can describe it. I reverted to the way I had reacted to other, though much less severe, situations: I walked. I really <u>wanted</u> to walk and never stop. I think I <u>could</u> have walked and never stopped. If I didn't stop, I didn't have to do anything; I didn't have to allow myself to let the horror that was surrounding me overtake me.

I could have seen Casey. She was in a room. But I couldn't. I couldn't. Steve did. He told me that she just looked like she was asleep. She was wearing her red shorts and a t-shirt, and he said she looked like she'd been playing ball, which she had. I've never second-guessed my decision not to see her. But I do envision what she must have looked like, and I do imagine holding her and rocking her in my arms. But how could I see my child, my Casey, dead? I didn't think I could, and I still don't think I could.

When we finally left the hospital, Thursday was over and Friday had begun. I didn't want to go back home, because Casey would not be there. It wouldn't be home anymore. Erin, Brad, Steve and I went to Steve's house in Knoxville. I never lived in my house in Oak Ridge again. Casey's dad took care of notifying Nikki in Nashville and making arrangements for her to fly home. We all met her at the airport later that morning. Then we all went to the funeral home. That night we all got together and looked at pictures of Casey.

The next days are a blur. So many people showed so much love for Casey and for our family. People stood in a long line at the funeral home on Saturday night to say goodbye. I still refused to look at Casey dead. Her dad and sisters stood by her casket, but I stood in another room. It never occurred to me at the time that people might think I was in another room because Casey's dad and I were divorced. We were way past that, and it had nothing to do with why I stood where I did. I just couldn't bear the thought of Casey in a casket, of Casey dead, and I would not look at her. People filed past Casey and talked with her dad and sisters, and then came to me. The next day, Sunday, the sanctuary at our church was standing-room-only for Casey's memorial service.

Then the "no days" started. That's what we called the days after Casey died. They were days of numbness and somehow functioning, unlike any other I'd ever experienced. Time was different. Everything was different. These "no days" went on for weeks actually. Yesterday filled my thoughts, not today or tomorrow. I couldn't even imagine a tomorrow.

It was as though a wall came down between God and me after Casey died. I couldn't even pray. I don't remember exactly how long that wall was there. But I do know it lifted. The "out-of-body" feeling that came over me as we were told that Casey had died stayed with me a long time. The shock enabled me to get through the next days, probably even months. It just couldn't last forever. That's when the hard stuff – grieving – began.

I have two major areas that I hope you can help me with. First of all: I cannot maintain peace for any length of time about how and why this happened. I read Psalm 139 that says all the days for Casey were written in God's book before she was born. I feel calm for a little while, believing it was God's plan that Casey would be here for only 14 years. I don't like that plan, but God knows better than I. But was this God's plan? Was it God's plan for her to die in that wreck? I just can't believe that.

Please tell me what you believe. Where is Casey <u>now</u>? Is she in God's presence? Did she go there immediately? Or is she sleeping and unknowing of anything until she will be resurrected? Were angels there with her when she died? Did they accompany her to heaven? Does she feel my presence as I feel hers? What is she doing?

I met with the pastor of my church weekly for a couple of months right after Casey died, but I'm sure I wasn't asking the questions so soon after her death that later came to gnaw at me. I met weekly with a psychologist at work for a few months. He sort of checked my progress in dealing with what had happened. I didn't ask him the questions I am asking you.

I am active in The Compassionate Friends, a national support group for families who have lost children. I am helped there through the friendships I have developed, and I hope I help others. But I don't ask them the questions I am asking you.

I attended "Beyond Grief" at church a couple of times, but I didn't want to be there. I didn't ask them the questions I am asking you.

Where is Casey?

The second part of my struggle is how to deal with the fact that it was my niece, my sister's child, who was driving the car that wrecked and killed my child. It took eight months before I felt like I finally knew what had happened. No witnesses came forward. Jennifer at first was barely alive, and when she was able to talk, she didn't remember. I felt like my sister and my mother were searching for reasons that it could not have been Jennifer's fault, even if it meant believing things that made no sense. But the Highway Patrol reopened the investigation at my request, and my questions about how and why were answered.

I am still so angry and resentful. I used to think if you just don't talk about stuff it will go away. But this is too big to ignore. It won't go away. And it's eating away at me. I feel guilty, but I am so hurt. What would God have me do? I don't feel very Christian because of the harshness I carry in my heart. This is not softening, the way I feel. If anything, it feels worse.

Question: If this was God's plan, then how do I reconcile accepting it as God's plan for Casey to live only 14 years with feeling the way I do? Did God use Jennifer as the instrument to bring about Casey's death? If He did, how could I be mad at Jennifer? If this was God's plan, then I must be so wrong to feel bad at my niece.

Please, please help me understand how I can get some peace in my heart and in my life.

❧

November 16, 1998
Dear Casey, I miss you so much. In so many ways I still can't believe you are not here. I miss you <u>so</u> much. I want to see you so badly. I know you are in heaven. I want to be there too. Love forever and ever and ever and ever. – Mom

❧

January 22, 1999
My Dearest Little Casey, The first letter I have written to you this year. But always I am communicating with you. Thoughts of you come no less frequently than last year or the year before. You occupy the greatest portion of thoughts and memories inside my head. I do miss you so much. I will always miss you. I so look forward to seeing you again – and I will. I must. <u>I must see you</u>.

Thanksgiving came. Christmas came. Valentine's Day will come soon. They just aren't fun anymore. I want you here.

I've been working for almost a year in an advertising agency. Yesterday at work I was looking through the photo library collection for pretty pictures to put in a brochure. I found an absolutely gorgeous shot of a red flower. It showed a fully blooming flower, with buds just below the flower that were getting ready to bloom too. It is one of the prettiest flowers (and pictures) I've ever seen, and I set it aside as a picture I would recommend be used. As I drove home from work, I was thinking about that picture. The thought crossed my mind that the flower itself has long since died, but the picture remains and it is just as beautiful today as the day it was photographed. You are like that, Casey. You are just as beautiful today as the day <u>you</u> captured my heart. My mind has a <u>captured</u> image of you that will always be beautiful and never die. I will always have you.

Today – it's ironic – I checked the date on the photo. It was made in 1982. The year you were born.

I love you so much, my precious, precious child. Until I see you and hear you and wrap my arms around you, I will be sad. – Love you forever & ever & ever, Mom

❧

June 5, 1999
Dear K-K, When we got to our room at the hotel after Ginger and Harry's wedding, the way the mirror on the bathroom door was positioned in relation to the wall mirror in the bathroom, I caught a glimpse of myself from behind and, again, for a second I saw <u>you</u>. I stood there and kept looking at the back of my head from various positions. I kept seeing <u>you</u>. I was so happy and filled with the wonderful feeling that you were there. Yes, I wanted to see you. I did see you. In me. That makes me happy. Casey, I do see you in me. Our thick hair, the backs of our heads, our shoulders. Before I colored my hair, your hair and my hair were exactly the same color. When you were little I could put our heads together and you couldn't tell where your hair ended and mine began. I love that. I'm so happy that that memory came back to me. You are with me always. My heart. My soul. And a little bit of my physical self reminds me of you. I love that. I love you, my little girl. – ❤*Mom*

❧

July 26, 1999
Tonight as I stood washing my face before going to bed, I looked into the
mirror and remembered Barbara Haun telling me on July 27, 1996, at
Weatherford's Funeral Home, "It never gets better, it never gets easier."
Barbara was right. She knows. She is a mother who lost a child. She
spoke the truth to me. Today, all day, I have relived July 26 three years
ago. Three years ago. But yesterday to me. I hate July 25. I hate July 25.
I hate July 25. I hate July 25. I hate July 25. I hate July 25. I hate
July 25. I hate July 25.

Judy Justice called me last night. She is so good to me. She always has
been. I told her I would be glad when the day was over. Now it's over,
and July 26 is almost over. But there's July 27 and July 28 to go. Every
day is a day that brings its own cover to lay over me. These days in July
make me feel like I can't breathe. That I don't want to breathe. I want
Casey. I want to go to sleep and wake up and Casey is here. I want
everything to be OK. It will never be OK without Casey.

❦

October 14, 1999
Today I noticed in the obituaries a memorial to an infant who had been
born October 14, 1957, and died November 21, 1957. The memorial had
the baby's name, birth date and death date and said: "Forever, I will
embrace the warmth of your love, the essence of your soul and the
presence of your spirit. We miss you." I was so touched. That little baby
was born and died 42 years ago. But he's still remembered and missed.

One Sunday when our senior pastor, John Wood, was baptizing babies,
he said these little ones would "outlast the stars." What a beautiful
phrase. What a beautiful way of looking at life. What a beautiful
assurance for me that my little one, Casey, will "outlast the stars."

❦

October 15, 1999
Dearest, dearest Casey, I am working back in Oak Ridge again, the city
that had been your home, our home. Today was a hard day. First, on my
way to work, I saw a green van like Brittney's dad used to drive. Second,
your friend Emma Drozdowski came by the office, and she had grown up
so much. Then, all the activity around the high school football field
caught me off-guard. I had to hear it and see it as I walked to my car
after work. And then tonight, Steve handed me an envelope that Donna

had given him that had Dustin's senior pictures for me. You would have had senior pictures too.

You should be here. I want to see you so much. I try so hard not to think – not that I don't want to think about you – but I try not to think about you being gone. I try to remember only happy times. I look at your picture in front of me at work and I say, "I love you, Casey," but I can't look long. I will go back down and fall apart if I look long. I miss you so much. How is it possible that you have been gone over three years? How is it possible that I have lived three years without seeing your precious face and hearing your precious voice. How?

I miss you. I miss you so much. – Love forever and ever, Mom

December 22, 1999
My dearest Casey, I haven't written anything to you for a while. Never are you away from my thoughts for very long though. I ask God to let me be with you again, and I ask Him to let you feel my love for you until the time when we are together again. It still takes my breath away and makes me feel like I can't breathe when I really comprehend that you are not here. I spent so long trying to figure out a way that what had happened had <u>not</u> happened, but I can't pretend any more. I know you are not here and that I will not see you again until I can come to you.

Casey, I love you <u>so</u> much. I never worry anymore about forgetting anything about you. I won't. I know that now. I just want new memories – which would mean you are here with me. That is what I want. I want you here with me. I love you. I miss you. – ❤ Mom

Christmas Day 1999
Dearest K-K Lou, It's Christmas morning and I just got up. I have been thinking of you and I feel like my head will burst. My heart literally aches. It feels sore in my chest. Aunt Hazel called me last night and told me a story of a little girl in heaven who would not join in the happy times her little group of friends were having because she knew her mother was crying. Tears are falling down my face, but I hope all you know is how much I love you. I miss you to the very depths of my soul! Aunt Hazel told me you would not want me to be so unhappy – but I

can't help it. I want you to be here so much. Life is not life without you.
Nothing is the same.

K-K Lou. I called you that so often when you were a little girl that you
answered to it. I wonder what you would look like now. I think you
would be tall and slim and beautiful. I know you would be beautiful.

I looked at your things in the bonus room this morning. Your tennis
racket reminded me of one of my all-time favorite times with you. Do you
remember when we played tennis in the rain at the Jackson Square
Tennis Court? We got drenched – and we laughed and loved it and had
such a happy time.

You gave us so many good memories. I've heard it said that "God gave
us memories so we can have roses in December." You are my little rose.
You are my precious little girl. I am so glad you were born and that you
are my daughter. Merry Christmas, K-K Lou. – With all my love, Mom

The year 2000 was a milestone, a touchstone of sorts. It was the year
Casey would have graduated from high school, the year she would have
turned 18, the year she would no longer have been at the high school
where I knew she was . . . the year she would have gone to college, the
first time she would have had the freedom of choosing "where" she was.
The four years she should have been in high school, I avoided driving
down Providence Road in Oak Ridge where the high school is located. I
no longer walked at the outdoor track at the high school (still haven't)
because she should have been there with me.

June 2000
The past few weeks have been especially hard because this past June 3rd
was Casey's 18th birthday. June 1st would have been the day she
graduated from Oak Ridge High School.

I had attended two other graduations, her older sisters', so I knew the
vicinity of where the graduates would be sitting at Blankenship Field. I
bought one red rose and walked to the field that afternoon before the
graduation began and before anyone was there. I imagined where the
"S" section would be, and where "Casey Shelton" would be in that "S"
section, and I placed her rose there. She graduated in my heart.

I don't know how to describe it exactly, but sometime after Casey's "graduation," I lost control. It was no different in some ways than the control parents of children who are alive lose. The years between her death in July 1996 and her "graduation" in June 2000, I knew where she would have been and basically what she would have been doing. She would have been at Oak Ridge High School, and she would have been playing basketball and fast-pitch, and she would have been running around with Elizabeth and Brittney, and she would have had a boyfriend, and she would be driving a car. But after her graduation in my heart, I didn't know where she would have been or what she would have been doing. I hope she would have been going to college, but which college would she have been attending? I hope she would have been preparing herself to be the oceanographer or vet that she always said she wanted to be when she grew up. But maybe she would have decided in those four years to do something else, to be something else. What would it have been? The first four years after her death, it was easy for me to imagine in broad strokes what her life would have been like. But after those first four years, I couldn't imagine anymore. That's when she became "stuck" as a teenager in my mind. I can't even imagine her being older. She was my baby. She always will be.

July 2000
July 25ᵗʰ will be here soon. July 25ᵗʰ marks the fourth-year anniversary
of Casey's death, and that's a terrible time for me.

Thanksgiving 2000
My dearest, dearest Casey, This is the fifth Thanksgiving away from you.
I miss you just as much now as I did four Thanksgivings ago. I will see
you again and be so very happy someday when we are reunited. You are
always in my heart and in my thoughts. I see you clearly and will never
ever let you go from my mind or my soul. You are always with me and
you always will be. I miss you. I love you, Casey. – Love forever, Mom

August 30, 2001
Dear dear Casey, I miss you every bit as much today as I did when you
first left my sight. You only left my sight – not my heart or my thoughts
or any other facet of my being. Today as I drove back to the office, a
truck was in front of me and in that truck sat a child about 10 years old

whose arm was outside the truck's window, feeling the breeze. It looked like <u>your</u> arm, like <u>your</u> hand. I wanted it to be you so bad, but I knew it wasn't. But I followed slightly behind the truck and pretended for a while that it was <u>you</u> in that truck with <u>your</u> arm stuck out the window. It's those little unexpected things that I see or hear that take my breath away when they remind me of you. I prayed that God would bless that child whose arm I saw, and I believe He will. So, see, that precious reminder of you has made a difference in some child's life – I hope a special blessing from God in your memory.

I love you, my little girl. Always my little girl. I cannot wait to see you again! I love you so very much. – Love and kisses and hugs forever, Mom

In early 2002, I became ill with what at first looked like lung cancer. After surgery, though, I was diagnosed with a rare form of pneumonia. I wrote the following letter as I recovered.

March 21, 2002
My dear sweet Casey, Here I am sitting on my porch, instead of with you. I thought a few times in the past few weeks that I may be with you soon – and maybe I still will be – but my diagnosis and prognosis improved, and I think God is not finished with me here yet. It's ironic – again, there's that word ironic – that my illness would be in my chest. The injuries that resulted in your death were injuries to your chest.

The thought of "suffering" really scared me, but never the thought of dying – because of you. I would be coming to <u>you</u>, and what a wonderful wonderful thing that would be. I get tearful and a lump in my throat even thinking about what a glorious reunion that will be.

I dreamed of you almost every night I was in the hospital. Then after I got home and got the first diagnosis, I semi-began to plan to die soon. Torn between being with my angel in heaven and my loved ones on earth – God would decide where I should be. And now it looks like it's here. I really love life and your sisters and Steve and the grandbabies and my friends. I know you understand that and will patiently wait for me to get

to you. We will be together then for eternity. I love you, my little girl. –
❤*Mom*

❦

September 3, 2002
As I walked into the Kroger store in Oak Ridge – where we used to shop – my heart was pounding. Why does this happen? The music playing on the store's intercom was "Yesterday."

❦

September 27, 2002
As I walked through the library at TTU, I saw students sitting in the computer lab and at the carrels where Casey colored while I viewed a video, and I thought, "That should be Casey sitting there. She would be a junior in college."

❦

September 29, 2002
Today I feel like I started another chapter in my life since Casey died. I went to Mom's for Sunday lunch and surprised everyone. I spent the day with my mother, my sister and my brothers. I am trying. I thought on Saturday about going to Mom's – then changed my mind, back and forth several times – before heading out to early church. I just said, "God, please lead me," and I tried not to over-think as I am so prone to do. On the radio on my way to church, there was a minister speaking about a "balm" to heal hearts and hurts – a Balm in Gilead. That was a song sung at Casey's memorial. A message for me? I think so.

❦

December 18, 2002
Dear Casey, Today I found a penny – heads up – as I got out of my car in Baxter. Then I saw one flower blooming in our front yard as I made a wreath for the porch. And then as I straightened your picture on the bookcase, a letter from your best friend Brittney (written January 21, 2001) fell into my hands. Oh, yes, one more thing happened today. As I got out of my car to go in Target, I noticed a new store. It's called "Casey's." I love that! (It's a "wine and spirits" store.) Four ways I felt you today. Always be with me. I love and miss you so much, my little girl. – Forever ❤*Mom*

❦

January 3, 2003
Today it occurred to me that I am OK with letting hurts that are unintentional and unnoticed by others just pass over me, with no need to

set things straight or explain to people who have not lost a child that they don't know what they're talking about. I do get tired, though, of people who <u>know</u> that I lost a child but who do not seem to remember it. For example, those who continue to ask, "Did you have a good holiday?" really bother me, but I just let it pass over me and don't try to explain anymore. Those who complain about trivial stuff really bother me, but I don't try to point out how insignificant their gripes are. No one (other than Steve and the girls and Kathy's mom) said one word that would make me even think they remember. I am learning – I guess I have learned – that it matters to me and always will – and that's all that matters. Would they remember or acknowledge it if I wore a sign that read "bereaved parent" or if I let them see my grief or if I talked about it? Is that what I want? There <u>is</u> nothing to make me OK. I don't expect it anymore, do I? What does it matter what others do or don't do, say or don't say? It doesn't. It changes nothing. It just hurts my feelings.

January 23, 2003
Out of the blue this afternoon, Casey's best friend Brittney called me. Brittney is now married, and she has a little seven-month-old son named "Brent." I asked Brittney if she knew that if Casey had been a boy we were going to name her "Brent Lawrence." Of course Brittney didn't know that. How ironic that she chose "Brent" for her son. And her son's middle name is Landen (the same middle initial). It was bittersweet talking with Brittney – more sweet than bitter – but it made me sad. How sweet that she still calls though. She said that Casey told her if anything ever happened to her that she wanted Brittney to promise that she would call me occasionally and that she would check on Granny to make sure she isn't lonely. Brittney said she told her husband about that conversation and she asked him if he thinks that some people sense that they're going to die early. I don't know. Maybe? Brittney said she thinks about going to see Granny to make good on Casey's request that she make sure she's not lonely, but she said she doesn't know what to say.

We talked about all the things Casey and Brittney used to do. She told me again that Casey would not ride her four-wheeler because I had told her not to, even though Brittney said she and her brother urged her to, saying I would never find out. We talked about the trampoline, the dogs, the go-carts. They really did have a lot of fun together. They lived and were so full of life. In Brittney's family the children were allowed to play and have fun. I'm glad Casey had Brittney for a friend. She really loved her.

As I read back over this note, I thought about the time Casey wanted to surprise Brittney by miraculously popping out of the opening in the back seat of our car. We did that. Brittney got in the car with me, wondering why Casey wasn't there, when suddenly Casey crawled from the trunk into the back seat. They thought that was just hilarious.

There's a picture of Casey and Brittney that ran in "The Oak Ridger." It was a picture of them with butterflies. How ironic. Butterflies. Lots of things are ironic.

❦

February 9, 2003
I have to rely on God.

❦

March 22, 2003
Today I went by the office early in the morning. As I drove back home from Oak Ridge, I felt so sad. And it occurred to me that moving to Knoxville really was the right and best decision for me. I miss my girls when I'm in Oak Ridge so much. I miss our life. I miss Casey. We should be there.

❦

March 25, 2003
As I write this, I am sitting in the parking lot at TTU. When I took a speech class at Tech, Casey and Erin helped me by listening and timing my presentations. I have pictures of Casey wearing my cap and gown and memories of her going to college with me. I also have pictures and memories of her playing basketball on the Vanderbilt court with Nikki, and pictures and memories of her at high school softball practices with Erin. High school and college with her sisters and me – it was like she got to do those things with us because she wasn't going to get to grow up to do them.

❦

April 2003
I'm always one day closer to Casey. Used to, I wanted to die. Now I want to live, content with knowing that in living each day, I'm still getting one day closer to Casey.

❦

April 24, 2003
Dearest Casey, You are on my mind <u>every</u> day. That is absolutely 100
percent the truth. This past week, though, it seems as if every other
thought in my head has been of you. You <u>are</u> with me, aren't you? I love
that. Last night, Steve, Granny and I went to the Gaither concert at
Thompson Boling Arena. What an awesome experience. While I was
sitting there drinking in the experience, I thought, "This must be what
heaven is like." Are you worshiping and singing God's praises? What
are you doing? I will be so happy to be there with you. Heaven, for me,
would be sitting there with you next to me (and then Nikki and Erin and
all our special little ones next to us someday after they've lived good
long years on earth) listening to the sounds of heaven. Steve will be
there too with Granny and Mimi and my dad and all the people we love.
You stay with me till I get there to you. – Love forever and ever, Mom

2003
Several years ago when I went to talk with my pastor, one thing he said
was that we can't know what Casey might have been saved <u>from</u>. This
thought came back to me when the war in Iraq started and Jessica Lynch
was taken prisoner. She was about Casey's age. I remember thinking,
"What if that had been Casey?" Later when Jessica Lynch was released,
I was so emotional; more emotional than I could have imagined being.

2003
Nikki doesn't talk about Casey. That sort of worries me, although I know
very well that everyone has their own way of dealing with problems and
hurtful events. Yet I worry about her. But sometimes I worry about the
way I deal with it too, because although I do talk about Casey – her life
and her death – I feel a scream just below the surface, wanting to erupt.
But I don't let it erupt. Sometimes I wish I could; sometimes I think I
should. But I keep it pushed down.

May 30, 2003
I'm having a test on Monday to find out what this heaviness in my chest
is. I think it is a huge scream of "No!" that I have choked down since
Casey died.

June 3, 2003
The book "Tragedy to Triumph" has been sitting on my bookshelf since 1996, given to me by Nancy Baldwin, a friend at work. For some reason, I hadn't read it. Why, today, on Casey's 21st birthday, did I get up at five a.m. and go straight to that book? And why is it meaning so much to me? Why are so many of the author's words and experiences touching a chord with me? I know why. Thank you, God, for comforting me today.

❧

July 5, 2003
The Compassionate Friends National Conference in Atlanta – As I held my candle in the air, I imagined Casey watching me and seeing her mom standing there in memory of her.

❧

July 9, 2003
I remember the first time I went for a long walk by myself after Casey's death. I remember exactly how the day felt. It was a Saturday in the fall of 1996, and I was home alone. I had lived in the neighborhood for only a few months so I didn't really know my way around very well. As I walked, my mind was on Casey and all the many things that went with that. I wasn't really paying attention to my surroundings. After a while, I realized I didn't know where I was, how I got there or how to get back home. I felt frustrated. Lost. Mad. Obviously I found my way home again, but that walk turned into a longer venture than I had intended. That was OK, though, because it let me expend some of my frustration and walk off some of the anger I felt at myself for getting lost and some of the pent-up anger I felt at this whole situation. I just looked up "venture" in the dictionary. It says in part that a venture is an undertaking "that risks a loss but promises a profit." I like that and am happy my brain had me use this word in the first place so that I would look up its meaning. "Venture" is just the right word. I did risk getting lost, but I profited from the walk. It was good to walk off some of my anger. Looking back, I see that I was filled to the brim with it. I had just begun to deal with some of it by walking.

I remember breathing that day too – and thinking, "This is the first time I remember breathing since Casey died." How had I been breathing? It's good breathing is one of those things you do without having to think about it. Thank you, God, for breathing for me.

I don't remember where I read these words: "You cannot fix this or make it better. For today just breathe." That was really good advice. Probably the best.

❣

July 19, 2003
I think for me it has taken seven years for the anger and bitterness and hurt to give way to just a deep sadness. This deep sadness is now a part of who I am. And I wouldn't have it any other way. Casey died and I am and always will be deeply sad.

❣

July 24, 2003
I haven't seen my baby girl since we said goodbye on July 24, 1996. Casey, where are you? I miss you so much, and my heart aches and hurts for you. I want to see you. Seven years. Seven years I haven't seen you. Please know that I love you with all my heart. I often pray to God that He will let you know how much I love you. I miss you, my baby girl. I miss you so much. I will miss you until the day I see you again, <u>and I will see you again</u>. I am going to hug you forever and never let you go. I am so glad you are my daughter. You made me happy. – Love forever, Mom

❣

July 27, 2003
Thursdays. I used to note how old she was by Thursdays. Thursday, June 10, 1982, she was one week old. Thursday, June 17, she was two weeks old. Thursday, June 24, she was three weeks old. And so on until I just naturally quit counting Thursdays. Years took the place of weeks. June 3, 1983, she was one year old. June 3, 1984, she was two years old. And so on and so on until June 3, 1997, when she wasn't here to celebrate with us the 15th year since she was born. That year a new count started . . . the first year she celebrated her birthday in heaven. But I mourned her first birthday she wasn't with me. Thursdays – a day I loved but grew to dread. She was born on a Thursday, but she died on a Thursday. For years, after Casey died, Thursday was a "feeling" I had. I was sadder, more tired, more everything on Thursdays. This lasted probably five years. All I had to say was, "It's Thursday," to my husband, and he understood immediately why I was behaving (without even consciously thinking) the way I was. Seven years later, I sometimes still feel the bruised spot on my heart especially on Thursdays.

❣

August 14, 2003
Sometimes the beauty of the area overwhelms me and I say, "Thank you,
God" as I'm driving along. Some of the things that come to mind:
Sunlight like a spotlight, yellow ribbons, red-white-and-blue flags, Dale
Earnhardt flags and "We'll miss you, Dale" signs, angels in cemeteries,
people who stop for funeral processions, cemeteries with profuse
displays of flowers on every marker, people being so nice to kids, funny
names like "Possum Trot" and "Frog Town." I was thinking as I drove
around today about how much this job has meant to me. It was a
godsend. It put me in touch with old friends and opened my heart again
to the beauty of nature. Working – particularly this *job where I get to*
travel and have lots of quiet time to think – has helped in my healing.

❧

October 23, 2003
Driving home today, as I passed the Memorial Park, it struck me and
took my breath away: I cannot believe Casey is gone, that she died. I
can't believe this happened.

❧

November 2, 2003
Today as I listened and watched the Children's Choir sing at church, I
had to rely on the "governor" that I seem to have on my emotions to
kick in and not allow me to go to a place that I cannot go. The little ones
signed as they sang. That reminded me so much of Casey as she
performed at Sycamore.

Casey's teacher at Sycamore, Mrs. Vickers, was just great. Casey
thought she was so cool because she drove a little red sports car, a
Miata. The highlights of Casey's day or week or month were the times
Mrs. Vickers forgot something from her car and had Casey run out and
get it. What a treat to get to retrieve something from Mrs. Vicker's car!

❧

November 3, 2003
I read an article in the newspaper that Trey McDonald is the punter for
Duke. Casey had liked him. She went to a dance in eighth grade with a
boy named Bret Hudson. I wonder what he does now and where he lives.

A funny memory of that time involved Steve. Casey was sitting in the
bleachers at Oak Ridge High School with Bret after her junior high

game was over. I think they were holding hands. Casey accused Steve of looking too much at them.

❦

November 5, 2003
Some days I am so pleased that thoughts and memories of Casey just appear to me all through the day. I love those times. I feel her presence around me so strongly. Then sometimes I feel she is so far away, and I miss her terribly.

❦

December 2003
For a long time, I wanted nothing to do with Christmas decorations – neither decorating or looking at them – but now in the eighth Christmas without Casey, I feel ready to decorate, because they're pretty. And that's OK.

❦

January 7, 2004
I don't think I'm superstitious, yet I put off as long as I could cleaning the fridge. I had done that July 25, 1996, AND the night before I had to go to the hospital with pneumonia in 2002. Cleaning the fridge frightened me because I associated that activity with sorrow and illness. Likewise, I wouldn't wear the clothes I wore July 25th or July 27th or July 28th.

I remember after I got home from work on July 25th, I cleaned the house and even the refrigerator. Little did I suspect that it would be the last time I would live in that house. I left the vacuum cleaner in the middle of the floor.

❦

January 10, 2004
Today as I listened to Bette Midler sing "From a Distance," I could see so clearly my little eight-year-old signing (yes, signing – not singing) this song as she and her classmates performed at Sycamore Elementary School. Oh, Casey, from a distance.

❦

January 14, 2004
I must write Casey's story, because if something happens to me, who else can write it?

❦

January 14, 2004

God. So big and so much I don't understand. But very much real and so a part of me. The longer I live, the more aware I become of just how big God is and how small I am. How can I ask of God all the things I ask of Him when He has so very many bigger and more important issues to be handling – wars, suffering people, earthquakes, grieving parents who've just lost their children? How can I make my requests? I'm selfish. Yet I'm told God does know and care about everything in my life. So He must be breathed into me. Ever present. And He takes care of me in so many ways that I don't even think about or petition of Him. How great He is. I feel so small and unworthy. As we drive along the highway or visit other locations or fly, I'm always reminded of just what an immense world there is and what a tiny fleck of that immensity I am. How does God keep up with all of us? But He does. I know He does.

January 18, 2004

Such a sad memory surfaced today. I remembered the Friday (July 26, 1996) when we went to the mall to get underwear and socks for Casey.

January 22, 2004

I love to make pictures. But after Casey died, I didn't even want to. I don't remember exactly when I picked my camera back up, but I know we have no pictures from the first Christmas after she died. And maybe the second, third and fourth as well. I still can't bring myself to get out the ornaments at Christmas that reflect the years we were truly a complete family. It's hard to imagine celebrating anything without Casey. But eventually we did begin to get back into celebrating – just in a different way – Christmas and Easter.

February 2, 2004

Tragic events that went on around me in 1996 didn't register. For example, the 1996 Summer Olympics were being held in Atlanta. Casey and I had watched the opening ceremonies together on July 19th. A week later a pipe bomb was detonated in Centennial Olympic Park, killing one and injuring over 100 people. It meant nothing to me because Casey had died that week.

February 26, 2004
I was walking in the snow, enjoying it – and then I heard the sound of children's voices. They were playing in the snow, like you used to do. I became sad again.

❦

March 14, 2004
It happened again today. As I pulled beside a car at a traffic light, a little girl in the backseat looked over at me and smiled. It reminded me so of Casey's smile and of Casey's eyes. It made me think back to the day several years ago when, at another stop, another little girl looked over at me and waved. It's like Casey was communicating with me. How I love those glimpses.

❦

March 22, 2004
Dear Casey, Today I ran into Kathy McGinnis, Lindsay's mom. We hugged and talked and caught up. She told me Lindsay is a senior in college this year in Mobile, Alabama. She plans to be a Christian counselor. She told me Lindsay has always kept your picture. Always. And she loved you so much.

I have been so out-of-sorts since I ran into Kathy. It was so good to see her, and so wonderful to know Lindsay still has you in her life, if only a picture. But I am so . . . I can't describe how I feel. Lindsay is 21 and a senior in college. That's what you should be too. – ❤Mom

❦

March 28, 2004
I thought today of how I miss the structure my girls gave my life. When Casey died, my structure entirely collapsed. When the girls were little, each day of the week had a special feel to it. Monday we do this, Tuesday, that . . . etc. In school, again the days had special meaning and so did months, holidays, everything. But after Casey died nothing was the same. One day was the same as the next, and holidays weren't special anymore and months were all the same. I was not ready to <u>not</u> be a mother and have my days defined by my children's activities.

The first time I met Mr. Wampler, he said, "It seems like it's been one long day." That's what it's been, it seems like, most of the time.

❦

From a note Nikki wrote to me in May 2004, with moonflower seeds she had given me for Mother's Day: *"I hope that these seeds will grow big and strong. I will always think of Casey when I see a moonflower. It is often said that we are reborn each morning that we awaken. It then follows that death is represented by nightfall. How appropriate it is that Casey's flower lies dormant during the day only to bloom a beautiful flower at night!"*

❦

May 29, 2004
Today I looked in my glove compartment and thought how "different" the glove box is in my car from what it used to be. It used to hold sunglasses and ponytail holders. Now it's tape, scissors, a clean cloth and bottle of water – for Casey's niche at the cemetery when I change flowers and shine her marker. I also think about what Mr. Edmond had written in Casey's memory book. Mr. Edmond has just died. Are they together today? Is she showing him the wonders she has discovered? I hope so. Heaven must be so great – but even more fabulous for Casey now that another special person is there for her. Wait on me, my little girl.

This is what Mr. Edmond had written about Casey, dated May 25, 1998:

"My memories of Casey are very pleasant. I loved Casey like a grandchild. She was so kind and considerate. I shall always remember her as a bright star that came into my life for a short time and made my life richer.

"I remember the little girl that moved next door. She would talk to me and ask questions about the things around her, the garden, flowers, snakes, turtles, etc. Always inquisitive, wanting to learn.

"I watched her growing into a lovely young lady with a ready smile. She shared things about school and sports. She could bounce a basketball. She would have excelled in any sport. She was special.

"I can remember wanting to share a soft drink or piece of cake with her. She would smile and say 'thanks' or 'I have had some.'

"Casey is in my Hall of Fame. I shall see her, again, one day. She will say, 'Mr. Edmond, I have been looking for you.' I'll see that sweet face and she will show me all of the beautiful flowers and 'wonders' she has discovered.

"I am glad Casey came into my life. – Love, Jim Edmond"

July 25, 2004
My dear sweet Casey, As I write this, it is almost eight o'clock p.m. Central time. Eastern Standard time, though, it's almost nine o'clock. That means it has now been eight years since you drew your last earthly breath. I hate this day. I hate this time. I hate the days leading up to it and the days immediately following it. I hate eight o'clock, and I hate nine o'clock. It was between those hours, the best I can figure, that you left me. Casey, how can it be that it's been eight years? How is it possible that I have lived eight years without you here where I can see you and hear your voice? You have always been and always will be a part of my life. That will never change. I think about you all the time. My tears don't come as readily as they once did – I rarely cry anymore about anything. That bothered me at first, but it doesn't now because I know it has nothing to do with not loving or missing you as much. I'll always love and always miss you.

Nikki, Kurt, Olivia and I went to Chandler Park in Tulsa today and released four balloons filled with Forget-Me-Not flower seeds for you. Did you see them? Did you get them? Did you feel the love we sent you?

Always know, my dearest little girl, how very much I love you and how very glad I am that I had you for 14 years beside me.

Until I see you, all my love and all my heart, forever and ever – Mom

August 8, 2004
Notes I made from Pastor John Wood's sermon on "Grief and Grace" today: Everything we do is like a wake. Our actions lift and float, or sink, the craft around us. God is tender-hearted toward us. God provides a way through our disaster. He makes a way of escape, an ark that lifts us up above the very waters that destroy. That ark is Jesus Christ. He doesn't just take us through it, He gives us a new start. God is so deeply

*involved in our life. Nothing our children do fails to bring joy or sorrow
to our heart. Same with God. We are His children.*

❧

*2004: For so long I haven't known what to do with the feelings bottled
up inside of me since Casey died . . . the deep sadness inside, so deep
inside . . . the anger . . . the disbelief even now after all these years. I
want Casey here. I want to see her. I want to hear her voice. I want to
know what she's like at 22. She was just 14. God, she was just 14! She
was a dream to me. Here for just a minute, then gone from me. It was not
long enough. Please, God, it was not long enough.*

❧

August 20, 2004
*Anxiety is my worst enemy. On one hand, the worst thing that could
happen to me <u>has</u> happened. My child died. On the other hand, the worst
thing that could happen to me could happen again. Sometimes this
makes me crazy. I know I must believe and have faith that it won't, but
it's a struggle for me. A real struggle. The grandchildren make me so
happy and glad to be alive. But they scare me. What if something
happens to them? I can let myself get crazy with that thought.*

*One time about two years after Casey's death, Erin was late arriving
home from a ball game and I was beside myself. I flipped out. Brad was
dozing on the couch and I woke him and got him all upset too. When
Erin pulled in the driveway, both Brad and I jumped on her. I blew the
whole situation way out of proportion, but that's what happens when you
find out that bad things don't just happen to other people.*

*When Nikki traveled in her job with a computer company, I was
especially anxious. I worried so much that something would happen. I
became obsessed. I remember one morning as I showered I was pleading
with God to protect Nikki and Erin and not let anything happen to them,
like to Casey, when I felt broken and said, "God, I can't do this
anymore." And I felt a peace come over me. It was as if God
replied, "You don't have to." How I wish I could keep the peace that
washed over my soul that day with me every day.*

*I would shudder at Compassionate Friends meetings when parents
introduced themselves as having two (or more!) children who had died.*

How could they stand it? And sometimes obituaries list more than one child who had died. How could those parents stand it? How???

❦

I don't know how many times when I was in the middle of what I can best describe as just vague anxiety, God's word kept popping up: "Cast all your anxiety on him because he cares for you." 1 Peter 5:7.

❦

August 21, 2004
Today it occurred to me for the first time that not only have I experienced the death of a child but I have also experienced the death of a sibling. I never thought of myself as a bereaved sibling, but I am. Why is it that that never really occurred to me till now? Could it be that it's because I was only a child myself when my newborn sister, Linda, died? Could it be because her death was rarely mentioned? Could it be because I don't remember seeing my parents grieve? I know they must have, and that makes me feel so bad for them.

❦

September 9, 2004
A couple of times in just the past few days, I've seen girls who look like Casey. Yesterday one little girl was sitting in the back of a Jeep at a traffic light. She had Casey's ponytail and body shape. I only saw her from the back, but it could have been Casey. But she looked about 14 years old, or maybe even younger, so it couldn't have been Casey, because Casey is 22 years old now.

❦

October 14, 2004
I dreamed tonight of Casey in her red Rams sweatsuit. She was dance-skating.

❦

December 15, 2004
Today I thought about how several times this month it has seemed like Christmas. I would get a reminder of the past, before Casey died. The remembrance would be in the form of cold air that reminded me of past Christmases, or a sight or sound would take me back to how it used to feel. For just a minute . . . a fleeting minute . . . but a minute. I thought, "Where have I been the past eight years during Christmas?" But I know.

❦

December 2004
Several families in the neighborhood where we had lived sent a beautiful big Ficus tree to me back in 1996. That tree became very special to me. I put white lights on it and kept it lighted year round. When it first arrived at the house, it went into shock. I called Mayo's to find out what I should do. It recovered and was beautiful for years, but then just gradually lost all its leaves. That happened over the course of seven or eight years. It was very, very hard for me to let that plant go. And the same story with other green houseplants that were given to us. I tried desperately to keep them alive. For some reason that was very, very important to me. Over the years they gradually dwindled down to just a few sprigs, but I still tried my best. It was a sad day for me when the last of the "funeral flowers" were dead.

March 18, 2005
Dear Casey, I had one of those take-my-breath-away moments today. "Almost spring" is in the air. I drove by the ballfield. You should be there. Not playing high school ball anymore but, at age 22, playing co-ed with your friends. You should be there. I feel you there.
   ❤ *Love, Mom*

April 8, 2005
This morning I got up early to watch the Pope's funeral. It came on at four a.m. It was so moving, an experience I will never, ever forget. I dozed off twice during the four hours I watched TV. <u>Both times</u> I dreamed of Casey. In both dreams, she was about 18 months old. In one she was running to me. I can still feel the anticipation of sweeping her up and into my arms. In the second dream, I was looking for her baby bed, but she had a big girl's bed. The dreams have left me so sad this morning.

Another thing that happened during the coverage of the Pope's funeral was that I saw a girl who looked like Casey in the crowd of mourners. She was a teenager, and the close-up of her face startled me. She looked so like Casey.

Watching all the people of faith mourn but celebrate the Pope strengthens my faith.

The three ties to Casey that I felt this morning make me sad but yet celebrate in my heart because she is already where the Pope just entered.

May 13, 2005
I have just awakened from a sad, scary, death dream. I feel so down. My throat feels constricted. It reminds me of how I felt so many times after Casey died. The constricted throat. In my dream, I could moan and cry out . . . but I could cry no tears. And I need to cry tears to help relieve the constricted feeling in my throat. I remember in my dream that I was clutching a box of ashes and rocking and holding them and moaning. I need to cry. I need to cry.

June 2005
She'd be 23 years old now. Where would she be working? Where would she be living? Would she be married? Some of her friends are now! Would she have children? Some of her friends do! My Casey, 23 years old – I can't imagine!

October 27, 2005
It occurred to me today that Thursdays, finally, are not as horrible as they've been since the Thursday Casey died. I had hated and been so out-of-sorts and sad on Thursdays. When Steve would sense something was wrong with me, all I'd have to say was, "It's Thursday," and he'd understand. It's softened.

December 6, 2005
It occurred to me this morning as I decorated Casey's Christmas tree that my subconscious has "accepted" that Casey died. I had a dream last night that Casey was dead. I was at a gathering of some sort where I was to speak about being the mother of a child who had died. In my dream I never gave the speech because I was trying to change clothes and I couldn't get the black sleeveless top I was wearing over my head to take it off. I tried and tried and struggled and struggled, but it wouldn't come off. I was getting so frustrated and claustrophobic as I'd pull it over my head. . . but it wouldn't come off. My arms were stuck, my head was stuck. The shirt was too tight and it didn't have buttons or a zipper to take it off. It had to go over my head, and it wouldn't. I was thinking about getting scissors to cut it off. That's when I saw that it was

my high-neck black silk top and I really didn't want to use scissors and ruin it. Then I awoke. I don't recall ever dreaming that Casey was dead. The frustration is still with me as I write this.

January 9, 2006
Today I was remembering how the moonplants – on their own – lined up last summer along the border of the front walk at our house. And how the dalmatian romped in our yard on Casey's 15ᵗʰ birthday. And how I met Bruce Hunter shortly before Casey died . . . and how he was then among the first to offer condolences when he heard what had happened to her.

Bruce's own 14-year-old daughter, Katie, died of an injury she received while playing soccer in 1991. The school (Robertsville Middle School) established the "Kathryn Leigh Hunter Award" in her memory, and Casey received this award on June 10, 1996. It was an award not for soccer but for being what I think of as an "all around good kid."

Bruce, Steve and I all worked at Y-12, and Steve introduced me to Bruce one day at work. I remember Bruce telling me how pleased he was that the school still presented this award in his daughter's memory and how pleased he was that my daughter was the recipient. Little did we know that just six weeks later, death would claim my daughter, just as it had his.

Casey and Katie . . . their resting spots are just across from each other at Oak Ridge Memorial Park. They never met in life, but I'd like to think they have now.

February 2, 2006
Last night I dreamed of my daughters, all three of them. It made me happy in recalling the dream that all three of them were in it. They were little girls, of course, in my dream. Always little girls. At Compassionate Friends I've found that we mothers usually dream of our children as little children.

February 8, 2006
Today at the mall I saw a kiosk selling gold teeth. What a kick Casey would get out of that. Not that she would want to buy or have gold teeth.

I just think she'd find that as funny as I do. You can buy gold teeth at the mall.

❦

May 10, 2006
As I took the box with "Casey" beautifully engraved on top from the chest of drawers beside my bed, my stomach flipped. I opened it. On top I noticed a newspaper clipping I had saved. It was a letter written to Billy Graham asking why children die. I shut the box quickly. I know below the Billy Graham column are the first "letters" I wrote to Casey. I remember writing those first letters to Casey on my lunchtime at work, with my door closed. Maybe I'm not ready to look in this box. It brings back memories of how I felt during those lunchtimes. It's already brought back the memory of the first day I returned to work after her death. I remember it took a lot of strength to get out of the car, walk down the hill and go into the building where I worked. I had lost 13 pounds in two weeks and felt so weak. I remember the first person I saw. I remember I started crying. I remember the pained look on his face. I'm starting to cry now just thinking about it. No, I'm not ready, even after almost 10 years, to revisit this box and all the memories it calls up.

So I closed the box and took a quick look around the rest of the drawer. There were the shoes she wore at her sister's wedding, the corsage she wore for the Robertsville/Jefferson basketball game, her "Fox and Hound" video, her backpack still packed with school things. I shut the drawer. The other three drawers have her things in them too. I don't want to look in them. I'll do that later. I have made it my 10th-year-after-her-death goal to look at her things, to maybe even watch the videos of her. I still have a little over two months till it's been "officially" 10 years. I'll look at these treasures (that still have her fingerprints on them!) another day. Maybe. It reminds me of the mother who wouldn't let the air out of the beach ball after her daughter died, because that beach ball held her daughter's breath.

I walked over to my closet and noticed the zippered case on the top shelf where I keep all the sympathy cards I received. I know another zippered case beside it, the white one, has the register from the funeral home in it. I don't want to see them just yet.

I thought about the love chest where I lovingly placed her favorite clothes and toys in the days after her death . . . and which I've never opened since. I think my children, maybe even grandchildren, may have to deal with that love chest after I'm not here. It has her purple pajamas in it. I don't think I could handle seeing those purple PJs.

❦

May 14, 2006
This morning the conditions and time of day were just right so that as our plane taxied down the runway and just as it lifted off, I could see the shadow of the whole plane just ahead and to the side of us. I looked at it and thought, "I'm on that plane." I could even judge, roughly, where my position on the plane was. I spend much of the time I'm on airplanes searching the landscape below for clues as to where we are. From high up, you can see the way things are laid out below. Squares. Rectangles. On the ground, though, it feels like a maze. This seems so symbolic of grief.

Airplanes are good for writing, for me. Wonder why.

❦

May 24, 2006
Mom and I went to the cemeteries today so she could put out her Memorial Day flowers. It reminded me that just two days before Casey died, she, Mom and I were at the cemetery in Wartburg where my friend Kathy was buried. There were little bunnies running around the gravesite. Then we stopped in Union at the cemetery where my mom's parents and other relatives are buried. I have such sweet memories of Casey at both places straightening up any flowers that had fallen over and dusting the grass away and being so reverent and caring of the graves. That was so her.

❦

July 26, 2006
Sweet little granddaughter Caroline is visiting today. It's like watching Casey play. From the back, Caroline favors Casey so much. Her head. Her body shape. Her movements. She talks about Casey, almost like she knew her. But Caroline's just four years old. Her mom (Erin) is keeping Casey alive. I love that.

❦

August 16, 2006
*Tonight I was going through some papers and I came across my
registration for Jordan, my 1992 Camry. I noticed that the license on it
was 213BBX. How interesting that my current 2006 Camry has the
license plate 448BBX. (2+13=15BBX; 4+4+8=16BBX) What are the
chances of that happening??? In keeping with what Casey started by
naming our 1992 Camry "Jordan," I've named the vehicles I've owned
since then "Troy," "Chipper," and now "Avery" after Casey's favorite
sports figures. Silly, maybe, but just important to me.*

September 17, 2006
*When Pastor John Wood gave the blessing at the end of the morning
service, I felt it and believed it. "The Lord bless you and keep you . . .
and give you peace." I still search for peace.*

October 29, 2006
*Today it occurred to me in church that for the first time since Casey
died, I can look at the children singing. I used to turn my head, read or
do anything to avoid seeing them. They were reminders of Casey. Of
how she looked when she sang with a group of children. But today, I
looked at the children. And they reminded me of my grandchildren. What
I have. Not just what I have lost.*

December 2006
*I want to go to church this month. For the last 10 years, I haven't
attended my church during the month of December. It's too hard. I can't
control the lump in my throat and the tears that sting my eyes and the
sadness that washes over me when I hear Christmas songs and see the
church decorated. But this year I want to go. And I want to decorate the
house and the yard. I want our house to "look" like the rest of the
houses in the neighborhood. I want to bake bread and give to friends
and neighbors. I want to celebrate. I want to do these things. Finally, I
want to. I still miss Casey though.*

*It's almost 2007, and I'm no closer to understanding if or how free will
and predestination can coexist. But it's not the pressing issue for me that
it used to be. People argue both ways, and both arguments are good. I
still wonder, but I don't have to know. It wouldn't change the outcome.
Casey is dead. I have a stronger faith that God makes no mistakes, and*

someday I hope to understand. There are so many things I don't understand, like infinity and black holes and space and stars that we see but which "died" long ago. How can this all be? But it <u>is</u>. And God <u>is</u>.

❦

December 8, 2006
Dear Casey, Today as I drove around doing errands, my mind seemed to finally establish or come to terms with what I <u>do</u> believe about predestination, and this is it: I believe as God's children we are <u>predestined</u> to live at least the 70 or 80 years allotted to us. (Psalm 90:10) The fact that some of us don't live that long – that you didn't live the 70 or 80 years ordained for you – was not what God planned. Rather, many lives are cut short by accidents, disease, wars, the actions of others and a myriad of other causes that are not really God's plan. God's plan is for us to live and prosper. It says that in Jeremiah 29:11. So I don't believe God intended that you live only 14 years, just as I don't believe it is His plan for so many children to die in war-torn countries or in countries where disease and the effects of poverty claim so many lives. Disease, poverty, accidents – all those causes of deaths of people under 70 – are not from God. The devil exists, just as God exists. God will conquer the devil and death. Being finally able to formulate what I do believe enables me to be more at peace with the scripture that reads "All the days ordained for me were written in your book before one of them came to be." (Psalm 139:16) Right or wrong, I believe God ordained 70 or 80 years for you, not just 14.

I feel a sense of relief that after more than 10 years I have reached a peace about this. I don't think God intended for you to live just 14 years. And I do believe that while God welcomed you home, He grieved with me too. He understands. He really understands.

I miss you this holiday season. I think about you all the time. – With love that will never end, Mom

❦

December 10, 2006
Dear Casey, I haven't cried much this year. It's certainly not because I don't feel sad and miss you; it's just the way things are after 10+ years. Before you died, I didn't cry easily. Then after you died, I couldn't stop my tears. Now, I seem to have returned to more like I used to be. But today . . . today, I couldn't stop my tears. Today was the 11th holiday

memorial service I have attended at The Compassionate Friends. I was doing fine, helping other people with their name tags, making sure their finger foods and loved ones pictures got in the right hands. Then I walked into the room where all the pictures had been placed with small candles in front of them. Pictures of beautiful children. Pictures of children just born. Pictures of teenagers. Pictures of young adults. A few pictures of middle-aged adults who were still someone's beloved child. Pictures of such beautiful children, so full of life – but now they're all dead. I saw your picture, and the tears began to spill from my eyes and down my face. And I couldn't stop them. I didn't even try. That's the way my tears are now. I think they're just right behind my eyes, waiting to be released, not asking for my OK, just happening. It breaks my heart that all those pictures were of children who have died. Most of all it breaks my heart that you are among them. I still can't believe it. I miss you so much. I love you, baby girl. – Love, Mom

December 13, 2006
Dear Casey, Today I went to the cemetery to replace your Christmas "decoration." I had put a basket of flowers on your niche earlier this month but, as on several other occasions, the basket was missing today. So I got another arrangement. It's funny the things I remember that I hadn't thought about before. Today as I drove past what used to be a farm just before you get to the cemetery, I remembered that at one time there had been a horse on that property. You had noticed it standing behind a fence, and you had wanted to stop and pet it. We didn't – and now I regret that. That was a long time ago. Never would the thought have even crossed my mind at that time that some day your ashes would be in that cemetery, just down the road from where you had seen that horse.

At the post office today, I overheard a young mother with two small children in tow tell the lady behind her that someone once told her that the days are long but the years are short when you're raising children. That's so true. And it's so true of grief. The days – and nights – are long, but the years are short.

It's been over 10 years since you died, and I'm still remembering new things about you. Still dreaming of you. Still missing you. Still grieving. I want to always remember everything I can about you. I want to always dream about you. I love (present tense) you so much that of course I will always miss you. And of course I'll always grieve. How could it be any other way? I wouldn't even want it to be. I love you, my little girl. – Love, Mom

Near the yew were tall flowering bushes – some kind of poppy, perhaps. But almost all of the petals had fallen off, so mostly I just saw a thousand tangled stems growing skyward. Then I realized that the stems were actually connected, and that they bore seeds that would flower again in the spring.

from *Bird by Bird* by Anne Lamott

Thoughts to Share

I heard something one time – I think it was from *The History Boys* – that the best moments in reading are when you come across words written by someone else that describe exactly how <u>you</u> feel. "It's as if a hand has come out and taken yours." I hope if you're grieving the loss of someone you love, you can feel my hand.

With a child's death, parents are bent as low as they can go. But we can, after time and a lot of grief work, straighten back up. I think we're made that way. And we're made to help others.

What have I said that hasn't been said before? Sadly, nothing. My thoughts and experiences are probably not so different from what grieving parents felt or said even eons ago. That is reassuring on one hand, but discouraging on the other. It occurred to me this morning that all the books in the world can be written for parents who have lost children – and you can get ideas for ways to cope in them – but really NOTHING can help you at first. NOTHING. The minutes, hours, days and months just have to pass. Then, without even realizing it, one day you might be ready to attempt one of those suggestions made by someone who has traveled the road ahead of you.

In many ways, as my letters to Casey reflect, I strive to keep the pain at arms' length as best I can. But then her birthday and the anniversary of her death come, and I can't hold it back. Because her birth month and day and death month and day fall just over six weeks apart, it's an intense six-week period for me. Those are always the worst days for me, and I expect they always will be. Every year when June and then July are over, I think, OK, I'm good to go again. For the first four years, back-to-school time was hard too. And of course holidays. So I always try to <u>do</u> something or <u>go</u> somewhere.

I've already written about some of the balloon releases we've had and about Casey's special Christmas tree, but some of the other things we've done include: planting black and red tulips that spell C-A-S-E-Y; planting a sunflower garden; planting a butterfly bush; providing a toy box at the local Legal Aid office for the children of clients (we call it

"Casey's Corner"); editing The Compassionate Friends newsletter and then putting together a book of articles and poems for TCF members; and writing Casey's friends and asking them to send me their favorite memories of Casey, which I then put in a special keepsake book. During the Christmas holidays, Angel Trees at work, church and the mall are loaded with names of children in need, so I pick an angel and think of Casey as I buy toys and clothing for this child.

My favorite way I've commemorated Casey's birthday was June 3, 2004, the day she would have been 22 years old. Steve was in Washington, DC, on business. I traveled with him and spent Casey's birthday walking all over the city and placing 22 tiny wooden ladybugs in 22 special places. I put them in the Botanic Gardens, House and Senate Office Buildings, the Library of Congress, the Supreme Court, the Capitol, the Smithsonian Air and Space Museum, Union Station, the Lincoln Memorial, the Vietnam Soldiers Memorial, the World War II Memorial, Arlington National Cemetery, the National Cathedral and even in a Red Trolley.

President Ronald Reagan died on June 5, 2004, just two days after I'd put Casey's ladybugs around Washington. As I watched his funeral services in the National Cathedral a few days later on television, I wondered if Casey's ladybug had had a front-row seat. Even now, I wonder if any of those ladybugs are still there.

It will soon be 11 years since Casey died, and I still struggle at times. It's still hard to accept she won't be coming back, that I'm not going to wake up to a different life. Although I know my subject matter – grief – this is not a how-to lesson. I don't have "the" answers. I just have some ideas that might help others. Here are a few things that helped me, that I would recommend:

❦ Just concentrate on getting through the next minute.

> *E.L. Doctorow once said that 'writing a novel is like driving a car at night. You can see only as far as your headlights, but you can make the whole trip that way.' You don't have to see where you're going, you don't have to see your destination or everything you will pass along the way. You just have to see two*

*or three feet ahead of you. This is right up there with the best
advice about writing, or life, I have ever heard.*

from *Bird by Bird* by Anne Lamott

I would add that this is good advice about living with grief, too.

❧ Take care of your heart.

My heart often physically hurt, especially at first. Whoever coined the
phrase "heartache" knew what they were talking about. I have felt my
heart ache. It's real. Grief lays heavy on your heart. It feels heavy. In the
February 19, 2006, issue of *Parade*, Marilyn vos Savant in her "Ask
Marilyn" column addressed this phenomenon:

> **Is there a medical explanation for the pain felt in the area of
> the heart when one is grieving over the loss of a loved one, or
> is the pain entirely psychosomatic?**
> *That condition, now called "broken heart syndrome" (stress
> cardiomyopathy), has a medical basis: When extreme stress
> causes adrenaline and other hormones to soar and stay at high
> levels for days, the heart may be unable to pump enough blood.
> (The hormones may cause small blood vessels in the heart to
> contract.) This can produce chest pain, shortness of breath, even
> fluid in the lungs – symptoms like those caused by a heart
> attack. Most people recover. But the same stress may trigger a
> real heart attack in those whose hearts are susceptible.*

❧ Do something physical to relieve mental stress. Do something mental
to relieve physical stress.

I think I heard this advice in a training class at work, but I've found it
applies to the journey through grief as well. Grief is what you *feel*; it's
internal. Mourning is what you *do;* it's your external reaction. For me,
walking helps relieve some of the mental stress of grieving; reading and
writing help relieve some of the physical stress of mourning.

❧ Accept that you may become self-centered and self-absorbed for
awhile.

I remember reading somewhere that grieving people are self-centered and self-absorbed. That sounded a little offensive to me. I felt like I seemed to spend a lot of energy trying to avoid making others around me feel bad. But I had to admit it had an element of truth. During those first intense stages of grief all I could think about was Casey and how terrible and sad and awful I felt. For a long time, I was both hypersensitive and insensitive. I was *hypersensitive* in respect to comments people made. For example, if someone said, "You seem to be doing better," or "You're looking better," I didn't say anything but I thought, "I'M NOT DOING BETTER! YOU DON'T KNOW HOW I FEEL! I'LL NEVER BE BETTER." And I would stew about it.

I was *insensitive* in respect to concerns of other people. An example of that is if someone told me what a bad day they were having for whatever reason, I would think, "YOU DON'T KNOW WHAT A BAD DAY IS! HOW COULD YOU EVEN BRING UP SUCH A MINOR, SILLY THING TO ME?" In comparison to losing a child, almost everything I can think of seems minor. I *know* what a bad day *really* is, what it's really like to be swallowed by a cloud. The sky *has* fallen.

❦ Recognize that you may develop a governor on your emotions.

There is an armor or shield around my heart now. I can't be as happy or as sad, and I can't be as touched or as moved by music or words or sights as I used to be. It's just different and hard to explain, and maybe it doesn't happen to everyone who loses a child. But for me, there's just a buffer there, a regulator on my feelings and their expression. Part of our grief work is working at being happy.

❦ Let others know you won't ever forget or just erase your child from activities or memories or recollections – as if your child was never there and a part of life – and you don't want them to either. In some ways this frees others to talk about your child and not be afraid they'll make you cry.

❦ Know that some of the people you would have imagined would be the ones who would rush to your side and "help" you are not always the ones who actually do.

In the beginning, I wasn't paying attention to who *wasn't* there. It was only later that a person or two crossed my mind and I remembered it had been "pre-accident" since I had seen or heard from them. I knew *they* knew about what had happened; wonder why they hadn't tried to get in touch? Why hadn't they said anything? That wasn't very nice of them. It even hurt my feelings. Then it made me feel bad about myself, because how many times had I been that person? I had known about someone's misfortune and I really cared. I really thought about them and even prayed for them. But I hadn't said anything to them. I hadn't visited the funeral home or attended the funeral or tried to get in touch. Ouch. A lesson there for me. So I couldn't let someone else's apparent disregard tick me off too much. Their disregard wasn't necessarily a lack of care. I've sure learned a lot of lessons the hard way in my life.

❦ Cut others some slack. Try not to harbor bad thoughts.

Wow, that was hard for me. Why do I have to be the one who cuts others slack? Yet I do, if I want to heal. People can have innocent motives, but bumbling actions. I'm only hurting, even poisoning, myself by dwelling on the mistakes of others. In her book *Traveling Mercies*, Anne Lamott wrote: *They say we are not punished for the sin but by the sin, and I began to feel punished by my unwillingness to forgive.* I think that happens.

❦ Share your faith.

After Casey died, I began to wonder why I was here. What purpose did God have for me? I wanted to die. After a serious illness in 2002, I began to believe God wasn't finished with me yet. I still had something to do with my life.

My faith makes a difference in how I have lived since Casey died. It's given me a foundation and a hope. I have had many experiences that have had no other explanation than God working in my life. Will others see by the way I am that God is in my life? I hope so. I don't often use my spoken words to tell others about God, but I hope my written words convey that God is alive in me. See what He has done for me. It's real. He loves me, and He loves you. Let Him.

❦ Heed the lessons you learn and become a more compassionate person yourself.

Before Casey's death I wanted nothing to do with death and funeral rituals. But I have reevaluated funerals, sympathy cards, flowers, expressions of sympathy and concern, visitation at the funeral home, food brought by others, just acknowledgment of the death. I have totally changed my attitude and what I do now. Those expressions of care are so very helpful and healing. I have learned that a person's mere presence speaks volumes. On Friday night, July 26, 1996, my childhood friend Margaret found me. I don't remember a lot about that night or what was said; all I know is she was there. And the next night her youngest little daughter made sure I always had a cup of water at the funeral home. Her name, appropriately, is Angel.

Ten years out, I can see that my behavior unknowingly and unwittingly fell into the general categories (or "steps") of grief. I went back and forth through shock, denial, anger, guilt and depression. I felt like everyone was looking at me. I didn't want pity. I didn't want sympathy. But I <u>did</u> want pity. I <u>did</u> want sympathy. Grief intensified everything.

Somehow, though, I did reach a turning point. There was restoration. Adaptation. Accommodation. The progression happened, even though at first I couldn't imagine ever being "restored," and I didn't want to "adapt" or "accommodate." I suppose I equated healing with being OK with the fact that Casey died, and I'll never be OK with that.

I saw this quote in the newspaper: "Almost every accident has multiple causes. 'The stars line up' is what they call it." Motor vehicle accidents are the leading cause of death among teens in Tennessee. It's a fact of life. But I can't help but look at statistics and think the population should be one <u>more</u> and fatalities should be one <u>less</u>. That crash should never have happened. Casey's death was wrong.

It was my niece who was driving the vehicle Casey died in. I felt compassion for her, but I also felt anger. At first, I wasn't sure sometimes whether I was going to implode or explode. I often thought it would be much easier if I had had a stranger or a drunk driver to lash out at. That would be more "acceptable." This was my niece. My family. It never felt right to feel the way I sometimes felt. But anger and resentment are a big part of my story, and I wrote about it sometimes. I haven't included those entries, out of consideration for my family. It has taken a lot of time to work through that aspect of my grief, and I don't want to un-do the healing that has taken place. It's been a difficult situation for all of us.

It was a long time ago that I first heard the expression "counting coup," but only recently that I wondered what it meant. I learned that this expression refers to a Native American battle practice. A warrior would sometimes touch or hit his enemy with a stick – a "coup stick" – then run away. This let the enemy know he was there and not afraid, that he could have hurt him if he had wanted to. By choosing not to hurt his enemy, the warrior could turn the situation around. He could turn his enemy's anger into something else, or even take it away.

I don't know why "counting coup" seems to speak to me. Maybe it's because in some ways my enemy, grief, seems to "count coup" with me. It approaches at both likely and unlikely times, touches me, then runs away. I know it's there and if we were to engage in hand-to-hand combat, I'd probably lose. On the other hand, I sometimes "count coup" with grief. I approach it, then run away. It takes work to let grief's energy change into something else. On a good day, my grief can be changed into help for others. As the years have passed, I have had more and more good days than bad. I've felt more like letting my grief be transformed.

The path my life has taken over the last 10 years is surely not one I would have chosen, because look what set me on this path: my little girl died. Her life was sunshine in mine; and my life has never been the same since the sunshine went away. Her death was my greatest loss and set the course for the remainder of my life. The path I had been on back in 1996 disappeared the day Casey died.

I'm not proud to admit that I did wonder why this couldn't have happened to someone else. It didn't seem fair or right that a person who hadn't done anything wrong would be the one to die. And I remember for a time feeling bitter that everyone else seemed to go on with their lives . . . but I couldn't. Yes, I know it probably appeared that I was. But

I wasn't. All I thought about was Casey. For the longest time I was obsessed with knowing the details. I was obsessed with imagining what her last minutes must have been like. Did she hurt? Did she cry? Did she know what happened? Did she call "Mama!" like she had the year before when she fell out of our canoe? I had been there to pull her back in. But I wasn't there this time, and the circumstances were so much more dire. I should have been there! I hated myself for not being there. My magical thinking allowed me to believe that if I had been there, this wouldn't have happened. If I had not let her spend the night at my mother's . . . if I had told her she couldn't ride in the car with her cousin . . . if I had picked her up *Thursday* afternoon instead of planning to pick her up Friday . . . if, if, if. I had failed as a mother. My child died.

But today, while I still cry, I still feel sad and I still miss Casey, somehow I have held it together. And for that I credit God, my family, and my old and new friends. My role models now are people who have lost children they love just as much as I love Casey. They are moms and dads who have gone on to help others – they helped me – and to honor the lives of their children. These are my heroes, someone I want to be like: Richard and Jean Dew, Ted and Frances Wampler, William and Rose Thompson, Tom and Margaret Baer, Verneen Holland, Barbara Wray and Judy Keiser.

The passing of time has helped too. When grandchildren came into my life, they brought a joy with them that had been missing since Casey died. Did Casey suit them up with that joy when they were together in "baby heaven" and have them deliver it to me? I guess I don't really believe it works that way, but it's a pleasant thought to let myself indulge in.

My relationship with Casey did not end when she died. It continues, and it will for the rest of my life. Casey's life and her death will always be a part of my life. My letters to Casey do not end with this book. I believe I'll always write Casey and always have things to tell her and memories to recall.

Dear Casey, I will always miss and always love you. – ❤Mom

Photograph Gallery

1982

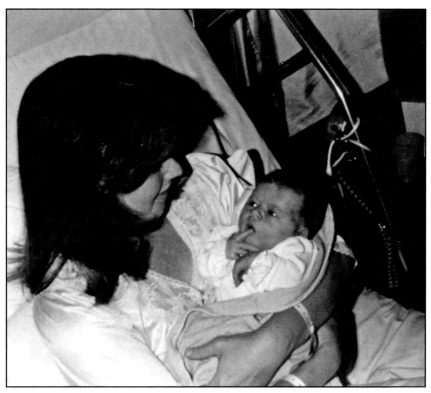

Welcome to the world, Baby Casey.

Sisters Nikki, Erin and Casey.

With big sister Nikki.

With big sister Erin.

Dear Casey . . .

Kicking her Easter purse
because she didn't like it.

With her dad Butch on
her second birthday.

1985

Two of my favorite pictures of Casey: one wearing what she called "spots, ruffles and flowers" and the other reading to her dog Barkley.

That's Casey, the little cheerleader on the left.

1986

Christmastime.

Casey with
the big blue eyes.

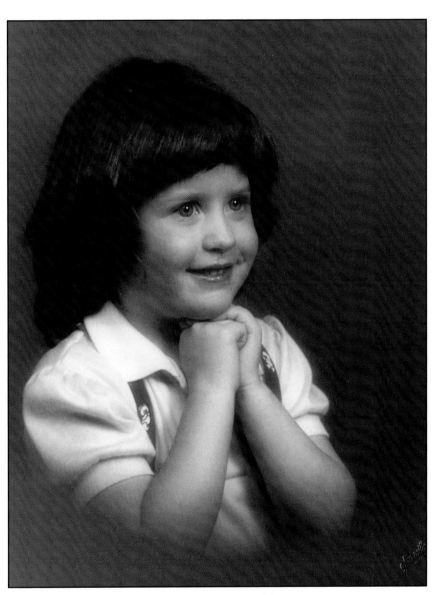

Just before she turned five.

Dear Casey . . .

Taking a break
from her soccer game.

At the beach.

Posing with the
picture that earned her
"Artist of the Week"
honors in first grade.

Halloween,
a favorite holiday.

Dear Casey . . .

With her beloved Ko-Ko.

Playing in the snow at Granny's.

1991

I always loved the
freckles across her nose.

Jessica and Casey, a/k/a
"Fudge" and "Spike" the dogs.

1992

Mother and daughter.

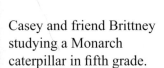

Casey and friend Brittney
studying a Monarch
caterpillar in fifth grade.

Cheering on her sister
at a cross-country meet.

Casey at 11.

Mother and daughters.
Nikki, Erin, June and Casey on Christmas Day, 1994.

1995

Steve Gibbs and Casey.
She said he could
marry her mom if
he'd get her a dog.

Fishing on her 13th birthday.

Visiting sister Nikki
at Vanderbilt.

Dear Casey . . .

Casey, #22, with her Robertsville Lady Rams team.

1996

Oak Ridge High School Lady Wildcats. Casey is fifth from left on the front row. Elizabeth Polfus, who did the artwork for this book, is second from right. (Both are wearing their hair in pigtails.)

Casey and her dad Butch on her 14th birthday,
just after a Lady Wildcats scrimmage game.

Casey helping sister Erin on Erin's wedding day, July 6, 1996.

Photo courtesy of Hancock Photography, Knoxville, TN

Erin and Nikki at Nikki's wedding. One of the most touching moments at the wedding was when a ladybug flew in and landed on Nikki's wedding gown, just above her heart. I called my daughters "Ladybugs" before ladybugs became so popular as decorations. Casey's brass plaque on the front of her niche at the cemetery reads, in part, "Daughter and Sister, Our Little Ladybug." So the ladybug that landed over Nikki's heart seemed to represent Casey's spirit for a moment for us. She belonged there with her two sisters.

2007

ABOUT THE AUTHOR

JUNE PATRICK GIBBS lives in Knoxville, Tennessee, with husband Steve. Daughter Nikki is an attorney in Tulsa, Oklahoma, and the mother of Olivia and Charlotte Vanderyt. Daughter Erin is director of the Parents Day Out Program at her church in Seymour, Tennessee. Erin and husband Brad are the parents of Caden, Caroline and Conlin Webb. The blended family also includes Steve's daughter Ginger, son-in-law Harry and grandson Jacob Cronogue of Somerville, Tennessee; and Steve's son Chris Gibbs of Powell, Tennessee.

June's first book, *Snow Blossoms*, was published in 2004, and she has plans for a children's book.

For more information about The Compassionate Friends, a national nonprofit self-help support organization for bereaved families, call the Knoxville chapter at 865-687-2117 or visit www.compassionatefriends.org.

Dear Casey

ORDER FORM

I would like to order _____ copies of *Dear Casey*. The purchase price is $19.95 per copy plus $5 shipping and handling. Internet orders can be placed at TVP1.com.

Please send check or money order to:

June Gibbs
8620 Belle Mina Way
Knoxville, TN 37923

Please send book(s) to the following address(es):

Name_____

Street or PO Box_____

City_____

State_____ Zip Code _____

Please list any special inscription you would like in the book:

_____

Name_____

Street or PO Box_____

City_____

State_____ Zip Code _____

Please list any special inscription you would like in the book:

_____